DEADLY SHORE

A Thriller

Andrew Cunningham

Copyright © 2015 by Andrew Cunningham
All Rights Reserved

No portion of this book may be reproduced in any form without written permission from the publisher or author, except as permitted by U.S. copyright law.
ISBN-13: 978-1515254294
ISBN-10: 1515254291

Books by Andrew Cunningham

Thrillers
Deadly Shore

Alaska Thrillers Series
Wisdom Spring
Nowhere Alone
The 7th Passenger
Lost Passage

Yestertime Time Travel Series
Yestertime
The Yestertime Effect
The Yestertime Warning
The Yestertime Shift

"Lies" Mystery Series
All Lies
Fatal Lies
Vegas Lies
Secrets & Lies
Blood Lies
Buried Lies
Sea of Lies
Maui Lies

Eden Rising Series
Eden Rising
Eden Lost
Eden's Legacy
Eden's Survival

Children's Mysteries (as A.R. Cunningham)
The Arthur MacArthur Mysteries: The Complete Series

As always, I couldn't do any of these books without the constant love, support, and ideas from my wife, Charlotte. Thank you!

To Christopher and Trevor
With Love … Dad

Prologue

July 5

The ladies of the Lifetime Book Club were among the first to hear it.

A rare Sunday afternoon meeting, they were—as usual—talking about everything except the selected book. The fact that the book club was named after a television movie channel said it all. At this particular meeting however, they were mostly complaining about the traffic. Traffic leaving Cape Cod on a Sunday in the summer was never good, but today it was the worst they had ever seen. Combine a beautiful Saturday 4th of July with a rainy and windy 5th, along with warnings of a hurricane heading up the Atlantic seaboard in the middle of the week, and the tourists couldn't wait to get home. But the narrow bridges were never meant for the onslaught of twenty-first century traffic. They were built in the 1930s when Cape Cod was an artsy place to visit and traffic jams didn't exist. Now, traffic was what it was all about. Cars would be backed up for miles on a Friday afternoon getting onto the Cape, and then the whole process would be repeated in reverse on

Sunday. Sometimes the traffic would be backed up all the way to Hyannis, more than fifteen miles from the Sagamore Bridge.

Today was special though. Today, people were looking forward to an eight-hour crawl along Route 6, as traffic was backed up all the way to the Harwich exit—a thirty-mile parking lot. Reports were that it wasn't any better on Route 28 heading to the Bourne Bridge.

The topic of conversation was intelligence—why people couldn't leave at midnight or even four in the morning to avoid the mess. Why they all had to wait until they'd had breakfast. Why was breakfast so important?

Eighty-four-year-old Claire was proudly explaining how she'd flipped off yet another tourist who didn't know how to drive a rotary when they heard it. It wasn't loud at first. Just kind of a *fwump* sound, followed by about five more. Then they couldn't help but to hear it.

The meeting was held at Gloria's house, just a block from the Sagamore Bridge. The house had a beautiful view of the Cape Cod Canal, that is, if you could see over the stalled traffic on the road that ran alongside the canal between the two bridges.

The new noise was deafening—a cacophony of screeching metal, car horns, and screams. Did they really hear screams? They ran to the window in time to see what was left of the bridge plummet into the canal. Dust and smoke choked the air as the ground on either side of the canal was torn up by the gigantic sections of bridge, and cars littered the area around the bridge. Those not burning were crushed beyond recognition.

The canal itself was a swirling deathtrap. Waves from the falling bridge swamped and, in many cases, overturned the few small boats that had ventured out in the rain. Two dozen cars were floating—or sinking—in the roaring water.

And then, except for the faint screams, it was quiet.

"Oh my God," said Gloria, the only one of the group able to utter a sound.

*****

Peter Clark had only been in traffic for an hour. He got on at Exit 2, expecting a short run to the Sagamore bridge. It had been anything but. Crawling at a snail's pace was bad enough, but his two preschoolers had been screaming from the moment they woke up, and Peter was frazzled to the core. But finally the bridge was in sight—not only in sight, but probably a minute away.

Suddenly the ground shook and a series of muffled explosions was heard over the roar of the AC. A moment later the bridge was gone. Disappeared. He was too surprised to even begin to comprehend what had just happened.

Everything stopped. No one moved. Slowly, people opened their doors. It was too late to try to take the exit immediately before the bridge; he was already boxed in. Besides, in their haste to take the exit, a five-car pile-up had just occurred, blocking any chance for anyone else to make a break for it.

No, they were going to be stuck there for hours ... maybe longer. Just Peter, his wife, and two out-of-control children.

*****

At the Bourne Bridge, Steve Jones had just pissed off about a dozen other motorists, driving along the narrow shoulder of Route 28 to bypass the non-moving traffic. A couple of cars tried to straddle the line to prevent him from passing, but he made it by somehow. When he arrived at the Bourne rotary that funneled cars onto the bridge, he pushed his way into the traffic, ignoring the horns and swearing of the other drivers. Now he was on the bridge, slowly increasing his speed and feeling pretty pleased with himself. And then the bridge started to shake.

He heard some of the explosions, but didn't connect them to the shaking. He never would. A moment later he was free-falling toward the water, and three seconds after that he was dead.

*****

Anyone looking from the Bourne Bridge toward Buzzards Bay would have seen the final structure plummet into the canal—the train bridge. Cape Cod was effectively cut off from the rest of Massachusetts. Those still on the roads weren't going anywhere.

Their vacations had just been extended.

One Day Earlier.....

July 4th

Chapter 1

"All eyes are looking to the tropics, where Chad has officially become a hurricane. At the moment a weak Category 1, it is expected to rapidly intensify before hitting the coast of Florida tomorrow as a much stronger, but still Category 1, storm. Hurricane warnings have been posted for all of southeastern Florida, with Hurricane watches for central and northern Florida and southern Georgia. After striking Florida, the storm track has it moving a bit out to sea, then slowly lumbering its way up the East coast. Most of the computer models have it eventually turning inland and severely impacting the Northeast on Wednesday, particularly Cape Cod and the Islands, where the early season heat wave has warmed the ocean water sufficiently to support a hurricane. It's still too early to predict the exact path of the storm and its impact on New England, but stay tuned..." The Weather Channel

July 4th in the summer vacation capital of the Northeast, and Marcus Baldwin was bored. He had been following Seth Wakeby for a week, only to determine that he had to be the least interesting person on the face of the earth.

It was apparent that Wakeby wasn't there to celebrate. There were no cookouts, family get-togethers, or sun-bathing in his Independence Day. As it turned out, there would be fireworks, but of the unplanned variety.

In the three days Wakeby had been on the Cape, the man had only ventured from his Hyannis hotel room half a dozen times—mostly to fast food joints for meals. Fine dining wasn't his strong suit. This dearth of activity annoyed Marcus to no end. But it was the life he had chosen, and while it lacked the excitement and danger he was once used to, it was also nice to go to bed at night without having to hide a gun under his pillow.

However, this was frustrating. He was sure Wakeby was on the Cape to meet someone, but it hadn't happened. And there was no chance that the contact had eluded Marcus. He was way too good for that.

He had been investigating Wakeby for a week, first doing the computer background work, and now the legwork. The problem was, he wasn't exactly sure what he was supposed to find. Marcus usually took high-end cases. His P.I. business wasn't in a dingy storefront and he didn't follow people named Knuckles. He worked out of his modest home in a Boston suburb, with a second home/office in the mountains of Colorado. His business was word of mouth—the mouths belonging to CEOs and billionaires. But this job was turning out to be low end—really low end.

It had come from one of his best customers, who happened to be both a CEO *and* a billionaire. The man was bothered. Wakeby worked for him in a somewhat lowly capacity, that of driver and all around gofer. Lately, Wakeby had become secretive, bordering on sneaky. That wouldn't usually bother someone of his client's stature. After all, he could just fire the guy or make him someone else's responsibility. The problem with Wakeby was that he was the client's nephew, and he had promised his sister that he would keep Wakeby employed. "Families suck" was how he put it when he asked Marcus to look into it. "Never hire relatives." It wasn't a problem for Marcus in his business—he had no close relatives and no employees.

So he grudgingly agreed to check into it, and now he was paying the price. Families *did* suck. He hadn't found any discrepancies in Wakeby's finances, such as they were, or his phone records. He was big into phone sex, hence the lack of finances. The guy didn't seem to be into drugs. He liked beer and bought a lot of it. But to this point, Marcus had come up empty. The idea that Wakeby had come to the Cape to meet someone was his one slim possibility. If this didn't pan out, he was going to have to go back and inform his client that other than having questionable moral values, Seth Wakeby wasn't guilty of anything.

And yet, why would someone come to the Cape during the busiest week of the year and do nothing but stay in his hotel room? Not to mention that he was staying in a resort hotel in Hyannis during peak season. Having seen his finances, Marcus knew that Wakeby couldn't afford it. Add to the mix the fact that you don't just appear at a hotel on Cape Cod the first week of July and expect to get a room that night. He had to have reserved it at least weeks in advance, if not longer. All the signs pointed toward something illegal. He was meeting someone and that someone was paying the bill. Chances were, that someone was also late or had left the meeting time flexible. Wakeby had probably been told to "hang out and wait for a call."

There was a sandwich shop and a Dunkin Donuts across the street from the hotel. The employees at both places had come to know Marcus pretty well. Both establishments had a clear view of the hotel and Wakeby's parking spot, so when Marcus wasn't sitting in his car—moving to different places throughout the day so as not to arouse too much suspicion—he hung out in one of the two eateries. He portrayed himself as someone a little down on his luck, the kind of person who could spend hours in one of those places just to pass the time without really being noticed.

But he was reaching the end of his patience. So when, midway through the day on the 4th, Seth Wakeby emerged from the hotel and strode to his car with a purpose, Marcus uttered a barely audible "Thank God," and started his car. The job might finally be leading somewhere.

Wakeby's ten-year-old Toyota Corolla let out a little puff of smoke as it pulled out of the parking lot and turned left. Marcus followed at a safe distance. Another left by Wakeby put him on Rt. 28 heading toward Falmouth. The ride was excruciatingly slow, clogged with tourists, but made slower by some orange cones put there the day before by a road crew fixing a crack in the pavement. While sitting in Dunkin Donuts, Marcus had heard people complaining about the state of the roads and how the extreme prolonged heat wave was wreaking havoc with all of the post-winter pothole fixes.

A half hour later, Wakeby took a right on Rt. 130 in Mashpee, the midway point between Hyannis and Falmouth, then made a series of turns on back roads. With each turn, Marcus dropped further behind his quarry in an effort to avoid detection. Finally, Wakeby pulled down a dirt path leading to a remote cranberry bog. Seeing no other car waiting, Marcus circled through the neighborhood and parked on a side road that gave him a good view of the bog entrance but still left him somewhat inconspicuous.

He didn't need to wait long. A late model Nissan Altima—probably a rental—entered the bog road and pulled up close to Wakeby's Corolla. A tall man got out and waved to Wakeby. Marcus figured the man to be about 6'5" and was skinny as a rail. In his late thirties-early forties, he had a protruding Adam's apple—the young Clint Eastwood look. Marcus got out of his car, camera in hand, and crossed the street into the line of trees along the edge of the bog and out of sight of the two men. He found a position that afforded him a good view of the impending meet. But while his position was good for viewing, he wasn't close enough to hear more than the occasional word.

He took several shots of the new man, and of the two men together, and then stopped. Voices were being raised. The friendly encounter wasn't so friendly anymore. Marcus looked around at the nearby houses and saw no movement. People were all at the beach or other celebratory gatherings. He laid his camera on the ground and took out his gun from a holster clipped to his belt under his loose-fitting shirt. He and his Sig Sauer 9mm had been together a long time. He had other guns for different situations, including a Walther P-22, a smaller caliber gun for close-up jobs, but the Sig was his favorite. With only a slight hesitation, he reached into his pocket for the silencer that he had taken from his bag at the last minute, and screwed it onto the barrel. It had been a long time since he'd had need for a silencer—back in his previous life—but the muscle memory of screwing it on came as naturally as if he had just used it the day before.

The conversation was growing more heated and Marcus made his way closer to the men. He heard Wakeby say in a whiney voice, "But I did everything you asked. I'd never tell anyone. I'd be in as much trouble as you." Marcus couldn't hear the man's response, but it wasn't what Wakeby wanted to hear. "You owe me that money. I need that money. I thought we were friends." If anything, Wakeby's voice was getting whinier. The man said something else. If he'd been talking in a normal tone, Marcus would have heard him, but he was talking softly. That raised flags for Marcus. It brought back all kinds of memories of his dealings with professional hit men.

"So what are you going to do?" asked Wakeby. There was a tremor in his voice. "Kill me?"

Of course he was, thought Marcus. He balanced his gun on a tree trunk and aimed it at the man. He was now less than fifty feet away, an easy shot. He waited to see what the man would do. He didn't have to wait long.

"Sorry Seth." Marcus heard that one. The man pulled out a gun and Wakeby took a step back.

Marcus fired two shots a second apart. The gun made two loud pops. Unlike in the movies, silencers weren't really silent, they were just quieter than an unsuppressed gun. However, being July 4th, hopefully they would be dismissed as firecrackers. The first shot got the man in the side, spinning him around, and the second caught him in the heart. He dropped to the ground in front of a bewildered—and scared—Seth Wakeby.

Marcus emerged from the woods and lowered his gun.

Wakeby, by this time, was wild-eyed and had a wet spot growing on the front of his pants. He looked at Marcus, then down at the dead man, and back at Marcus again.

"Who are you?" It came out as barely more than a whisper.

"Today, I guess I'm your guardian angel." Marcus looked back up toward the houses. Still no activity. It would have been hard to see this spot clearly—a momentary advantage—but he would have to act quickly.

Marcus was now faced with a dilemma. He had just killed a man. Legally, as a P.I., he should call the cops. But questioning Wakeby would reveal who his uncle—and Marcus's client—was, and Marcus couldn't allow that. The confidentiality of his clients was sacred. He wasn't overly worried though. His former profession had allowed him a tremendous amount of leeway when it came to rules and laws, so stretching another one wouldn't bother him.

He looked at Wakeby, who had sunk to the ground, his whole body trembling. "Stay here," he ordered. Wakeby didn't move.

Marcus put on a pair of latex gloves—something he was never without—and searched the dead man's pockets for his keys. He went back to the man's car and moved it out of the middle of the dirt path and closer to the tree line. He went back to the man, took his wallet, and put it in his pocket. He would look through it later. He approached Wakeby.

"Who are you?" Wakeby asked again, shakily getting back to his feet.

"We have plenty of time for that. Here's what you're going to do. You're going to get back in your car and drive back to your hotel…"

"How did you…"

"Not now. Right now, you do as I say. No questions. I need you to move quickly. Think you can do that?"

Wakeby nodded dumbly.

"Then get back in your car and go. I'll follow in a few minutes and meet you there. Don't even think about going anywhere else. I can find you in a second. I've been watching you for days and I'm probably the only one who can keep you alive."

Marcus just threw in that last sentence. Frankly, he had no idea what was going on, but he figured that if one person wanted Wakeby dead, there were probably more who did as well.

"Move!"

Wakeby moved. He ran to his car, turned it around, and started up the path. Marcus held up his hand for Wakeby to stop. Wakeby rolled down his window.

"What's your room number?"

"211."

"I'll be there a few minutes after you. My name is Marcus Baldwin. I'll knock and let you know it's me. Don't open the door for anyone else. Also, take your time. Don't speed. Don't give the cops any reason to stop you. Got it?"

Wakeby nodded and took off.

Marcus went back into the woods and found his shell casings, then went over to the body and searched it further. No cell phone. Interesting. He checked the car. Again nothing. He'd been there long enough. It was time to go. He took one last look and headed back to his car.

Well, he thought, at least he was no longer bored.

Chapter 2

Sara Cross had been watching the guy for an hour. Her instincts told her that he was up to no good, and her instincts were good. No, her instincts were superb. The problem was, all she could do was observe. And then what? And then nothing. There was nobody on Cape Cod who would believe anything she said. So why was she bothering to watch the guy? Maybe, she figured, old habits just die hard.

A former MP in the Marines, Sara had done her job well, so well that she was the recipient of a fistful of commendations. When she had had her fill of life in the Marines, she applied to police forces around the country, receiving numerous offers for her services. She had settled on the town of Barnstable, which included—of Kennedy fame—Hyannis. The choice wasn't hard. She was a New England girl who had spent many summer vacations on the Cape. Barnstable offered her a bit of excitement due to its fairly high crime rate. As in so many areas, the drug trade had overtaken the Cape in recent years, and the sordid underbelly of the vacation paradise was hard to resist for someone with her skills.

Now approaching forty, she had risen from patrol officer to lead homicide detective in ten short years, winning the accolades of fellow officers and her higher-ups. Her conviction rate was amazing. She had her career and her future set. And then it had all come crashing down.

A year earlier, she began having problems with her boss, Captain Chandler. It was the usual stuff a female in a predominantly male profession had to deal with. He had come on to her and she had rejected his advances. His male ego took a major hit and he resented her for it. From that point on, her life there had become hellish. She complained to the chief, and while he investigated, he found nothing to support her claims. Her boss had covered his tracks well. But Sara was a fighter and wasn't going to give up that easily—the Marines had taught her that.

Chandler's vindictiveness, however, knew no bounds. Six months later, a stash of coke was found in her car. Chandler said he had received a tip that Sara was dealing on the side. He made sure he investigated it by the book so there would be no questions asked. But Sara knew he had orchestrated the whole thing. He included the chief in the process and made sure someone else did the search. When confronted with the findings, Sara said she was being framed by Chandler. Based on her reputation, everything was done to prove her innocence, but in the end, nothing could be found to support her claim. As honest and thorough as she was, her boss was just as thorough and totally dishonest. He had won the war. While they didn't convict her, the evidence was more than enough to get her fired.

Sara had spent the last six months trying to figure out her life. Police work was her passion, and now she was a pariah. No police department in the country would hire her with that stain on her record. When she ran across her former fellow officers, some would look the other way rather than having to acknowledge her. This one man had shattered her life, and as much as she wanted revenge, she knew it wasn't going to happen. But in the six months since her firing, she still had no idea what she was going to do with the rest of her life. She owned a condo, but if she was able to sell it, she wouldn't have a chance of breaking even, and she was going through her savings faster than she thought possible, with no income source in sight. She had hit rock bottom.

Now she was at her storage locker, cleaning out the last of her belongings. She could no longer afford the monthly expense, so what she didn't donate she would have to fit into her small condo. The guy she was watching had a locker down the row from her. What had caught her attention was the gun in his belt when he leaned over to pick up a box. There were all kinds of valid reasons for carrying a gun. He wasn't a cop on the Cape—she would recognize any of them—but he could simply be a citizen with a carry permit. But there was just something about his manner that bothered her. He was loading his cart with boxes of all shapes and sizes, but none had any markings. There were probably a hundred valid reasons for that too, but there was just something … something that didn't feel right. He seemed to be going to great lengths to appear innocuous. Someone who is truly innocuous doesn't look the part, he just is.

She had most of her stuff strewn about in front of the locker as she sorted it out. Part of the reason was to give her some space to go through it, and part was to be able to watch him surreptitiously. Why? It wasn't like she could do anything. In fact, there was a part of her that purposely didn't want to do anything. A big "fuck you" to her former employer. Still…

He was done. He locked up the now empty locker—she had noticed that it was almost empty during her last trip to her pickup—and walked up the corridor. She had a decision: Follow or ignore. She had timed her own work so that she finished a few moments before him, so she knew the answer to that one.

She followed him out, dragging a box behind her. He knew she was behind him but didn't offer to help. When they got outside, he loaded the last couple of items onto the truck and locked the back, then got into the cab. It was an old U-Haul truck that had long ago been put out to pasture. The U-Haul logo was painted over with white, but she could still see it beneath the paint.

Follow? Sara asked herself. No need. He only drove the truck across the parking lot away from the loading dock and into a real parking space. She was puzzled now. She very slowly loaded her pickup with the last of her items, all the while keeping an eye on the guy. He got out of the truck, opened a flip phone, and pressed one key. Obviously a stored number. He said a couple of words and hung up.

Sara was deep in the back of the pickup fiddling with nothing in particular, with just enough of a space to see him without him being aware of it. He looked around, especially at Sara's truck, then let the phone drop from his hand. It hit the ground and he stepped on it, grinding it with his foot to make sure it was good and crushed. Then he picked up the remains and threw them in a dumpster. He walked over to a late model Altima—clearly a rental, she observed—and started the engine. By then she was already in the cab of her pickup starting her own engine. He backed out of his spot and made his way to the road, turning right out of the parking lot.

She waited. She knew the roads around there as well as anybody, so she wasn't concerned about losing him. Slowly she backed out. When she thought he was far enough down the road, she followed. He got onto Rt. 28 toward Falmouth. When he reached the town of Mashpee, he took a side road, then another, followed by a few more. She was able to stay way behind. She knew this area like the back of her hand.

He was now in a neighborhood that had only one road in and out, so she waited before following him in. When she had given it enough time, she drove in. His car wasn't in any of the driveways, or parked on the side of the road. Suddenly she knew. He was heading for the cranberry bog. When she got close, she pulled into a small side street and turned off her engine. She got out of her car and walked around the corner. There was a car, a Nissan Pathfinder, parked on the road out of sight of the bog. Somehow, it seemed out of place, but she wasn't sure why. Instincts.

Why was she doing this? Once a cop always a cop? But she wasn't. Not anymore. She had absolutely no reason to be there. It was sheer curiosity.

She saw her guy get out of his car next to a crappy old Corolla. A young guy was standing there. Prematurely balding and pudgy, he didn't seem to belong with the guy she'd followed. Clint Eastwood! That's who her guy reminded her of. That had been bugging her from the moment she'd first seen him. Wait, there was a third guy. He was just going into the bushes from the road. She watched him set down a bag, pull out a camera, and start taking pictures. A Fed? A P.I.?

Definitely not a local cop.

Voices were being raised. The guy in the bushes didn't like the turn of events. He set down his camera and pulled out a gun ... and something else. A silencer! This was heavy-duty stuff. And there was nothing she could do. In addition to her job, she had lost her license to carry. She still had a gun, but it was locked in a safe in her condo.

Clint Eastwood pulled out a gun and pointed it at pudgy guy, but that was as far as he got. The guy in the bushes double-tapped him and he went down. She could see that pudgy guy had wet himself. Bushes guy stepped into the open and was talking to pudgy guy. They didn't seem to know each other. Bushes was ordering Pudgy to do something. Bushes was a decent-looking guy—not tall, about 5'10", and well built, with slightly graying hair. Maybe fifty? He looked like he kept in shape. He moved Clint Eastwood's car, then said something to Pudgy.

Pudgy guy got into his junk box and took off. Bushes guy stayed around a bit longer. He went back into the bushes and collected his camera and was looking around. Shell casings! The guy was a professional—but a professional what? He headed up from the bog toward the Pathfinder. Her instincts were correct. She went over to her pickup and got in, but didn't start the engine. He looked around before getting into the Pathfinder. She saw him look hard at the pickup. She knew what it was. Her car wasn't there when he first arrived. Definitely a pro. He got into his car and took off. She started her engine. She had no choice now. She had to follow him.

What had she gotten herself into?

Chapter 3

Marcus had time to think on his way back to Hyannis. It wasn't a drug deal. Nothing changed hands. Wakeby thought he was meeting the guy to get paid, so obviously Wakeby's role was completed. Clint Eastwood must have felt that Wakeby was a liability, and to be willing to kill someone to silence him meant that this wasn't some minor job. Wakeby had gotten himself involved in something way over his head. It was time to inform his client.

He dialed the number. He had access to the client's private line, one of the stipulations in taking a job. None of his clients objected, as his services were crucial to them.

"Hi Marcus, what have you found out?"

"I'm afraid your nephew is involved in some deep shit."

"How deep?"

"I just killed a guy who was about to kill Seth."

His client let out a long, low sigh. "Holy crap." There was silence. Marcus let it sink in.

"So what's he involved in?"

"No clue yet. I told him to go back to his hotel and wait for me."

"Think he will?"

"Seth isn't the shiniest penny in the pile, but he'd have to be dumb as a post not to."

It showed Marcus's status with his employers that he could talk straight with them, even if he said things they didn't want to hear.

"Yeah, he gets his brains from his father. It's why my sister divorced him. You never met a stupider man." He went silent again, then said, "You think there are others involved?"

"I would definitely bet on it. What I have to determine is how much danger Seth is in. Will there be others coming after him or will they cut and run if they hear about the other guy's death?"

"When are you bringing him back?"

"Tomorrow. I'm going to stay with him in his hotel tonight to see if anyone else tries to contact him."

"Okay, I know you'll keep in touch. Hey Marcus, do me a favor?"

"Yeah?"

"Smack him over the head with a baseball bat. Put us all out of our misery."

Marcus smiled. "Gladly. Talk to you later."

He pulled into a parking spot at the hotel, and sat in his car and waited. He knew what he was waiting for, and there it was, the pickup he'd seen near the bog. The driver was good at tailing, but not good enough. Marcus had picked up the tail five minutes earlier.

Marcus got out of his Pathfinder and walked into the lobby of the hotel, and immediately out the back entrance. He walked around the side of the building and peeked around the corner. Oh how nice, he thought. The pickup was parked in the end spot closest to him. The spaces were angled so that the front of the truck was facing away from him. The truck's engine was off and the windows were open so the driver could catch a breeze—what little there was. The driver was still in the truck. Marcus could see his hands on the steering wheel. The only odd thing about the scene was the stack of boxes and other items in the back of the pickup. Pretty much household items, it looked like the person was moving. So why was the guy following him?

He pulled his gun out and hid it beside his leg, and then he moved. He was at the passenger-side window in three strides, too fast for the driver to react if he saw him in the side mirror.

Correction: She. Marcus put his gun in the window and pointed it at her. He was impressed by her reaction. Instead of screaming or jumping, she left her hands on the wheel, lowered her head in defeat, and just said, "Shit."

"Mind telling me why you are following me?"

She was cool. "You know, you don't have the silencer on your gun anymore. You shoot me and everyone will hear it. They'll catch you in no time."

"I'm pretty good at staying hidden. Besides, I don't think I'll have to kill you. Who are you?"

"Who are you?"

"I asked first."

"Sara."

"I need more than that. Why were you following me?"

"I was curious. I haven't actually witnessed a homicide in progress before today. Seen a lot of homicides, but always after the fact. Although, my guess is you were protecting the other guy. You a P.I.?"

He had to tread lightly. He reached in and pulled out his

license and showed it to her. "Marcus Baldwin. I'm guessing you're a cop, the way you talk."

"Ex-cop. Homicide. I was following the guy you killed. Don't ask me why. It was none of my business anymore. I just didn't like what I saw. Do you mind putting the gun away?"

He holstered it. Marcus had spent a career making split-second judgments about people, and he couldn't think of any that he had gotten wrong. Not only did he believe her, but since she had been following Clint Eastwood, she might actually be able to fill in some of the blanks. "So you saw me shoot the guy, but you didn't call the cops. Any particular reason?"

"A lot of particular reasons." Silence. That was all he was going to get for now on that subject. "Still none of my business, but would you mind telling me what's going on?" she said.

"I don't know what's going on, but I'm about to find out. I still know nothing about you, though."

"Fair enough. Sara Cross. Former chief homicide detective here in Barnstable. I was unceremoniously canned about six months ago, reasons for which are none of your business. I was cleaning crap out of my storage locker when I saw the dead guy loading a truck from a locker close to mine. Something wasn't right about it, so I followed him."

"Where's the truck?"

"That was the other odd thing. He filled the truck, then left it at the storage facility and took the car you saw him in."

"And why didn't you call it in when you saw me kill him?"

"As I said, a lot of reasons, none that concern you. Besides, I knew there was more to this story and I wanted to see what it was. How about you?"

"I was hired to find out what the other guy had gotten himself into. He's an employee and relative of my client. The killing part came as a surprise."

"So I'll ask the same question: Why didn't you call it in after you killed him. It is your responsibility, after all. You know that, right?"

He gave her a look to tell her that he knew exactly what he was doing.

"Never mind," she said.

"Seeing as how we are both involved in this, would you like to come along and see what Mr. Seth Wakeby has to say for himself?"

"I've gone this far. I may as well see it through," said Sara. "Hopefully he changed his pants."

Chapter 4

He had, but he wasn't yet calm. Marcus was pretty sure this experience would stay with him for a long time. He answered the door at Marcus's knock, but only after Marcus had identified himself. When Marcus and Sara entered the room, he slumped into a chair.

Marcus wasted no time. "Seth, this is Sara Cross. She's helping me. I was hired by your uncle to find out what's going on with you, so my question is simple: What's going on?"

Instead of answering, he put his head down to his chest and began to cry. They gave him a minute, then Marcus repeated his question.

"I have no fucking clue what's going on," he finally said. "I was just meeting a guy to get paid."

"For what?"

"A job."

"Maybe I should've let him kill you. Try it again."

"If I tell you, you'll tell my uncle."

"That's kind of how it works. He pays me to find some information, and when I do, I give it to him."

"He'll fire me."

"An hour ago you were almost dead."

His head went back down into his hands. "Shit, shit, shit,

shit."

"Still waiting," said Marcus.

"I like your bedside manner," said Sara.

"One of my strong points." He looked back at Wakeby. "Now!"

"Okay, okay." He lifted his head. His eyes were red and puffy. "You know my uncle owns a lot of different businesses, right?"

Marcus nodded and turned to Sara. "All legal," he said. "In case you were wondering."

"I'm not a cop anymore. I really don't care."

"I do. I don't work for crooks. One of my rules."

"As you know," continued Wakeby, "Some of them are retail, including a small chain of electronics stores. When I'm not driving my uncle, I work in the warehouse. He's got a whole mess of phones, you know, the disposable kind. So I took some. They were the old flip phone type. I didn't figure my uncle would even notice."

"How many?" asked Sara.

"Sixty."

"Who did you sell them to?" asked Marcus.

"Just a guy."

"He bought all of them?"

"Yeah ... except that I guess he had no intention of paying me."

"Did you find him or did he find you?"

"He found me. An old friend of mine put them onto me. He was looking for phones, and the friend knew what I did for a living, so he hooked us up. I figured he was going to re-sell them on eBay or someplace."

"You don't try to kill someone over stolen items on eBay. You kill someone to shut them up. You said 'them.' More than one?"

"That's usually what 'them' means," answered Seth in the most smart-alecky voice he could muster.

Marcus slapped him hard across the face and Seth fell off the chair.

Seth crawled back on the chair and looked at Marcus with a defiant expression. "I'll tell my uncle you did that. I'm sure that wasn't part of the job. He'll fire your ass."

Marcus hit him again. "Actually," he said, "your uncle wanted me to use a baseball bat." After Seth had once again crawled into his seat, Marcus said, "Let's get something straight. I have very little tolerance for bullshit. When I want an answer, I expect to get it. You are in no position to get cocky. You'd be dead now if it wasn't for me, so let's start this again. How many people besides the dead guy?"

Seth looked at the floor. "I don't know. My friend is one. The guy I met to hand over the phones was with this guy. So there were at least two more of them, but he also said something about his friends, so I gathered there were more than that."

"When did this happen?"

"About a month ago. After that, he called me a few more times, asking me to get him wire, duct tape, various types of little electronic shit ... stuff like that."

"Why did you come here?"

"About a week ago, he told me to come down to the Cape and check in here. He said the room would be waiting under my name. He said he might have more use for my services, then said there would be a big payday in it for me at the end."

"End of what," asked Sara.

"Don't know, but they said to stay here and that they would contact me. He warned me that it might be a few days. Today, he called and said that they wouldn't need anything else and to meet his friend to get paid."

"You didn't get suspicious when they wanted the meeting in such a remote place?"

"Not really. He was always pretty mysterious about everything. I just figured it was more of the same."

"And you have no idea what they needed everything for?" asked Marcus.

"None."

"I know what they needed the phones for," said Sara. "Short-term use. Probably just a few times and out. The dead guy dropped a phone and ground it into the pavement before he got into his car to come and meet Seth. He threw the pieces into a dumpster."

"We should check out that truck," said Marcus. "This could be a simple drug trafficking deal, or something else."

"You're thinking terrorism," said Sara matter-of-factly.

"Definitely possible." He turned to Seth. "You stay here. Like before, you don't open your door to anyone except me."

"Okay."

When they were outside, Marcus said, "You still in? I could go look at it myself."

"For six months I've been driving myself crazy with boredom. I need this."

"Let's take my car," said Marcus. "Yours looks like the Beverly Hillbillies truck with all that stuff in the back."

"Sorry, this wasn't in my plans for the day."

The storage facility was only a few minutes away.

"Why were you canned from the police force?"

"I said before that it was none ... oh, never mind. My boss hit on me, didn't like my response, and made it his goal in life to make me suffer for it. He planted drugs in my car. My word against his. You can see who won. Turn here. It's on our left."

Marcus pulled into the lot.

"Gone," said Sara. "Truck's not here."

"Not a good sign," said Marcus. "We're not dealing with drugs."

"So terrorism."

"It fits. The disposable cells, the wire and electronics, and the attempted murder of Seth point that way. And the different shaped boxes you saw being loaded on the truck. If it was drugs, the boxes would be similar in shape and size."

"I don't know why, but I got the impression that cleaning out that locker was the end of something. The way he threw the boxes into the truck made me think they were leftover pieces."

"Supplies for explosives, possibly."

"And the target?" asked Sara. "The president?"

President Landau was on Martha's Vineyard for his summer vacation. He and his family had arrived on the 2nd and were planning to stay the week. News of the possible impending hurricane had reporters questioning whether he would be heading back to Washington early.

"I can't imagine. Security is so tight between here and the Vineyard, it would be next to impossible for them to carry out an attack over there. If I had to guess, I'd say it would be something on the Cape."

"Next step?" asked Sara.

"Maybe the FBI can put two and two together from the dead guy." He pulled out a cell phone and dialed. "Blocked number and totally untraceable, as are the bullets in the dead guy."

"I'm assuming you have an interesting background," said Sara.

Before he could answer, his phone call went through. "Federal Bureau of Investigation. How may I direct your call?"

"You can just listen. I know this is being taped. There is a dead body by a cranberry bog in Mashpee, on Cape Cod." Sara gave him the street name and he passed it on. "He has two bullets in him. It's a strong possibility that he is a member of a terrorist organization, and there is evidence that they are planning something soon on the Cape. That is all the information I have, but I suggest that someone take it very seriously and try to make a connection. His driver's license gave the name George Olson, but I'm sure it's a fake. You are also looking for a seventeen foot former U-Haul truck painted white. Also, look at unit…" He looked at Sara, who told him the storage business name and unit number, which he repeated. "You might want to check it for traces of explosive. That's all I have for you." He hung up.

"Time to go babysit Seth for the night. If no one makes contact, I'll take him back to his uncle tomorrow and wash my hands of him."

"And the possible link to terrorism?"

"The FBI has the resources. They know as much as we do now."

Sara wrote something on a piece of paper and handed it to

Marcus. "My phone number. If anything comes up tonight and you need help, just give me a call."

He gave her an amused look and she turned beet red. "I know how that sounded. It's not what I meant."

"I know. I will. Here's my card. You have nothing to gain from this. At least I'm getting paid. What's your angle?"

"Boredom. Total boredom."

Chapter 5

"Where the hell is he?" Mason looked at his watch for the fifteenth time in the space of an hour. "He should have been back long ago."

"I tried calling him a few minutes ago," said Holt. "No answer."

"You did what?"

"I figured a quick call wouldn't hurt anything."

Mason gave him a withering look. "You screw up one more time and I'll strap you to one of the bridges myself. Listen up all of you. I know we all come from a generation that can't live without our cell phones, but I've gone to great lengths to make sure we leave no trail whatsoever. That means cell phones are used for quick calls to me—and only me—with coded messages. After three calls they are destroyed. Why is that such a difficult concept?"

There was silence. Mason looked around him at the motley crew that made up his organization. Organization, ha! It was a ragtag group of young rednecks that he recruited from survivalist groups all over the country. It took him months, but he finally settled on the six pawns he needed for his scheme. They were all under the ridiculous notion that they were the root of a movement that would eventually take over the government. Stupid, all of them. All of them except Tanner, the missing man. Tanner was Mason's partner in crime. The two of them thought up the whole thing two years earlier. It was Tanner's idea to recruit the disposable fanatics. Get the right people with the right skills, feed them some bullshit propaganda to appeal to their misguided patriotism, and when it was all over he and Tanner would be long gone and the morons would be left trying to explain their actions to the authorities—if they weren't dead. At least, that was the plan that he had worked out with Tanner. What Tanner didn't know was that he was also a pawn. Mason only needed him for his organizational skills, his ability to help him procure the items they needed, and his help in recruiting the morons.

And now Tanner was gone. It was supposed to be a simple job—do away with Wakeby. Tanner chose to do it because he knew he was the only one who could point a gun at someone and actually pull the trigger. Fanatical as their hired hands were, Mason and Tanner seriously doubted that any one of them had the ability to kill someone. Well, that would all change tomorrow, although it was a hell of a lot easier to kill someone remotely than face-to-face. To these guys, it would be little more than a video game.

Tanner was different. With his background, doing away with Wakeby would be a walk in the park. When he was younger Tanner was involved in all kinds of covert jobs and killing was a way of life. How hard could it be to take out a scared guy who possessed absolutely no survival skills whatsoever? But obviously something had happened. This wasn't the end of the world. In fact, if somehow Tanner had gotten himself killed, all the better. Tanner's job was over. It would save Mason from having to do away with him. That was going to be the tricky part anyway.

Right now it was time to sit back and wait. Everything was in place for the next day. If Danielson and Packer, the explosives guys, did their job right, everything should go off like clockwork—literally—and the next step of the plan would take place the following day. Let the panic kick in tomorrow. The fun would really start on Monday.

There was only one thing that could screw up their plan—Hurricane Chad. Whoever heard of a hurricane this early in the season in New England? He'd have to watch it carefully. They had worked on this plan for two years. They had every base covered. They had backup plans, and backup plans to the backup plans.

They didn't have a plan for a hurricane.

July 5th

Chapter 6

Several hours before the bridges collapsed into the Cape Cod Canal on July 5th, Hurricane Chad hit Miami-Dade, Broward, and Palm Beach counties in southern Florida in the early morning, with a ferocity they hadn't seen in a storm in many years. The weather reports predicting it would hit as a Category 1 were very wrong; it intensified quickly before reaching land and hit as a Category 3. The devastation was complete. The residents of south Florida did everything they were told in order to prepare, but it wasn't enough. The smart ones had already set aside their supplies of drinking water and non-perishable food at the beginning of hurricane season. Really smart folks also had plywood for their windows, and fuel for generators. Those who preferred to wait until the last minute stood in line for hours at the gas pumps, the grocery stores, and the Home Depots.

As forecasters suddenly found Chad increasing in strength and magnitude, residents were urged to leave the area and head north and away from the coast. Few took the advice. But it wasn't belligerence or even laziness on their part. They just didn't have the time. They were expecting a Category 1, not a Category 3. In fact, the change in forecast took everybody by surprise, including the forecasters themselves. There was very little to indicate that the sudden strengthening would take place until it was too late.

As a result, the death toll mounted quickly. Whole trailer park communities were flattened. Houses and condo units made of concrete fared well structurally, but flooding did the job the wind couldn't, making many of the homes uninhabitable. Trees by the thousands were uprooted and countless numbers of cars were crushed. Drivers stupid enough to be on the roads quickly hit flooded sections, stalling their cars and putting them in the direct path of the massive wind-driven floods. People drowned trying to escape their partially submerged cars.

When the falling of the Cape Cod bridges was announced a few hours later, it had little to no impact in southern Florida. The reason for this was two-fold: For many, their lives were already in shambles due to the storm; and for others, the widespread power outages completely isolated them from the outside world.

The storm exited quickly, but not before the damage was done. It left behind hundreds dead, thousands of ruined lives, and millions in property damage.

As devastating as it was, however, forecasters huddled around computer printouts and radar screens were even more frightened for the future. The little bit of strength it lost by making landfall, it quickly gained again as it headed north. It was predicted to miss most of the rest of the coastline—the Outer Banks being the exception as it brushed by—allowing it to gather strength and develop into one of the worst hurricanes in history. The Outer Banks was already in the process of being evacuated, so the concern of the experts was its next landing spot as it eventually veered back toward land—toward Cape Cod and the possibility of a direct hit. And now, because of the terrorist attack, evacuating the people would be nearly impossible. The numbers of dead in Florida from Chad would be a drop in the bucket compared to the final tally on Cape Cod.

Chapter 7

Ann Lawrence watched the receding tail lights of the Truro police car. This visit was a pleasant one, but she knew the next one wouldn't be so friendly. Officer Parker was just doing his job. She knew that. In the event of an impending storm, the local police visited all of the outlying homes, in case they hadn't heard the warnings. Of course she had heard them. She may live in the boonies, but she knew what was happening in the world. Hurricane Chad was coming. It was the big news on all of the Boston stations. People living near the water were being encouraged to seek shelter inland. It was being suggested that visitors to the Cape end their vacations early and go home. That was the best news she had heard in a long time. Good riddance. All they did was clog the roads and make it impossible to get groceries.

In the forty years she had lived in her house on the dunes, she had dealt with hurricanes, nor'easters, and blizzards, and only once—her first year there—did she let someone convince her to go to an evacuation center. What a mistake! Screaming kids, an overwhelmingly stench of body odor permeating the place, and the need for people to babble incessantly. After that, every time the police came to warn her, she thanked them graciously, but said she had no intention of leaving her house.

They were upset, but it was her house and her life and they couldn't tell her what to do.

The last hurricane was Bob, back in '91, which she came through just fine. But she had an added incentive not to let Chad drive her out. Chad was the name of her husband, the one she threw out more than forty years ago. His name was appropriate, because it rhymed with what he was; a cad. When she was still married to him and would have a day out with her friends, one would always ask how Chad the Cad was. It was funny at first, until he lived up to his name and slept with one of the friends. Ann kicked his ass out faster than he could say, "It didn't mean anything." That was when she stopped meeting her friends for lunch, and about the time she bought the place on the dunes.

You could still get beachfront property pretty cheaply back then. She had a little money from an inheritance, and bought the place with the intention of working on her art. She had already begun to build a name for herself with her paintings and decided she would give herself two years in Truro to make it a venture she could live on. If not, she would head back to Boston and get a real job. Back then, Provincetown, Truro, and the rest of the Outer Cape was full of artists who lived the storybook life, owning their own artist shacks. Sadly, she thought, all of those "shacks"—those that were still there—were now worth a fortune, and most of the artists had sold them. Living there was no longer cheap, and artists who flocked to Provincetown were shocked at the cost to "live the dream." Ann was lucky. Her art caught on, and for many years had been providing a good living.

So no hurricane named Chad was going to drive her away.

She wasn't stupid though. She would do everything she needed to make her house secure. Now that she was eighty, it wasn't quite as easy as it once was, but she knew the routine. She had the plywood in the shed for the windows, and she would pull in all of her chairs and assorted junk from outside. Over the years, she had had a fair amount of work done on the place to make it stronger than the average dune cottage, so she wasn't worried. She was also a good 200 yards from the beach. It would have to be one hell of a storm to bring the water up that far.

The phone rang. No need to guess who that would be. Her niece Marie would be checking in on her. This would be fight number one. Although not her daughter, Marie was almost a daughter to her. Marie had spent a lot of time with her when she was young, often visiting Ann for weeks at a time during summer break from school. She had picked up Ann's love of art, and had become something of a sculptor. As Marie got older, married, and started a family, they didn't see each other as much, but the closeness was still there. They talked on the phone or on Skype several times a month. This phone call, however, wasn't going to be easy.

"Hi Ann." She had begun calling Ann by her name from an early age, at Ann's urging. No "auntie" for her.

"Hello dear. I know why you are calling, and you know my answer."

"But they are saying that this is going to be a big one, and it's aimed right at the Cape."

"They always say it's going to be the big one. How many times have we heard the term "storm of the century," and it fizzles out?"

"I think this one is different."

"Has that hunk from the Weather Channel, Jim Cantore, come yet? That's always a good sign."

She heard her niece sigh. "I don't know Ann, but I'm really afraid this time…" She tailed off.

"Marie, are you still there?"

"Hold on." Ann could hear the TV in the background, and then an "Oh … my … God" under Marie's breath. "Ann, are you watching this?"

"I don't watch daytime TV. What is it?"

All she heard was another "Oh my God."

"Marie, you're scaring me. What's happening?"

Marie got on the line. She was crying now. "The bridges. The bridges are down."

"What are you talking about?"

Marie tried to compose herself. "The bridges to the Cape, all of them. They've all fallen down! They all came down at the same time. They suspect terrorists. A lot of people are dead. All those people stuck on the Cape, with a hurricane coming. What are they going to do? What are you going to do?"

Ann knew what she had to do—get to Stop and Shop before the hordes converged on it. She hung up with a distraught Marie and went to her closet where she kept a revolver. She put it in her pocketbook as she left the house.

She was thinking one thing. All hell was about to break loose!

Chapter 8

Dead silence. Almost. Every few minutes a fire truck or ambulance would scream by, heading to the bridge on the wrong side of the road—the only side that was passable—but for the most part, it was silence. An unnerving, frightening silence. It had been ten minutes since the bridge had gone down and drivers all along Route 6 had turned off their engines and gotten out of their cars. Smoke and dust still hung in the air. The jokes about the highway being a parking lot on a Sunday had become reality.

Finally, people began to talk. Theories were being bandied about, everything from an earthquake, to the poor infrastructure of the roads and bridges, to terrorism. Mostly terrorism. Radios were turned up to hear the latest updates. But there weren't any updates, just the same news being reported over and over. All three bridges connecting Cape Cod to the mainland had gone down. Hundreds were presumed dead and a terrorist attack was the most likely cause. More news when it became available.

The time for mourning had passed. It was time for action. All along the highway drivers started their cars and were turning across the median onto the opposite lanes to head away from the bridge. For a long stretch of Route 6, trees separated the eastbound and westbound lanes, so the crossover could only happen in designated areas, adding to the near impossibility of it all. Voices were raised as drivers in the right lane had to wait for drivers in the left lane to cross over, and then had to deal with other drivers cutting them off in their haste to turn around. For many, they could see the futility of it all and just abandoned their cars altogether and started walking, and in some cases, running. Where they were running to was somewhat unknown. What had been a quiet, almost reverent scene a few minutes earlier was now one of chaos.

No police cars arrived. Those that weren't at the bridges were trying to keep order in the towns, where people crammed the police station parking lots looking for answers or had thought ahead and were flooding the supermarkets for supplies.

*****

At the Shoot Zone, a gun store on the outskirts of Hyannis, owner Rodney Sinclair ushered his two customers out the minute he heard the news on his police band radio. No loss, they were window shopping anyway. He was smart enough to know what was coming next—a run on the gun store. It would be a mob scene. Everyone would come, each looking for a gun and/or ammo and he couldn't sell to them. He could only sell to Mass residents with valid permits. There would be no way most of those looking for weapons would have Mass licenses. There were just too many tourists on the Cape, not to mention local residents who shouldn't be within ten feet of a gun.

He could see where this would go. It would start out

calmly enough, but when people heard that he couldn't sell them weapons, it would get ugly. He could either sell people guns who had no legal right to own them, which would get him in massive trouble with the authorities, or he could just throw open the doors and watch his stock walk out the door, which would result in financial ruin. Two lose-lose scenarios.

So he closed up shop, locking the doors and pulling the bars over the doors and windows. And then he sat in a dark, quiet corner, gun in hand, waiting for the onslaught.

*****

The Barnstable Police headquarters was no different than anywhere else on the Cape—chaos reigned. The chief of police was on vacation in Montana, which left Captain Bryan Chandler in charge. In his twenty-five years on the job, he had never experienced anything like this. The phones were ringing off the hook, the line of terrified civilians spilled out into the parking lot, and his own officers were in and out of the station, looking for guidance.

Guidance wasn't Chandler's strong suit. Technically, he was a good cop. As a beat officer he always had good reviews from his superiors, leading to him becoming a detective at an early age. His arrest record was exceptional in his years as a detective. Unbeknownst to his colleagues though, he often cut corners and was even capable of planting evidence when the need arose. Eventually he was made captain, a perfect example of the Peter Principle. He was not cut out to be a leader of others and found it harder to cut the corners he was once so good at.

The low point of his career was the Sara Cross episode. He made a major mistake with her, and if he could take it back, he would. She was a good cop. No, she was a great cop, one of the best he had ever seen. She was also honest to a fault. The thought of her ever planting evidence like he did was ridiculous. He envied her for that quality. She was able to close out her cases based solely on her abilities. Chandler never resented her for that. In fact, he admired her for it—deeply admired her. In a way, he even found it sexy, which is why he made his mistake with her. Why he could even think that she would be attracted to him was beyond him ... now. At the time though, he was so obsessed with her that he was able to delude himself into thinking she might be interested.

When she turned him down, it devastated him and it angered him. Most of all, he was embarrassed. If he had bowed out gracefully it would have blown over. Sara would have moved on. All he had to do was apologize to her and he couldn't even do that. His manhood was threatened. For weeks after the rejection he couldn't think of anything but revenge, eventually leading to his planting of the drugs in her car.

Cross was fired and ostracized. In reality, he knew that very few of her fellow officers believed that she was capable of dealing drugs. He wasn't even sure the chief believed it. But the fact was, Chandler had never been caught when he planted evidence as a detective, so there was no reason he would've been caught this time ... and he hadn't. But things hadn't been the same in the department since her firing. He had lost the respect of his officers, and he knew it. Lately, he had considered retirement. Looking around him now at the bedlam, he wished he had gone through with it.

"Captain, we've gotta do something. It's all gotten out of hand." It was Scarputo, one of his senior officers. The guy wasn't scared, he was just overwhelmed by it all. Well, thought Chandler, who could blame him? Scarputo was also one of the many who blamed Chandler for the Sara Cross situation. "We've gotta get these people away from the station so we can do our jobs."

"Suggestions are welcome."

"Get on a bullhorn. Tell these people to go home. Tell them to gather supplies. Whatever. Tell them something to get them out of here."

Scarputo was right. Chandler had to do something. He looked around at some of the younger officers who had gathered. He saw fear in their faces. He had to do something for their sakes. Ironically, the person he needed most now was Sara Cross. She was always calm, and possessed a massive amount of common sense. Well, that ship had sailed and it was his fault. Nothing he could do about it now. He heard Scarputo taking the responsibility himself and making the announcement to the crowd to gather supplies and go home. It had two effects, neither one positive. The first was the panic of the locals who suddenly realized that they were wasting their time at the police station. It resulted in a series of fender benders as they fought to get themselves out of the parking lot. Two more accidents—more serious this time—occurred on the road when the drivers escaping the parking lot ran out of patience with the traffic and tried to force their way into the flow. It resulted in the parking lot being blocked and the eastbound lane of the road becoming even more clogged.

The second result was an uprising of tourists who had

already left their rentals for the week and now had nowhere to go. As one, they demanded that the police help them find alternate housing. When Scarputo explained that the police were being stretched to the limits and couldn't help in that area, some of the more hot-headed in the crowd expressed their anger by swearing and screaming at him. Scarputo knew that physical conflict couldn't be far behind.

Chandler watched from the window. If it's this bad now, he thought, only a couple of hours into the crisis, what's it going to be like in a week, with the stores cleaned out? There were about a half a million people on the Cape. How in the world would the authorities get supplies here? He could only imagine a total breakdown of society. And that was without factoring a hurricane into the equation.

"We're fucked," he said to himself.

Chapter 9

It should have been a run-of-the-mill trip. For many, it meant the end of their vacation. For others, it was just a trip on the ferry from the Vineyard to the Cape for the day. For all, it was the beginning of a nightmare.

The ferry from Martha's Vineyard to Woods Hole was nearing its destination. In another couple of minutes they would be entering the mouth of the harbor. Richard and Julie Price couldn't wait. They were just returning from three days at a get together of Julie's family at the family's summer home on the Vineyard. It only took them a few hours on the first day to remember that, in fact, they didn't like her family. Richard took the blame. He was the one who pushed Julie to join them for the 4th, despite her reminders to him of the awful childhood she'd had with her parents. "Get over it," was his response. After all, he explained, most people had difficult childhoods. There came a time to forgive and forget. Plus, they now had Sophia, who, at four, had never met her grandparents on her mother's side. So after three days of being told what they were doing wrong—not just by Julie's parents, but by her older brother as well, a really arrogant know-it-all—they couldn't wait to board the ferry and get out of there. "Summer playground, my ass," said Richard, when they were safely on the boat.

Overnight, a storm had descended on the northeast. All of the forecasters, who were surprised by the intensity of the storm, insisted it had nothing to do with Chad, which was still days away. But to the passengers on the ferry, it sure seemed like it did. It had been a rough trip, and because of the rain and the rocking of the boat most people were below deck. All the seats were taken and many of the passengers were standing. Some lost their patience with the crowds and heat and found the rain and wind preferable, leaving the claustrophobic atmosphere inside for the fresh—but wet—air outside. Rumor had it that the Steamship Authority was going to suspend service between the Vineyard and Woods Hole after this trip until the winds died down a bit. Because of that, Richard and Julie were extra grateful they had made this crossing. Even a few more hours with her family would have resulted in an act of satisfying violence by Richard.

They had gotten on the boat early and had secured enough space for the three of them to sit comfortably. Now, in a few minutes they'd be in Woods Hole, taking the bus to the parking lot to pick up their car, and then back to Connecticut. The further away from her family they got, the better.

However, this was anything but a normal trip. A few minutes earlier, word started to go around about the falling of the bridges. For the first minute, there was the expected buzz as everyone had to tell everyone else what was happening, even though the people they told already knew. Eventually though, it quieted down as the TVs on board were tuned to local Boston stations and passengers' tablets, phones, and laptops were connecting to various news outlets.

And then the boat stopped. Rather, it stopped moving forward. It was still rocking sideways from the waves. People looked at each other in fear until the Captain's calm voice came over the boat's PA system.

"Ladies and gentlemen, may I please have your attention. As most of you have probably heard by now, the Cape has suffered a catastrophe of epic proportions, with the Bourne Bridge, Sagamore Bridge, and train bridge all collapsing. With this in mind, for the safety of everyone on board I have been instructed to turn back to Vineyard Haven."

Richard looked at Julie, unsure of what concerned him the most—the falling of the bridges or the realization that, like it or not, they were stuck with Julie's parents for an indefinite length of time. There was nothing he could say. Julie just held Sophia in her arms, comforting her daughter who was suffering from a mild case of seasickness, and looked back at Richard with fear in her eyes.

Others had no problem voicing their displeasure, however. There were many angry voices from those who lived on the Cape and were just going home and from others whose travel plans had just been disrupted (as if the falling of the bridges wasn't disruption enough). The captain, who probably anticipated the outcry, waited a few moments before continuing.

"I know this comes as a major inconvenience for many of you, and I sincerely apologize, but already the dock is clogged with people wanting to leave Woods Hole and get off the Cape while they can. The fear is that if we dock, the ship will be overrun by the crowds, putting everyone's life in jeopardy. I can't allow that, so it is my decision, and that of my superiors, to head back to Vineyard Haven until things have calmed down. I..."

An explosion rocked the ship. Mass hysteria took over as passengers crammed the doors and stairs to the decks. With all the ferry accidents around the world over the years, the thought of it tipping over was foremost in everyone's mind. Smoke filled the passenger cabin and those on deck could see it billowing from the engine room area below deck. People were praying or screaming—some passengers doing both simultaneously. Crew members were trying to calm the passengers, with little luck. A few jumped overboard, thinking they were close enough to land to swim, not realizing that the strong currents of the Woods Hole passage, especially today, extended that close to land. Some were swept under, while the stronger swimmers made it to the rocks. Richard and Julie, watching the bedlam in the stairwells, chose to stay in their seats for the moment. Other than the movement from the waves, the ship didn't seem to be listing.

After a few minutes, the captain came back on to announce that the ship was, in fact, not sinking, and to please calm down. It took a while, but eventually people quieted down enough to listen to the captain.

"The explosion happened in our engine room, totally incapacitating our motors, but not compromising the integrity of the ship's hull. There is absolutely no danger of sinking, but I'm afraid that we are going nowhere. Judging by what is happening on shore, you are actually safer staying onboard the..."

Once again the captain was interrupted by explosions, but this time they weren't emanating from the ship, but rather from shore. One by one the docks collapsed into the waters of the harbor, and once again there was silence aboard the ferry as the passengers stared in horror. Those who were crowding the docks either died instantly from the blast or found themselves in the water fighting for their lives. From the distance, on the other side of Woods Hole, they heard more explosions.

From the bridge, the captain also viewed the situation with grave concern, but he was also thinking ahead. Destroying the docks meant that no ferries would be able to make it into Woods Hole. The other explosions would have been the docks at the Coast Guard Station Woods Hole. Whoever was doing this had planned well. A minute earlier he had heard on his radio that the same thing was happening in Falmouth harbor and Provincetown, and in Hyannis harbor where the ferry from Nantucket had suffered the same fate as his and was sitting dead in the water. Unlike his ship, however, the Nantucket ferry was stranded farther from shore in the middle of Nantucket Sound, being punished by the waves and the elements twice as badly as his ship was. He hadn't heard any news of it happening anywhere else in America, so for some reason, Cape Cod was the target.

They had lost electricity from the explosion, but the backup generator was working, supplying power to the radios and essential lights. The toilets were still working for now, but they would fill up fast. The captain wasn't worried about food or water, as that could be delivered to them, assuming, of course, that the weather calmed down a bit. While it would be inconvenient—and would become more so over time—in some ways the passengers of his ship might be safer than those on land. He would let them know that fact to calm them down.

Even if they had to stay there a few days before being unloaded and taken back to the Vineyard, they could do it.

And then he remembered the hurricane.

*****

About thirty miles away at the Barnstable Municipal Airport, people were already flooding the terminal trying to get flights to wherever they could go that would get them off the Cape.

Not exactly the busiest airport in the world, it was quickly overwhelmed by the crowds. Hearing the news about the bridges and the ferries, airport officials quickly made the decision to cancel any remaining commercial flights for the day. Featuring small regional airlines, Barnstable Municipal Airport had found its niche as a laid back, small town airport, catering to vacationers, businesspeople, and tradesmen, and servicing mostly Nantucket and Martha's Vineyard with a bevy of ten-seater propeller planes. Over the years, as the demand warranted, some of the larger carriers signed deals with the airport to provide service to Boston, New York, and various other northeast cities. A Jet Blue flight to Boston had just taken off, leaving the airport without any larger planes on site.

Seeing the crowds forming, and noting their general state of panic, the airport officials suggested to the local carriers that any remaining flights on the ground quickly take off—minus passengers—and head over to Nantucket until further notice. Their thinking was that if the airport had no planes available, maybe the crowd would disperse. So in rapid succession, six very empty planes took off, much to the chagrin of the hundreds of onlookers who never would have made it onto the planes in the first place.

The quick thinking by the airport officials ended up potentially saving many lives. Twenty minutes after the last of the six planes took off, a series of explosions rocked the airport, sending the screaming crowds that were inside the terminal racing for the exits. The first of the explosions destroyed the tower. The second, third, and fourth targeted the refueling trucks, sending fireballs hundreds of feet into the air. The last two explosions were the most damaging, as these were in the runway itself, creating large craters in the tarmac and rendering the runways—and in turn the airport itself—useless. Had the officials not closed the airport to incoming and outgoing traffic, express flights from both Boston and New York, in addition to several local commuter flights, might have been casualties of the attack. However, nothing could save the men and women working in the tower.

One of the first questions asked was how this could have been carried out. How could the terrorists have gotten access to the trucks and the tower? An even more concerning question was how they could have rigged charges in the runway without anyone seeing them. Down the line, airport security would once again get looked at, analyzed, and talked about endlessly, and new measures would be put in place to make sure it never happened again. But for now, the concern was a more immediate one: dealing with the dead tower workers, putting out the fires, and clearing the airport of the panicked masses before any further casualties resulted.

*****

In the police station a couple of miles away, Captain Chandler heard the explosions and knew exactly what it was. So when the call came in moments later, he was expecting it. He found himself shaking and quickly made his way to the bathroom, where he threw up. He had never felt fear like this. First the bridges, then the ferries, and now the airport. For whatever reason, some group had successfully cut Cape Cod off from the rest of the world. Whatever their intentions, they were now in complete control. Not knowing what was coming next was just plain frightening. Were the police stations next? Was he about to be blown to kingdom come?

He washed his mouth out with water and composed himself. Whatever was coming next, he still had a job to do. He opened the door and surveyed the utter chaos around him, with phones ringing off the hook, officers running back and forth, and crowds still packing the lobby.

Where the hell was he going to start?

Chapter 10

Doyle had hit the big time. Finally. This wasn't just some run-of-the-mill low-class break-in. No, not this time. Those days were over forever. He had just joined the big boys. The elite. The cream of the crop.

Well, except for the little problem with the car. By now they probably knew who he was. Okay, so maybe it was more than just a little problem. The fact was though, he had just ripped off one of the richest men on Cape Cod, Emerson Flint. One of those self-made millionaires who grew up on the streets of Boston, Flint was now the owner of numerous transport companies and real estate; the guy made the rest of the millionaires on the Cape look like paupers, people who should be selling pencils on the street. He had always heard that expression. Did they really sell pencils?

And yet, Doyle ripped him off. How comical was that? And it was easy. It just cost him about $20,000 in seed money. Of course, he didn't have the money, so he had to get it from a loan shark. Since he got the loan a couple of months earlier and hadn't paid any of it back yet, his tab was around thirty grand now. And, he had to tell Murphy—the loan shark—sort of what it was being used for, and Murphy demanded a cut in addition to the loan. Ten percent! What an asshole. Oh well, he figured he had to have scored a mil at least, so he should have no trouble paying back Murphy and giving him his cut. The nice thing? It was all cash. Nothing to fence. Plus, he could hide half of it, not tell Murphy, and pay him a smaller amount. He'd have to do it soon though. He was supposed to do the job a week ago, but Flint's schedule changed and screwed him up. Now Murphy was on the warpath for his money. No problem. In a few hours, he'd walk right into Murphy's office and drop a bag of money on his desk. He couldn't wait to see Murphy's face.

If he ever got there. Problem was, he was stuck in traffic. Route 6 was a parking lot all the way to Harwich. He wasn't going anywhere soon. He looked in his rearview mirror. He had done it about a thousand times, but so far hadn't seen anyone following.

The $20,000 was to pay off one of Flint's right-hand men. Turns out Flint was cheap. Really cheap. He paid his staff shit. He figured the prestige of being able to say that they worked for the great Emerson Flint would be worth its weight in bragging rights. But you can't live on bragging rights. His nickname amongst his staff was Skinflint. Behind his back they all called him Skin. Like, "What's Skin up to today?" Twenty grand to one of them was six month's salary—tax-free! Add to that five percent of the take and the guy jumped at the chance. Doyle assured him there was no way Flint would know it was an inside job. That was a lie. Of course he'd know, but by then Doyle would be long gone, sipping drinks with umbrellas in them on a tropical island.

Flint was in his eighties, but looked about a hundred and fifty. He was a ruthless sonofabitch and was pretty sharp for a man of his age, but he was beginning to forget the little things, like people's names, and unimportant things, like the combination to his safe—the same safe that contained a million in cash. It was suggested by those who knew his condition that he write down the combination and keep it in a secure place. His answer was simple: he'd forget where he put it. Others suggested that he get a safe that responded to his fingerprint, but he had no faith in that. Give him a simple combination lock any day, he said.

The upshot was that he entrusted the combination to his aide Vincent, the one person who was willing to sell him out. Despite his cheapness, there were many on his staff for whom bragging rights must have been important, and who were loyal to a fault. Or maybe they just hoped he'd remember them in his will. Vincent wasn't one of them.

Doyle robbed Flint during the fireworks. Flint had his own celebration to which he'd invited many of Chatham's elite. The house was pretty deserted, with everyone outside for the show. Robbing the safe was just about the easiest job Doyle had ever pulled. The problem came an hour later when he cleaned out his hotel room only to find his car dead. He knew it was coming, but why now? It was the transmission. AAA wasn't going to be able to help him. He couldn't steal a car—getting caught in a stolen car would ruin a great heist. He couldn't take a cab without arousing suspicion. And of course, none of the rental agencies were open. He'd just have to sit tight for the night and hope that they didn't break Vincent. Luckily, he had the room rented for another week—insurance if the robbery didn't go off when planned—so he just moved his stuff back in for the night.

Doyle and Vincent had devised an elaborate plan whereby, after the money was stolen, Vincent would play with the old guy's mind, convincing him that he had told others the combination as well. Doyle didn't have a lot of faith in the plan, but he also didn't care. He wasn't going to tell Vincent that. Let him get caught. Less money Doyle would have to pay out. He had already given Vincent the twenty grand, and had arranged to meet him at Fanueil Hall in Boston in a week to give him the five percent. Now he was reconsidering that. Hey, the guy got some money out of it, he can't complain. No, it was time for Doyle to skip town. He'd deposit the money in a couple of banks in Boston, take some spending money, and head to a Caribbean island.

He looked in the rearview mirror of his newly rented Malibu again. He'd lost most of his morning waiting for one of the rental agencies to open up. Flint would know by now that he'd been robbed. He'd call the police, of course. If they didn't get Vincent to cough it up, Doyle was safe from the police. But it wasn't the police he was worried about. Flint had his own security guards (a lot of good they'd done the night before). They weren't overly intelligent, but there was a lot of muscle among them. They'd be more than happy to find Doyle and deal with him before turning him over to the police.

So the sooner he was off the Cape, the better. But "soon" wasn't a word he'd be using today, not with this traffic. And his day was about to turn from bad to worse. A breaking report on the radio detailed the falling of the bridges. His heart stopped. The first question that ran through his mind was: *"Are we being attacked?"* The second was a little bit more immediate: *"Where can I possibly go where Flint's men and the police can't find me?"*

All of his euphoria from the night before was gone. Now he was simply scared. He had a million dollars and no place to go.

Chapter 11

They were out in hordes, like locusts descending on a cornfield—the cornfield in this case being the North Truro Stop and Shop. Ann had never seen it like this. She had lived through countless storms and hurricanes, but had never witnessed the fear consuming those around her now. She grabbed one of the last remaining carts and hurried to the water aisle. The water wasn't yet cleaned out, but give it five minutes and it would be.

She put as many gallon containers into her cart as she could fit. Already she was exhausted. At eighty, she had a lot of stamina, as well as a good deal of arm strength, but the combination of having to work fast and sensing the frenzy surrounding her tired her out quickly. A young woman pushed by and took two of the waters from Ann's cart.

"Hey," Ann yelled. Yelling was the only way to be heard. But the woman had already disappeared.

It was then that Ann realized the danger she was in. Sure, a hurricane was possibly coming, and a major one at that. But this was different. The bridges were down. Getting supplies to the Cape was going to be a nightmare for many months to come. People knew that. And then add the word "terrorists" and rules and courtesy went out the window.

Now she was scared. She wasn't without food at home, so she had to get out of there as quickly as possible. Besides, the canned food aisles were jammed with carts. If she left hers to grab some cans, she'd come back to find her cart gone, and the water was more important. She passed an endcap loaded with canned pineapple, so she threw as many as she could into her cart. Another endcap had pasta and sauce. She could live on pasta for a while, so she loaded up her cart.

Enough! Time to go. The store was getting more crowded by the minute. A few people were just walking out without paying. So far, they were the minority. Most were still willing to pay, but it wouldn't be that way much longer. Panic was setting in. The line she was in wasn't too bad yet—most people were still stocking up—and she got to the checkout counter without too much delay.

Suzie was at the register, and she looked terrified. Unmarried and in her early sixties, she had worked for Stop and Shop for almost twenty years, first in Hyannis, and now here.

"Oh Ann, what's going to happen?" she asked.

"The minute chaos breaks out, you get out of here. Do you have supplies?"

Suzie leaned over and whispered, "The manager put a pallet of water aside for the employees to take home. He moved the water and some canned goods into one of the spare rooms and locked it. He said if people start going into the storeroom to grab things, ours should be safe."

"It's only a matter of time before things get out of control, so watch yourself, okay?"

"I will, Ann. You too."

As Ann was pushing her cart toward the door, two Truro police officers—one of whom was Parker, whom she had seen earlier at her house—came in the front door with a bullhorn.

"Attention shoppers. This is the police. Calm down now. Panic will only make things worse. Be considerate of those around you. Anyone trying to steal food will be arrested. It's a tough situation, but none that we can't handle. No one will go hungry…"

He was still talking when Ann left. She wheeled the cart to her Jeep in the pouring rain and opened the back. Suddenly a young guy stepped from the shadows and grabbed her cart.

"Sorry lady, but I'm taking this." He began to wheel it away. All Ann could do was stand in shock.

No it wasn't. Clear thinking kicked in. She reached into her purse and pulled out her revolver. Her hand was shaking as she lifted it and pointed it at the back of the robber.

"Stop!" she cried out. He kept on without turning. Now she wasn't scared, she was angry. She was still shaking, but not as much.

"You've got one second to stop before I put a bullet in your back."

He stopped and slowly turned around, a mixture of fear and surprise on his face.

"You wouldn't really do that," he said.

"Sonny, I've been shooting since I was a little girl. I'm very good. Would I put a bullet into someone cowardly enough to rob an old woman? You'd better believe it."

In fact, Ann had never shot a gun in her life. The revolver she was holding belonged to Marie, who insisted that Ann have one for home protection, living as far out in the boonies as she did. It was against the law for Ann to even have it. She had only taken it to appease Marie. But in case she ever did need to use it, it was nice and simple—point and pull the trigger.

It was enough to convince the punk. He let go of the cart and ran off. She retrieved her supplies and, pleased with herself, mumbled under her breath, "Dirty Harry's got nothing on me." She put the gun back into her purse and finished loading the Jeep. A minute later she was back on Rt. 6 heading home. The road was the busiest she had ever seen it, cars going in both directions in a wild scramble to locate supplies. She had a picture in her head of a thousand mice being let go on a kitchen floor and scampering in a thousand different directions. The problem was, there just weren't enough stores down Cape to support the number of people desperate for supplies. She wasn't even sure if there were enough stores on the whole Cape. Oh, it was going to get ugly.

She got to her road and made the turn. It was nice to be off the main road. She now felt safe. But how safe? She'd be okay for a while, but eventually she would have to venture out into civilization—such as it was—to replenish her supplies.

And then there was the hurricane. If the power went out, the pump on her well would stop working and she'd be without water for washing, much less drinking. She also couldn't charge her cell phone. Her landline should continue to work—she had an old rotary phone someplace—but things would get bad fast. She would be totally cut off, communication-wise.

The hurricane didn't scare her before all of this. Now it terrified her—seriously terrified her.

Chapter 12

So close. Doyle was so close to making it over the bridge and on his way to freedom. Whoever brought them down couldn't have waited a few more hours? That would have sealed his escape. Well, there was no sense in sitting in this unmoving traffic. He was in a good spot to make a U-turn, so he turned back the way he had come.

He had to think. Hopefully, Flint's men would assume he made it over the bridge and not try a pursuit, especially now with so many other things to think of. So he was stuck on the Cape, maybe for a long time. Where should he go? All the hotels would be sold out by now. He could live in his car, but not someplace downtown. Way too crowded and dangerous. He had a gun, but little good it would do him around so many people. No, his best bet was to head further down Cape—Truro, Wellfleet, or the outskirts of P-Town—somewhere not so crowded. Of course, this was Cape Cod on 4th of July weekend and everything was crowded. But it would be less so down there. He could live in his car near the beach. He'd have to get some supplies, but he could do it. Then again, what if the hurricane hit? One problem at a time.

Everyone was making U-turns. Probably most had no idea where they were going to go, but they obviously knew that the bridge wasn't it. Others stayed in line. Most likely, they didn't have their radios on and hadn't yet heard the news. Well, between cell phones and word of mouth, they'd know soon enough.

People were already getting crazy. Cars trying to reverse direction were slamming into cars speeding away from the bridge. He felt like he was playing bumper cars. Somehow, though, he was managing to avoid an accident. This went on for many miles, until he reached Orleans. After that, it lessened up. Why would that be? At that point Route 6 became a much narrower road. You would think it would be the opposite. And then it hit him. Supplies! People were heading to the Mid-Cape in search of supplies. That's where they would find the Home Depots, the warehouse stores like BJs, and more supermarkets. Also more gas stations. Well, he had news for them. By the time they got there, those places would be cleaned out.

He looked at his own gas gauge. Half full. Half empty would be more like it. He'd have to find a place to park to wait this thing out. But not in his car. What if it took a couple weeks or more to get supplies here? He'd never make it.

He had to find a house. Preferably an empty one that still had some food and water. It was changeover weekend. The people taking summer rentals by the week would be leaving today, and hopefully the people renting for the next week were still on the mainland. If he could find one of those, he'd be golden.

Five hours later, he had come up empty, which was exactly where his gas tank would be if he didn't find something soon.

The news on the radio was dire. The death toll from the collapsed bridges was in the hundreds. Homeland Security had been called in to investigate, but hadn't arrived yet. No one had claimed responsibility as of yet. Something was also happening at the airport in Hyannis, as well as with the ferries in Hyannis and Woods Hole. More explosions, he thought. But the news was sketchy. What the hell was going on? Had we just entered World War III?

Doyle was scared. This was big and he was in the middle of it. Even worse, he had a million dollars of stolen money on him with—he could be pretty sure—a pretty incensed old man pulling out all the stops looking for him. What if they broke Vincent and he gave up Doyle's name? He didn't care about it before because he'd be a long way away. Now he was practically right around the corner. This was not good. Maybe he should return the money. Nah, they'd still want to kill him. Not good at all. He had to find a house, the more remote the better.

Luckily he was in Truro now, one of the more remote areas on the Cape. He was slowly traveling down a back road, aware now that a warning light had been blinking on the dashboard for a while. Time was about to run out. And then he passed it—the perfect hiding place. A narrow dirt road—actually, more like a sand road—led off into the dunes. In the distance through the rain he saw a house. It was more like a shack, but it had been fixed up nicely. In front was parked a Jeep. Someone was living there. That could be problematic.

Problematic or not, he no longer had a choice. At that moment his car died and slowly came to a stop. He got out and looked around in the mid-evening gloom. Fifty feet up the road was a small turnout. Putting the car in neutral, he pushed it toward the turnout. Once it was safely off the road, he retrieved the knapsack of cash and headed back toward the dune house.

Like it or not, whoever lived there was going to have a visitor.

Chapter 13

President David Landau sat in the makeshift Situation Room on Martha's Vineyard. What a vacation this turned out to be, he was thinking. Frankly, he hated the Vineyard. Way too crowded for his liking. The mountains of his home state of Wyoming were more his speed. But, despite what most people thought, a president couldn't make too many of his own decisions—especially when it came to vacations.

He had two things working against him: The mansion in which he was staying belonged to his largest and most influential campaign contributor. He had promised the man two years ago that he would stay with him at his Vineyard house, and he couldn't very well renege on the promise. It was important for his … something … self-esteem, maybe … that he be seen hosting the president at his home. And you don't piss off your biggest supporter, especially if you planned to run in the next election.

The place was ugly to boot. Ostentatious to the extreme. There was nothing homey or comfortable about the house. He had been there only a couple of days, but already it seemed like a month. He almost felt embarrassed staying there.

The second thing—or person—working against him was his wife, Debra. As much as they tried to hide it, it was no secret that they were having marital problems. It had never been a marriage of love. They had both been ambitious, and ambition was a turn-on for each of them. It was more a business deal than a real marriage. Oh, there had been some times in the early days that David might have seen as love between them, but that was a long time ago. They settled on a fondness for each other, and it had worked ... until recently. Debra didn't like some of his decisions and David didn't like some of the causes she supported. The fondness had begun to disintegrate, and the press was beginning to pick up on it. He didn't honestly know how he was going to survive a re-election campaign with her at his side. He thought about divorcing her—after all, they had no children—but those in his innermost circle advised against it.

So the upshot of it all was that she loved the Vineyard and had insisted that they vacation there—for the second year in a row. The first time had been nightmarish enough, staying with wealthy friends of her family. To have to suffer through it for a second year was just too much, but if he put his foot down and said no, the repercussions would have been more than he wanted to deal with.

He looked around at the crowd that had gathered in the basement of his donor's house: his chief of staff, representatives of the FBI, NSA, CIA, and who knows what other organization ... the Girl Scouts, maybe? And of course, all of the military heads were there. Is this where the term "talking heads" came from? Because they were all talking and he wasn't catching a word of it.

"Is there anyone in this room," he said slowly and forcefully, and the crowd went quiet, "who has actually heard what someone else is saying? I get the feeling that you are all too concerned with getting your point across. To whom, I have no idea, because like you, nobody is listening. Does someone want to give me a quick and painless breakdown of the situation? How about the FBI?"

"Well, Mr. President," began a mousy-looking man in an ill-fitting suit, one of the only suits in the room. The usual FBI representative was out of the country on vacation, so his assistant got the honors. He was understandably nervous and cleared his throat. "An hour ago we wouldn't have had anything for you, but the terrorists have just started communicating with us by email through the Boston newspapers and TV stations. We have issued a gag order to all of the outlets involved and deployed agents to each one to enforce the gag order and to let us know the minute they contact us again."

"Why the media?" asked Landau.

"We can only assume they wanted to go through a media outlet to get their message across to us, maybe for the exposure. The Boston outlets seemed the most logical."

"What do they want?"

"The usual. Money. They want a billion dollars dispersed to a bunch of numbered accounts across the globe."

"A billion dollars?"

"Yes sir. They also want land."

"I assume they don't want Cape Cod."

"No sir. We are still evaluating it, but it seems to be some land in Wyoming and Montana."

"And if we don't give in to their demands? I'm sorry, what's your name?"

"Merle Wiggins, sir."

"Okay, Mr. Wiggins. What are they threatening?"

Wiggins looked more uncomfortable. "They say they have anthrax."

"Aw, shit," said the chief of staff. "Not anthrax again. Can they prove it?"

"They don't have to," answered Wiggins, gaining a little confidence. "In a period of about an hour, they just isolated Cape Cod from the rest of the country. They've already killed hundreds of people. I think we have to take the threat seriously."

Landau turned back to Wiggins. "What kind of time frame are we talking about?"

"That's the interesting part. We think the email, the initial one anyway, was pre-written, written to be disseminated at a certain time. We've only received the one so far, so we don't know if any future ones will be more real time."

"Why do you think that?" asked Landau.

"The time they gave. They said they would let it loose into the air on July 8th."

"And?"

"The 8th is when Hurricane Chad is supposed to hit. Assuming you're going to distribute this by air, you can't let anthrax go in the rain ... and it *will* be raining hard. It'll just get washed into the soil."

"It's raining now. What's the forecast for the next few days?"

"Rain, rain, and more rain. This front came in ahead of the hurricane. Chad will eventually push it out, but I doubt if we will see any break in the rain. It will just go from steady rain to hurricane conditions. Thursday, the 9th, looks to be the next clear day. Being the day after a hurricane, it stands to be windy, which would be optimal to disperse the anthrax."

"Can it be delivered any other way?"

"Through the drinking water supply, but we don't think that will happen. They specified the air in the email. Also, it would be harder to do that on the Cape, since most of their water supply comes from wells. The smart money is on an airborne release."

"Smart money ... right," he mumbled. "So do we have the source of the emails?"

"Yes and no. It's coming from an email account associated with a man named Seth Wakeby, but it's going through so many servers in so many countries, we can't track it. They could have made up an email address, but they used one linked to a real person. We're not sure why. We've tracked down Wakeby—or at least we've discovered some things about him. He's the nephew of Peter Singleton. If that name doesn't ring a bell, it should." Wiggins was beginning to enjoy his moment in the sun. "Singleton is a billionaire who runs a half a dozen corporations. As far as we've been able to determine, he's clean. Seth Wakeby is his nephew and he works for Singleton in some pretty lowly positions. I just got off the phone with Singleton a few minutes ago. He was suspicious of Wakeby and hired a P.I. to track him down and find out what he was involved in. He heard from the P.I. last night that he had found Wakeby and that he had to kill a guy who was about to kill Wakeby. The FBI field office confirms that they got an anonymous call from an untraceable phone telling them where the body was and that the person might be involved in planning some sort of terrorist attack. Agents found the body, but so far haven't gotten very far."

"So the terrorist could be dead?"

"An operation of this size would require a lot more than one," said Wiggins. "We do think we know who called it in. The P.I. assigned to find Wakeby is ex-CIA." He looked at the CIA representative. "And from what we have gathered, quite a star in your agency."

The CIA rep took over. "His name is Marcus Baldwin. He retired with honors a few years back and became a hot-shot P.I. He only works for the richest and most secretive clientele and has an excellent reputation. If we can contact him, he'd be a good asset on the ground. But getting in touch with him is a problem. Already, cell phone service is being affected with the towers being overloaded. We figure by tonight they'll all be down."

"Something I don't understand," said Landau. "An operation this big, why didn't we get wind of it? Was there no chatter? And who is it? ISIS?"

"Not a word," said Wiggins. "Not even an inkling. And no, we don't think it is ISIS or any Middle-Eastern group. There would have been something out there. Our best guess is home-grown. Whoever they are, they've avoided social media and electronics of all kinds. They did this under the radar, so to speak. Low-tech. And that makes them that much harder to find."

"Well, I suggest we use the military airfield on the Cape and start bringing in troops. Maybe we can even start getting some people out…"

"Excuse me sir, but we can't do that," said Wiggins.

"Why?"

"The other part of their message. If we attempt to land troops at Otis—actually, if we attempt to land anything anywhere on the Cape—they said they would start killing mass numbers of people."

"How?"

"They didn't say, but if they use anthrax, they can target individual buildings from inside and not have to worry about the rain. And again, we've already seen what they can do with explosives."

"So we can do nothing?" said the president. "What about the local authorities?"

"The State Police are almost nonexistent on the Cape today. All the local police departments are trying to deal with the mobs and the looters. They'll be of no help."

President Landau felt paralyzed. He thought back a year to a terrorist situation in a mall. He authorized an assault and ended up with thirty innocent people dead. It was the low point of an otherwise illustrious career. Now he was faced with a similar situation, except that the potential death toll could be exponentially higher.

"Suggestions?"

"I suggest we hold off making any provocative moves for now," said Wiggins. "I'm sure we can get a few agents onto the Cape secretly somehow, but anything we plan to do has to be well thought out."

"Can we assume they won't do anything on the 8th?" asked the president. Wiggins nodded. "So best case scenario is that we have until the 9th. He looked around the table. "I want a plan in my hands by tomorrow morning, because, by God, no terrorists are going to hold this country hostage. Not while I'm president."

Well, that sounded good, he thought as he left the room, but he was troubled. The incident at the mall had shaken him, and now he questioned if he had the courage to make the right decision.

The mall situation wasn't even supposed to be his call. The final decision should have been the FBI's to make, and they certainly wanted to make it. His chief-of-staff, however, saw it as the perfect opportunity for the president to show that he had the ability to make the tough decisions, a criticism of him since taking office. And so he bullied his way into the situation, citing all kinds of legal precedents. The mall was a large one outside of Washington D.C. that was taken over by a street gang trying to prove something. He forgot what exactly what it was. He had some memory of other members of their gang being in jail on what they said were trumped up charges. Until they were released, they would hold the mall hostage. Frankly, their demands weren't of interest to him. He wanted to make a point, the point that he was done letting the scum in this country run things, especially in the cities. Besides, they would never have the nerve to carry out their threats. He ordered the mall taken.

It turned out that the gang did have the nerve. When the siege was over, thirty men, women, and children were dead. The FBI was assigned the blame—Waco all over again—and he managed to skate through with only minimal damage. Psychologically though, it did a job on him. Now in front of him he had a real crisis, and one he couldn't hide from. He was going to be seen as front and center in this.

The lives of a half a million people rested in his hands, and he didn't know if he was up to the task.

Chapter 14

Marcus looked at his watch. *Well, that was smart,* he thought. He didn't intend to leave so late. It was Seth who made them late. He had been awake all night in the bathroom throwing up. He said he must have picked up a bug, but Marcus knew better. He had had too much experience with death and how it affected people. Sometimes the reality of a situation didn't show up until long after the incident. Seth's brush with death hit him late in the evening.

They were still sitting in traffic somewhere west of Hyannis, with Seth still looking a little green around the gills. During the night he had asked Marcus a half dozen times how he was able to kill someone so easily. Marcus changed the subject a half dozen times. Now Seth was silent, exhaustion having set in. Marcus hadn't slept either, but he was used to it, having spent much of his adult life catching sleep in bits and pieces. Other than Seth's becoming intimate with the toilet bowl, it was an uneventful night, with no uninvited visitors. Marcus wasn't surprised. Getting rid of Seth was nothing more than taking out the garbage, tying up loose ends. If it didn't work the first time, there was no way they were going to chance it a second.

He wondered how many were involved in the mess Seth

had made for himself. Were they terrorists? It looked that way, but who was to know. It could be that the guy Marcus shot was the ringleader and it would now fade away. That would be the ideal situation. Well, it wasn't his problem. He gave the information to the FBI and he saw online that a body had been found in a bog in Mashpee. It was up to them now.

He thought about Sara. Cool, capable, smart, attractive, and obviously hurting. Her career and passion were ripped out from under her. It wasn't going to be easy to come back from that. And it didn't appear that she had anything else in her life. It was clear that she wasn't in a relationship. He sensed that she was a private and solitary person. She had a hard road ahead and he felt for her.

A police car passed them in the breakdown lane, siren screaming. It was followed a minute later by several fire trucks and ambulances. Add an accident to the Sunday traffic and it was going to be an excruciating drive. He would turn around and try it again later, but with Seth by his side it would be just as bad. A lose-lose situation.

His phone rang. It was Sara.

"Hey," he said.

"Where are you?" No preamble.

"Stuck in traffic just outside Hyannis. Got a late start."

"So you haven't heard the news." She said it as a statement.

This didn't bode well.

"No. Our friends?"

"Seems so. They've just brought down the bridges to the Cape."

Holy shit.

"Can you turn around?"

"Looks like I'll have to," replied Marcus. "When did it happen?"

"Just a few minutes ago."

"Okay, we're turning." Marcus saw his opportunity up ahead, a crossover with a sign: *Official vehicles only*. No one would care at this point. Word must have been getting out. A number of cars were doing the same thing. Marcus rode up the narrow grass area alongside the fast lane—that was a misnomer today—and turned at the crossover. Traffic on the other side was light, but the cars heading back to Hyannis were traveling at faster than normal speeds. Panic. Another half hour and it would be sheer chaos.

"Done," he said. "Thanks." He may have sounded calm on the phone, but he had no doubt that this was just the beginning of a disaster in the making.

"Need a place to stay? I assume you checked out. You'll never get back in there now."

"I guess we do. You offering?"

"I am."

"Appreciate it."

"No problem." She gave them instructions to her condo, then said she was going to see what she could get from the news.

They saw the beginnings of the panic on their way to Sara's: lines outside the gas stations, parking lots of the supermarkets already full, fender benders at an alarming rate, and people ignoring red lights. Not good. Marcus thought about some of the hotspots of the world he'd seen. In many of those places, bombs would be going off every day and people would be calmly going about their business. Here, in a place not known for its everyday violence, at the first hint of conflict, they lose all sense of civility. He couldn't blame them, though. It must be frightening for them. An hour earlier they were on vacation. Now their lives were completely turned on end.

Amazingly, they arrived at Sara's condo accident-free. Marcus parked in a visitor's spot in the virtually empty parking lot. Word had already gotten out and the residents were trying their luck at the supermarkets. Sara's truck, now devoid of her storage belongings, was the only other vehicle.

Sara met them at the bottom of a set of stairs that led to a second floor containing three units. She was dressed in shorts and a sleeveless top, and was barefoot. It looked like she was ready for a day at the beach. She had her shoulder-length sand-colored hair pulled up, loosely held together by a large clip. For the first time, Marcus could really study her, and for the first time in a very long time he felt the stirrings of desire. It wasn't just that she was physically attractive, she had an air of confidence about her—a confidence based on experience. She could probably handle herself in almost any situation and Marcus appreciated that quality. There had been numerous women over the years he'd been attracted to physically, but they had always lacked the strength he found so important. All except one.

A few months earlier, in a rare moment of reflection, he realized that he had never actually been in a real relationship. Mostly, he had only ever had a series of one-night stands. Just once did he ever feel that things were becoming serious with a woman. In his previous profession, he had worked with a woman named Skyler on three consecutive missions. By the third, they both knew that a strong attachment had been formed between them, but neither had a clue as to what to do with it. They couldn't very well settle down to a peaceful life in the suburbs. They were both too high-strung and intense for that. They also both realized that they had become too suspicious—not suspicious of each other, but of the world and the people around them. They were both meant to be operatives and clearly saw that a real relationship was out of the question. So when they parted after that third mission, it was with the understanding that what they had was the best it would ever be—a few intense nights together once or twice a year.

That never happened, however. Eight months later Skyler was dead, assassinated in Turkey by a contract operative for a foreign government. A laptop containing the names of American spies had been stolen from a section head. Even though the list was coded, it was easy enough to hack. Two of the operatives, one being Skyler, were assassinated and the rest were in imminent danger. Marcus's name was on that list. Of course, he wasn't known as Marcus back then. It was decided for his own safety that his time in the agency was finished. He was offered a desk job, but they knew as well as he did that he would never be happy sitting at a desk. So he left.

In all honesty, Skyler's death had affected him more than he thought possible. Even though it was the only job he had known for most of his adult life, he was ready to leave. Using contacts he had formed over the years, he started his P.I. business. That was ten years ago. He didn't miss his old life at all. In times of loneliness though, of which there were many, he thought about Skyler and the closest he had ever come to being in love.

"We appreciate this," said Marcus. He didn't know if Seth appreciated it or not, as he hadn't said a word since getting in the car at the hotel. But he really didn't care what Seth thought.

"My pleasure," answered Sara. "It'll be a bit tight. One of you can have the couch and the other the air mattress, but we'll make it work."

"What have you heard?"

"It was just the bridges at first, but the latest report just a few minutes ago indicated that the ferry docks might have been hit. That would correspond with the explosions I heard from the direction of the harbor."

As she was bringing them up to date, a series of explosions shattered the relative quiet—if you discounted the constant police and fire vehicle sirens—and immediately after that a plume of black smoke could be seen rising above the rooftops.

"And that would be the airport," she said with a calm she wasn't at all feeling.

"Bridges, ferries, and airport," said Marcus. "That pretty much completes the picture. For whatever reason, these people want to keep everyone here."

"The ferries and the airport are overkill," said Sara. "They couldn't get anywhere near enough of the people off the Cape anyway. The bridges were the best way off for the majority of the population. I wonder why they went that route."

"Fear," said Marcus. "You're right, it would hardly make a dent in getting people off, at first anyway. Given a few weeks it might, but I doubt if the terrorists mean for this to go on that long. No, I think the purpose in getting the ferries and airport was fear, plain and simple. They want the panic to be heightened. They want people to feel that there is no way off.

They want to instill total fear."

"Well, it's working," said Sara.

Chapter 15

And working, it was. A few hours earlier, it was a normal crazy Sunday on Cape Cod. Those who were leaving were in the usual end-of-vacation grouchy moods, enhanced by the rain and the anticipation of many hours on the highway crawling to the bridge. Now, with the realization that no one was going anyplace for a long time, the craziness was no longer normal. Any semblance of civility had disappeared. Looting had begun in earnest, but unlike the riots in so many cities over the years, the looting wasn't done by thugs. These were normal people, who, hours before were living normal lives. They were just trying to think ahead and gather anything that might help them survive. At first they felt bad for the owners of the hardware stores and corner markets that were being cleaned out, but over time the survival mentality kicked in and they just did what they had to do. They knew that by nightfall there wouldn't be a loaf of bread or gallon jug of water left on the Cape. They didn't like being looters, but they had no choice. They rationalized their behavior with the assumption that the store-owners would be reimbursed by their insurance companies. Whether that was true or not didn't matter. As long as they didn't dig too deeply into the thought, they were satisfied.

It wasn't only food supplies, gas, and large items like

generators. Guns were high on the list. There was only one gun store of any significance on the Cape, The Shoot Zone in Hyannis. When the crowds arrived at the store, they found it closed and barred, but that didn't stop them. Some welder's equipment was found and an attempt was made to melt through the bars of steel. However, haste led to carelessness and the building caught on fire. Within minutes, thousands of rounds of ammunition were exploding and the building was engulfed in flames. An hour later, it was a pile of rubble. Unbeknownst to everyone, the body of Rodney Sinclair, the owner who was just trying to follow the law, lay at the bottom of the rubble, having made the wrong decision for the right purpose.

Add to that the underlying fear felt by most: What was next? Could it be that all of this was preparation for setting off a nuclear device? Was all of their running around and law-breaking for naught? Were they all going to die anyway?

Those who didn't get off the highways leading to the bridges right after the bridges went down were now going nowhere. Major accidents in a dozen places on the westbound lanes stopped the retreat of traffic. People abandoned their cars and began to walk—most having no idea where they were going. Frantic cell phone calls were placed to hotels and motels all over the Cape in the useless attempt to find a room. An hour after the attacks the hotels had stopped answering their phones altogether. People were stuck. Word of the schools used for hurricane shelters started to get around. Maybe they would open for this disaster as well. There was no indication that they had opened, but it at least gave people something to aim for. Parents carried their crying children, trying to reassure them that everything would be okay, when even the parents themselves weren't so sure.

Emergency vehicles were no longer seen. It wasn't because they weren't working—they were working as hard as ever—but because things had gotten so bogged down, they were just as stuck as the people they were trying to help. Six ambulances were in line at the Cape Cod Hospital ER to deliver victims from the various bombings. But with the ER already bursting at the seams with patients, there was nowhere to put everybody. Finally a tent was hastily set-up in an empty space behind the hospital and the paramedics were able to deposit their patients and attempt to go for more victims.

Further hampering rescue missions, and attempts by displaced tourists to find shelter, was the rain. By mid-afternoon, what had been a drizzle in the morning was now a steady downpour. The rain was a system totally unrelated to Hurricane Chad, but the timing of it couldn't be worse. It only helped to fuel the pervading fear and frustration.

*****

Near the site of the former Sagamore Bridge, Gloria had had enough of her book club friends. Her house was small, and the thought of housing all eight additional women for an indefinite time was already taking its toll. The bridge had fallen only seven hours earlier, but between those who were crying incessantly and those who were talking incessantly, she was ready to throw them all out. A couple of the women were good friends, but the others were once-a-month acquaintances who showed up just to talk books (which they never did) and consume vast quantities of wine and food (which they always did). Gloria was quickly seeing the other side of some of these women. And they were all ready to kill octogenarian Claire, who was boring them all with her theories of who was responsible and how the U.S. was going to "kick their butts" as soon as some group claimed responsibility.

The problem was, none of these women had anywhere to go. Five of the eight lived on the other side of the now nonexistent bridge, and the other three lived down the choked highways in Falmouth and Hyannis. These women weren't going anywhere for a long time. If something didn't change soon and she couldn't figure out how to get rid of them, Gloria just might have to slash her wrists and call it quits. Anything would be better than this.

*****

Only seven hours into the ordeal and the resources of the Barnstable Police Department were already at their breaking point. Captain Chandler looked around at what was once an orderly station and he wanted to throw up again. The men and women under him had never dealt with anything like this. Hell, he never had either. Every year they all participated in terrorist drills and emergency preparation exercises, but they were nothing like the real thing. The real thing involved seriously panicked citizens, many more incidents—criminal and accidental—than the department could handle with their limited manpower, and the officers themselves worried about their own families. Many of the families had been brought to the station for their own safety, but they all knew that it was a short-term solution. In a couple of days the reserves of food and water in the station would run out and they would be in the same boat as the rest of the citizens.

The crowds outside had diminished significantly once they realized they'd get no help standing there. But those who were still camped out in the parking lot were a vocal crowd—an angry vocal crowd—and Chandler was afraid they were going to get out of hand and he would have to deploy tactics that could result in many injuries or deaths. Why couldn't they just go and prepare like everyone else was doing? He asked them that over the bullhorn, only to get back a jumbled mess of rants, threats, whining, and pleading.

"It's your responsibility to take care of us..."

"Where do you want us to go?..."

"Do your job..."

A few left when he announced the locations of the shelters and informed them that the shelters would be open by morning. He didn't really know if this was true. Yes, it was definite that they would open, but he didn't know how many supplies were available or how many volunteers would be manning the shelters. This wasn't like a hurricane—*Shit, that might be on its way, too*, he thought—where they had days to prepare. This was unprecedented and he was way out of his league.

As he was walking back into the station, he was hit in the back of the head by a rock. Another one caught him in the shoulder. He got in the station and closed the door just as another rock shattered the front window. It was time. Leaving one man on guard, the rest of the officers followed him to the gun locker. He opened it and passed out riot gear and automatic weapons. They all solemnly put on the bullet-proof vests and helmets, loaded their weapons, and made their way back to the lobby.

Chandler hoped to God that the sight of the riot gear would be enough to calm the crowd, but if not, he was ready. In fact, he was becoming angry. People were supposed to be helping others, not becoming troublemakers. Well, desperate times called for desperate measures, or so the old saying went. If it meant that he had to pick off a few of the leaders to disperse the crowd, then so be it.

The situation had just been knocked up a notch.

Chapter 16

They were idiots, thought Mason. How he had been able to mastermind such an elaborate plan with morons was beyond him. Maybe it just gave credence to the assumption—his assumption anyway—that he was a genius. Nobody else would have been able to accomplish all of this with the group he had. He was definitely a genius. Some might have said that a real genius would have picked men who weren't morons, but they'd be wrong. He knew that he needed men who would be easily led, and men who had more passion than brains. That's why he picked them from survivalist groups. Passion was what they were all about. There was danger in picking people with too many smarts. You ran into the possibility of someone wanting to take over the group. He needed people he could keep in line with stirring anti-government speeches and the promise of riches in the end.

Finding them hadn't been hard. Tanner had ties to survivalist groups all over the country, so they visited a few of them to pick their men. There were dozens of willing bodies, all of them insisting that they were the perfect choices. They smelled blood and were anxious to be a part of something violent. Tanner and Mason only hinted at the job, but they knew how to sell it. Their problem was picking the right people. They had made a decision not to pick two people from the same group. The last thing they needed was a palace coup down the line. They also had to be loyal and hard-working, but not especially bright—men who would do what they were asked without needing too much explanation. They had to be men who had been off the grid for a while—and who didn't have police records. They absolutely would not tolerate any drug use. Those last two items narrowed down the choices drastically, but they were able to find four men from four different areas of the country. He wasn't much older than the four, but he had a maturity far beyond any of them.

The only intelligent ones in the group—besides himself— were the two explosives guys, Danielson and Packer, as well as the late Tanner. He didn't actually know that Tanner was dead, but it didn't matter. Dead, hurt, or in jail, it made no difference. Tanner was gone, and all the better for it. He had recruited Danielson and Packer through a network of disaffected former soldiers he belonged to. He needed men he could rely on for this part of the job, and they came highly recommended. Unbeknownst to the other members of the crew, Danielson and Packer were being paid for their work—a small advance with the promise of a big paycheck from a secret fund when completed, a fund that didn't really exist. But he wouldn't have to deal with the fallout when they came looking for their nonexistent paychecks, they'd be dead in a couple of days with the others.

The idiot part of the rest of his crew was on full display, and he was about to put a stop to it. He showed up at an apartment that had been rented for two members of his crew, only to find four of them there. Yet another breach of protocol.

Only Mason could call them all together, and he always found private, out of the way places for his meetings. He looked around as he walked in the door. Holt and the rest of his survivalist buddies were having a grand old time, drinking beer and celebrating their success. Luckily, Danielson and Packer weren't a part of it. Those two took the job seriously and were back at their own apartment waiting for orders. Well, it didn't matter. He only had to keep these four in line for another couple of days.

They saw Mason come in and raised their beer cans to the air in salute.

"Hail the conquering hero," said Holt.

The group took one look at Mason's face and went silent.

"What are you doing?" he asked.

"Celebrating, boss," said Holt.

"Celebrating what?"

"Our success."

"What success?"

Holt hesitated. "The bridges and ferries?" He said it as a question.

"So you think we're done?" asked Mason. "We can go home now?"

"Well ... no. But this was big. Look what we just did."

"You morons get any louder and all of your neighbors will know what you did." Mason brought his voice down to a near-whisper. "This is only the beginning. The next few days will be the crucial time. This is not the time to party."

Seeing their crestfallen faces, Mason thought, *what a bunch of children*. He backed off a little. The last thing he needed was for his crew to lose their confidence.

"Look," he said more softly. "What you guys did today was monumental. You did something no one else has ever done. You've been able to hold a whole island—which is essentially what it is now—hostage. Other than private boats and small planes on private airstrips, there is no way off. These people are stuck here. They are terrified and they are panicking. This is exactly what we wanted. You should all be commended."

He saw them perk up and knew he had them where he wanted them.

"But we're not finished. The first set of demands were already emailed out. Tomorrow, we will follow-up those demands with ultimatums and we will bring this government to its knees." *Well, not really*, he thought. He just needed them to think so. Even Danielson and Packer, the demolition guys, didn't know what it was really all about, but they didn't care. As long as they got paid big money, they would just do their job.

"Having a party when all hell is breaking loose might just bring attention to yourselves, wouldn't you think?" They nodded. "That's why I rented two places for the four of you, so it wouldn't draw any attention. And that's why we don't all meet at your places. That's why we don't communicate via text or emails. That's why our telephone communications are short and coded and we go through so many phones. I've taken great pains to do this as anonymously as possible, so don't you think that having a fucking party on the day the bridges come down is a little inappropriate?" He raised his voice with the last sentence to make his point.

It was made. They hung their heads.

"So here's what we are going to do. When I got here, I

checked out the other apartments in this building and they all seemed empty. Probably all at the store getting supplies. I don't think any damage was caused by this shindig of yours. We are all going to leave and you two," he motioned to the two who shared that apartment, "will take a drive to a supermarket. Obviously you don't need anything, since we planned for this, but it's important that you see what's going on in case a neighbor wants to talk about it." He looked around at the others. "You will all do that. Try to buy something, but don't worry if you can't. Then head home and lay low until I call. You need to seem as normal as possible and not draw attention to yourselves. And it would be normal for you to be out trying to scrounge supplies. Think you can do that?"

"Okay boss."

"Then let's go. The next few days will be crazy and your main part in all this starts tomorrow and will be critical, so lay off the beer and get some rest."

As he walked to his car, he couldn't help but to feel nervous. So far, everything had gone as planned. Bringing civilization on the Cape to a halt was easy. The hard part was going to be convincing the government that they were capable of something even more monstrous. When word of what he had in store for them filtered down to the people, they'd go crazy. Good. That was exactly what he wanted. More importantly, he wanted the government to see just how scared the people were. And when they did, he could allow the last part of the plan to kick in—the part his men didn't know about, and never would until it was too late.

As he pulled out onto the main road and into the absolute chaos the Cape had become, he had to allow himself a smile.

Even though it wasn't exactly his true purpose, he really would bring the government to its knees.

The old saying was right: Power *was* intoxicating.

Chapter 17

Doyle studied the cottage. Being dusk, the lights were on inside the house and he could see an old woman inside. He hadn't seen anyone else and had to assume she was alone. It was a good and bad situation. On one hand, taking over the house would be a piece of cake. On the other hand, he didn't want to be the cause of her having a heart attack. He was a thief, not a murderer. He'd have to approach the situation subtly. Subtly? How subtle could he be telling an old woman he was taking over her house? But what if he didn't tell her that? The news broadcast on the radio said that there were thousands of displaced tourists looking for lodging. Officials were encouraging people to open up their houses. He seriously doubted many would. It wasn't that they didn't want to be good neighbors. If it was a natural disaster of some kind, they would do it knowing that disaster relief couldn't be far behind. It was easier to share when the end was in sight. But with this one the very future was questionable. With the bridges down, the docks blown to kingdom come, and the airport unusable, they were going to have to resort to shipments by helicopter and airdrops, just like in third world countries. And everyone knew how successful that was. Things were going to be bad for a long time to come. He was going to have to charm this lady.

Well, good luck with that.

He could see another cottage further up the road, but it was falling down. The roof had collapsed in on itself. Probably from the bad winter. This one looked sturdy.

He saw her go into the living room and turn on the TV. The news was on. He had a feeling the news was going to be on constantly for a long time to come. He picked up his backpack with the million dollars and slung it over his shoulder. He was learning that a million dollars was heavy. Upon reflection, he set it back down on the ground and took his gun from his belt and put it in the backpack. He might be able to con the lady into letting him stay, but if she accidently saw the gun in his belt, things might get ugly.

He didn't always carry a gun, but knowing who he was dealing with in trying to rob Flint, he felt safer with it. If he ever got caught with it by the police, he'd go straight to prison. An ex-con wasn't allowed to possess a gun. Ten years earlier he was caught breaking and entering some rich couple's home on the Cape. The place was massive and they only used it a few weeks a year. They weren't even supposed to be there, but, Doyle's luck being what it was, they were. The police were there in minutes, as they often were for rich people, and instead of being charged with breaking and entering, he was charged with home invasion, a much stiffer penalty. It was also his second brush with the law, so he went to prison. It could have been worse. He was out in three years. It was made abundantly clear to him, though, that one more time and he'd be in for a long time. Of course, with the current situation, good luck with catching him—or any lawbreaker for that matter. Crimes were going to be committed all over the Cape and very few of the criminals would be caught. The police were already spread dangerously thin. He didn't have much to worry about. If he couldn't con her into letting him stay, he'd force his way in. Either way, this was going to be his home for a while.

He started up the driveway to the house. Was he going to be presentable enough? Not that he needed to be, but it would help. He smelled his armpits. Whoa, they were ripe. He hadn't changed in about twenty-four hours, and sitting in the car all day didn't help. He wished he had some deodorant and a clean shirt.

He got to the door and could hear the TV. He listened for a moment. She was tuned to one of the Boston stations. The newscasters had on their disaster voices. If he could see the TV, they would also be sporting the corresponding faces. To give them credit, most probably weren't in the business in 2001 for 9/11, so this kind of situation was new to them. The closest that they had probably ever been to a serious local emergency was the marathon bombing. Doyle figured the newscasters lived for moments like these and they were probably trying their best to sound more professional than their counterparts at the rival stations.

He knocked. The TV volume decreased slightly.

"Who is it?" The voice had a tremor to it.

"Ma'am, I'm sorry to bother you, but I'm really stuck. My car ran out of gas and I have nowhere to go. I called AAA, but there is no gas available. I hate to impose, but is there any way I could use your floor for the night? I know it's a lot to ask, but the whole world has turned upside down. I'd be happy to pay you."

Silence. Doyle could almost hear the wheels turning in her

head. She had a moral decision to make.

"They've set up shelters in town," she answered. He could tell she was having a hard time with this decision.

"Yes, ma'am, but that's miles away and I'm now on foot. Besides," he added, not really knowing if it was true, "they aren't opening until tomorrow."

More silence.

"If it's any consolation," he added, "this is just as awkward for me as it is for you. It would just be for the night. I can walk to a shelter tomorrow. It'll be easier walking in the daylight."

That did the trick. The locks turned and the door opened slowly. He was met by the close-up version of the woman he'd seen through the window, a short lady probably in her late seventies or early eighties with the appropriate gray hair and wrinkled skin.

"Okay," she said. "I guess you can come in. It wouldn't be very friendly of me to deny a traveler a place for the night, considering all that's going on, would it?"

"I totally understand," he said as the door finally opened enough for him to step in. He held out his hand. "Joe Doyle."

She reluctantly took his outstretched hand. "Ann Lawrence." All the while she was cursing the fact that he had ended up on her road. The last thing she wanted, even if he was perfectly harmless, was a visitor. She had her routine set out—even in an emergency like this—and didn't want to share the moment with anyone. After all, there was a reason she was living out in the boonies alone.

"Please come in," she said graciously. "I apologize if I seemed rude."

"I understand perfectly," said Doyle as charmingly as he

could. "I was on my way home after a week's vacation and got caught up in the traffic. After the thing with the bridges, I figured I'd better find a place to stay. I couldn't find any place, and then I ran out of gas. Again, I'm sorry to impose."

Ann studied her uninvited guest as he entered her home. He was pretty average-looking in her eyes, almost nondescript. He was the type who could have a five minute conversation with you and if asked to describe him later, your mind would go blank. He was of average height and weight, dark hair cut short. She noticed he was balding on top. A lot of men these days cut their hair short so as not to draw attention to the bald spot—better than the days of comb-overs, she thought. He was dressed in jeans and sneakers and a Hawaiian shirt.

He looked like someone on vacation ... and yet, he didn't. There was something about him that didn't ring true. The weather had been unbearably hot, and yet, he was wearing jeans. Even now in early evening it was in the high eighties. She supposed she couldn't judge. Maybe he had a skin condition on his legs and couldn't wear shorts. Maybe he didn't like to wear sandals. There could be a million reasons. But there was something else. He was dressed to look like a tourist, but it was almost like a costume, like he was trying too hard to look the part. He was carrying a backpack. That didn't look like vacation luggage. She shook her head. Just her suspicious nature. Probably the rest of his luggage was in the car.

"Come in and sit down. I was just watching the news for updates."

"Thank you." As he walked past she wrinkled her nose. He was ripe. But if he was in his car all day, especially with the stress of the events, she could understand. "Anything new?

"Not in the last few minutes. Can I get you something to drink?"

"A water would be great. Thank you."

She ran some tap water into a glass. *Typical old person,* thought Doyle. He was expecting a cold bottle of water from the fridge, but she probably didn't believe in buying water, so he got barely cool tap water. Well, he was thirsty. He'd deal with it.

"As I'm sure you know, besides the bridges, the ferry docks are gone and the airport is unusable. People are looting the stores. The locals would never have done that. It's the tourists." Then, realizing that she was talking to one, she apologized.

"No need," he said. "You're probably right. The tourists don't live here. They just don't care the same way a local would. Any news on the hurricane?"

"It walloped the east coast of Florida this morning. Things are pretty bad there. Almost all the models—you know, all of those strings of different-colored spaghetti they always show on the weather—almost all of them have it hitting the Cape head-on on Wednesday. It's going to be bad."

"Are you going to a shelter?" He said it hopefully. If she went to the shelter, he could sneak back into her house and ride it out. Chances were, she wouldn't get back for a while. But no such luck.

"I think I'm safer here. I've ridden out many storms in forty years. With all else that's going on, I'd rather stay."

"Probably smart."

Over the next hour, Ann got her "guest" something to eat and pulled out an air mattress she kept for when Marie would visit, and a spare sheet and pillow. At nine o'clock she asked him if he needed anything else, then announced that she was going to bed. She doubted she would get much sleep with a stranger in the house, but she was sure she was just feeling paranoid.

"Good night, Ann. I really appreciate your hospitality. I promise I'll be out of your hair in the morning."

A promise he had no intention of keeping.

Chapter 18

It didn't take long for Flint to have the name of the person who made off with his million—and the other thing, the more important thing. Vincent broke like a piece of fine china. He gave up Joe Doyle's name in the first five minutes. That didn't stop Flint's men from spending the next hour working him over, even though it resulted in very little additional information of substance. By the end of the hour Vincent was still alive, but he wished he was dead.

The one piece of information they gleaned from the session was that Doyle most likely never made it off the Cape. Doyle had made the mistake of mentioning to Vincent that he had to pay off a loan shark in Boston. Flint worked his sources and within an hour found the name of the scumbag who had loaned Doyle the money. At first the guy wouldn't give up the information, but once Flint offered to pay what Doyle owed him—and having heard of Flint and knowing the man's reputation for getting what he wanted—the guy provided Flint with everything he needed. Yes, Murphy had loaned Doyle the money. No, he had no idea what it was for—just some sort of scheme. Doyle was supposed to deliver what was owed that day. A quick phone call from Doyle said he was stuck in traffic and would bring the money as soon as he got off the Cape. But he never showed. That meant to Flint that unless he was one of the unlucky ones on the bridge at the time of its collapse, he was still on the Cape. He just had to figure out where.

Money and power got things accomplished, and Flint had loads of both. In no time his men discovered where Doyle had been staying and what he had been driving. They found his car in the hotel parking lot, and at first assumed that Doyle was still staying at the hotel. But after checking his room and finding it bursting at the seams with a family of eight, they gave his car a going over and quickly determined that it was a junk box that had bit the big one. Logic told them he rented a car, which would explain why he didn't escape the previous night and why he never made it off the Cape—nothing would have been open. A short time later Flint's men had the rental information. It was now just a matter of time.

No one on the Cape was going anywhere anytime soon, and that included Doyle. Flint had no doubt his men would find Doyle. They had the time and they had the manpower. The Cape wasn't that big. They would find that car, and when they did, they would find Doyle.

Flint just hoped Doyle wouldn't understand the significance of the other item he stole with the money. If that happened, it would change everything, and it was the only thing on earth that scared Flint.

*****

Flint wasn't the only one who was scared. After saying good night to his new roommate and hearing her lock her bedroom door behind her, Doyle took a moment to breathe.

Since the robbery the night before and then the problems with his car and with getting off the Cape, Doyle had been in a constant state of panic. He had no idea what his normal blood pressure was, but he was sure it had skyrocketed. Enough to give himself a stroke? Probably not, but he needed to breathe. He had heard somewhere that breathing calmed you down. Hey, at this point, he'd give anything a try.

It was working. He was becoming a bit calmer. He took that time to tell himself that he was safe. Even if Vince talked, they would think he was off the Cape by now. No way would they be looking for him around there.

Oh shit, he'd forgotten about Murphy. He had to call the guy and let him know he was stuck on the Cape. Murphy was going to be pissed, big time. He'd probably demand more money. Hey, if it would keep Murphy off his back, he'd pay him. He'd still have plenty left.

He looked at the bars on his cell phone. He actually had service way out here. Then he noticed he had a message. It must have come in when he was in a bad service area and his phone didn't ring. It was Murphy.

"So where are you, you little dirt-bag? You better not be running out on me or you'll be looking over your shoulder for the rest of your miserable life … your short miserable life. Call me."

He dialed. There went the blood pressure again.

"What."

"This is Doyle. I'm stuck on the Cape. I never made it over the bridge before it came down. Don't worry, I have no intention of running out on you. I just don't know when I'm going to get out of this place."

"You know that every day adds to what you owe me."

"I know."

"No, I don't think you get the picture. I'm doubling the daily amount. Whatever you stole, it better be enough for you to be able to pay me."

"C'mon, Murph. That's not fair. I'm stuck here. I'd bring it if I could."

"And that helps me how? You want me to triple it? Look, we'll see where this goes. Maybe I can get a boat down there to pick you up."

"That would be great."

"You should know," said Murphy, "that the guy you stole from is looking for you, and he probably knows you're stuck there."

Doyle felt as if a knife had been shoved into his heart. That changed everything. If they knew he was there someplace, they wouldn't stop looking until they found him.

"Normally, I wouldn't bother telling a piece of crap like you," continued Murphy, "but you owe me a lot of money, and I want it. Stay out of sight. I'll call you." He hung up.

Doyle slowly laid his phone on the coffee table. No way was he going to leave the old lady's house now. His best bet was to lay low and hope they didn't get lucky and find him there. He picked up his backpack and set it on the couch. He glanced at the bedroom door and reached in and pulled out the bag containing the loot. He took out the piles of banded $100 bills and laid them on the coffee table. That cheered him up somewhat. At the bottom of the bag was another item. *Oh right*, he thought, he'd forgotten he'd taken that as well. It was a box. About eight inches long, it was an inch thick. He was thinking it was probably a piece of jewelry. He didn't like stealing jewelry—too hard to fence—but he might get lucky with this one.

He opened the box. Not jewelry. He stared at it for a moment and then recognition set in. He began to tremble and he set the box down on top of the money and almost reverently withdrew his hands. No, he wasn't going to get lucky.

He was going to get dead.

Chapter 19

Things were getting tense in the Barnstable Police Station. Chandler had reached out to the other departments on the Cape and determined that they were dealing with the same problems he faced. The State Police were of little help simply due to manpower. Most of the units stationed at the Bourne Bridge barracks were on the other side of the bridge when it came down. In fact, there were only six State police cars on the entire Cape, and all but one were still helping out at the sites of the downed bridges. The sixth one was stuck in Falmouth, having been rear-ended by a panicked driver.

Stories were coming into the station from the officers on the road, describing the horrific scene in downtown Hyannis. Almost every store in the middle of town had been looted. The mall had tried to close its doors, without success, and was in the process of being cleaned out.

How could people act like this, Chandler wondered. What made them do things that they would never before have done? It was fear, he concluded: fear of the unknown. They had no idea who was behind all this, or how many of them there were. Were they planning on detonating a nuclear weapon? Would it become like the Middle East, with random beheadings? When fear was involved, people changed.

And then he thought of Sara Cross. What he did to her was no different than what the people out there were doing. While some of his actions were based in anger and embarrassment, he had to admit that fear was the overriding reason he did what he did. He was afraid she would report him to the chief, or laugh at him and tell her co-workers. That wasn't her style, and he knew in his gut that she would never have done any of that, but fear makes a person rationalize his behavior, and Chandler had certainly taken rationalization to a new art form.

He wished Sara was there at that moment. He needed her common sense, her intelligence, her courage, and most of all, the respect the others gave her. Well, that ship had sailed. He had to get a grip on the situation. His people needed a leader, and like it or not, it was up to him to assume the role he had been given.

"Everyone gather around," he said.

Very quickly—illustrating the fear his own men and women were feeling—the talking in the room stopped and he was surrounded by officers in riot gear.

"It's a mess out there and it's up to us to somehow put a lid on it." He counted. Including him, there were thirty-six officers. Most of the 100 or so members of the police force were already out on the front lines, in many cases on foot and alone. "I don't want any more people going out there alone. You work in pairs. Number one concern is to assist any of our people in trouble; number two concern is to help any member of the public in trouble. Pick and choose your battles. Most petty crimes can be ignored. The same with traffic violations. We're certainly not handing out tickets. Use your common sense. If a situation is bad, take care of it, otherwise move on. We're going to get a lot of shit from the citizens when this is all over, but all we can do is the best we can do. Worry about the safety of your fellow officers and the safety of the public. Beyond that, there's not a whole lot you can do except be a presence. I'll stay behind with three others, just in case some idiot decides to storm the police station. The rest of you get out there, but be careful."

Chandler noticed that they seemed anxious to get out on patrol. Feeling vulnerable and disliked, as he had ever since the Sara Cross incident, he wasn't sure if they were anxious to be out there or just anxious to be away from him.

For the twentieth time that day, he wished the Sara Cross thing had never happened. He needed her by his side.

And for the twentieth time that day he wondered where she was and what she was doing at that moment.

Chapter 20

At that moment Sara was also wishing the incident with Chandler had never happened. She loved her job and the variety that went with it. Yes, she was the lead homicide detective, but homicides—despite the ever rising crime rate—weren't an everyday event in Hyannis. As a result, she often found herself involved in practically every aspect of police work, helping out in every department and even mentoring some of the younger officers. It wasn't easy at first. A police force is a predominately male-oriented club, and there were many who resented her presence in the beginning. But Sara came from another male-oriented profession—the Marines—and had proven herself equal to (and usually better than) many of her fellow MPs. She knew that it would take some time. In fact, it took very little time. Two years into the job in Hyannis she had already won over ninety percent of the force with her skill, calm demeanor, and intelligence. The few who were still biased against her were mostly old-timers who eventually dropped away through attrition.

A situation such as this was ideal for someone like Sara. Ten minutes after the fall of the bridges, she would have already anticipated the response from the citizenry and would have had everyone placed in strategic positions to quell trouble before it began. In short, she would have taken over, and it would have been with the blessing of everyone concerned—the patrol officers because they needed guidance, the chief because he recognized her skills, and even Chandler, who would have been grateful because of his own deficiencies.

Now all she could do was observe. Or not.

She went to her gun safe and pulled out her 9mm. She checked the magazine to make sure it was full and put it, with two more loaded magazines, in her handbag.

Marcus was eyeing her with amusement. She caught the look.

"What?"

"Nothing. Just seeing where this is going."

"You expect me to just sit around while all this is happening?" she asked, glaring at him.

"Hell, no. I was actually wondering why it took you so long."

Since he and Seth had arrived at Sara's, the evening had been somewhat awkward, watching the now nonstop newscasts from every station. When they got tired of the talking heads sitting around the table on CNN, they tuned back to a Boston station. Sara's condo was far enough from the main part of town so that they couldn't hear much of what was transpiring with the looting.

The awkwardness came from several fronts: 1) Sara wasn't used to having visitors and Marcus could sense it loud and clear; 2) Marcus realized soon after arriving that the attraction he felt for Sara was mutual on her part, creating a mild sexual tension; 3) And with that in mind, having Seth there as the third wheel was unwanted by both of them. In this case, Seth was the worst kind of third wheel. He hadn't said more than two dozen words all day and still felt sick to his stomach. If he wasn't his client's nephew, Marcus would have jettisoned him long ago. Frankly, his client would have been onboard with that plan—he obviously regretted ever having employed Seth in the first place.

Sara sat down on the couch and was silent while she fondled her gun like the old friend it was. Seth had gone into the bathroom for the third time since they arrived, and they both appreciated his absence. Finally she looked up at Marcus with tears in her eyes.

"I don't know what to do," she said in a whisper. "I don't fucking know what to do."

Marcus could see that the indecision was killing her. She was used to being in charge of a situation, not the effect of it.

"I want to help. I want to be out there," she said. "Fucking Chandler. Why did he do this to me?"

"You don't strike me as someone who wallows in self-pity," said Marcus.

"I'm not. But I'm also not someone who can sit still while the world around me goes up in smoke."

"Going out tonight would be a bad move," said Marcus. "It's chaos, and without the police force behind you it would be dangerous—gun or no gun. How about we settle in for the night and take this up in the morning?"

"And do what?"

"Go after the bad guys. Try to figure out who they are and what they want. Maybe Seth knows more than he thinks he knows."

"And what do we do if we find them?" asked Sara.

"Get word to the FBI, I guess."

"You said that grudgingly," said Sara. "You don't like going through channels, do you? When you worked for the, I assume, CIA," Marcus nodded, "you were out there on your own a lot, weren't you?"

"All the time. I got my assignments and I did them. My contact with the agency was by computer or in person with other field agents. They pretty much gave me free reign."

"And you got the job done."

"Most of the time. No such thing as one hundred percent success rate in that business. You succeeded when and where you could."

"Why did you leave?"

Marcus told her the story of Skyler, downplaying the romance part, and of her death and of his identity being compromised. He needn't have bothered downplaying the romance.

"The agent who was killed, Skyler. You were in love with her, weren't you?"

He was silent for a moment.

"None of my business. I'm sorry."

"No, it's fine. In that life nobody ever used the word love. Life was too fragile. But yeah, I suppose you could call it that. One way or the other it was never destined to succeed. That life would have made it impossible. For her to die though, it was…" He let the sentence trail off.

At that moment Seth returned from the bathroom, looking no better than he did when he went in.

"You okay?" Marcus asked him.

"Fine," he mumbled.

It had been a long day and everyone was exhausted. They finally turned off the TV and made their way to their beds—Marcus's bed being the air mattress on the floor and Seth's being the couch. Sara set the house alarm, bid the two men good night and closed her bedroom door. Marcus looked longingly at the door for a few seconds, imagining the scene on the other side as Sara got undressed.

Nothing was said between the two men as Seth laid down on the couch and turned his back to Marcus. That was fine for Marcus. He was ruing the day he'd accepted this job.

At 2am, the house alarm suddenly began to screech. In a half second Marcus was up with his gun pointed at the half-opened front door. A moment later Sara appeared, wearing running shorts and a baggy t-shirt. Her gun was also pointed at the door. After a quick survey of the scene, she walked over to the alarm box and entered her code. The sweet sound of silence took the place of the alarm.

Marcus put his gun in his belt. It only took a second to know what had happened.

"Seth is gone," he said.

*****

A long silence followed, Marcus and Sara both evaluating the situation. Marcus plunked down into a chair, exhausted, with Sara, feeling the adrenaline of the moment beginning to dissipate, easing herself down into the chair opposite. They both avoided the couch, somehow not wanting to sit where Seth had just been sleeping.

Marcus glanced at the door.

"It's still raining out," he said.

"Windy, too. And dark."

"He could be anywhere," said Marcus.

"And I'm tired," added Sara.

"Frankly, it's been a long day. A long week, for that matter. I'm really sick of anything to do with Seth Wakeby."

"The next couple of days will be intense and Seth isn't going anywhere. I'm betting a little sleep will help prepare us."

"Uh huh." Marcus suddenly realized that he was staring at Sara's legs. He looked up and caught her looking at him with an amused smile. "Sorry," he said.

"Nothing to be sorry for. How long has it been?"

Marcus was caught off-guard by her comment. "Uh, not exactly sure."

"That long?"

"I guess so. Skyler, a long time ago. My work is kind of solitary. I don't get out much. How about you?"

"I was married to my job. I never got out. It's been a long time."

Now the silence was awkward, neither wanting to be the one to make the move. Finally, Sara stood up and reached her hand out. Marcus stood and took it and then followed her to the bedroom. As they walked into the bedroom, their clasped hands gently moved back and forth as they searched out each other's touch in anticipation of the next several hours.

Clutched in their free hands were their guns.

July 6th

Chapter 21

After slamming into Florida, Hurricane Chad slid off the coast and began to strengthen, preparing for its next target, the Outer Banks. The residents of northern Florida, Georgia, and South Carolina breathed a collective sigh of relief knowing that they had escaped the worst of the storm. They were happy to deal with high winds and rain if it meant avoiding the brunt of the hurricane.

By midday, the Outer Banks were almost totally empty of people, the tourist season going on hold. Longtime business owners knew that the magnitude of Chad wasn't going to just disrupt the tourist business for a week or two, it was going to destroy it for the rest of the season. Without the storm having even hit yet, they knew that when it did come, cleanup would take at least weeks, and by the time it was done the tourist business would be tepid at best for the rest of the summer. If the storm hit with the predicted fury, the tourist trade wouldn't return at all, resulting in many millions of dollars in lost revenue.

Homes and businesses had been boarded up the day before. They knew what they were doing, and had done it many times before. *Just another hurricane* was the rallying cry of the old-timers. But even the old-timers were nervous about this one and sensed that when they returned from the shelters on the mainland, their homes might very well be gone.

For Cape Cod it was a different story. The meteorologists looked at the ever-narrowing of the spaghetti strings that signified the hurricane's path with a mixture of excitement and horror. The excitement came from the very reasons they became meteorologists in the first place. The horror came because they were human and they could foretell the devastation that the Cape would suffer. And unlike the Outer Banks, there was no escaping it. There would be no mass evacuation, and for some, no place to hide. The damage would be catastrophic. Those who thought of the lost tourist trade because of the storm knew that it really didn't matter. That ship had sailed the moment someone decided to bring down the bridges. The tourist trade on Cape Cod would be non-existent for years to come.

The computer models had the storm bouncing off the Outer Banks and slowing down, where it would once again gather strength in the record-warm waters of the Atlantic. By the morning of the 7th, it would resume its trek to New England. All the estimates had the storm slamming into the Cape by midday on the 8th, at least as a Category 3—and very possibly a Category 4—hurricane, and exiting many hours later.

The black humor circulating at the National Hurricane Center was that the terrorists who had brought down the bridges couldn't have predicted the weather. Chances were that they were going to be stuck on the Cape with all of their half a million hostages. Served them right.

But humor aside, the growing sentiment from

meteorologists across the country was very simple: *God help them all.*

Chapter 22

July 6th started out as ugly as the previous day had ended, weather-wise. The rain wasn't as heavy, but the wind still hadn't let up. The Cape was quiet. The looting of the night before was over, not because everyone had suddenly come to their senses—although many had, long after the damage was done—but because there was little left to loot. Supermarket shelves were empty, mom and pop stores (what few there were to begin with) were empty, most likely never to open again, and gas pumps had either run dry or had been locked by the owners. Two gas stations on the Cape had erupted in flames when fights broke out and carelessness took over. News helicopters buzzed the area by the dozens, reporters expressing their shock at the aftermath. No one could blame riots only on inner city anger any more. The vast majority of the violence and damage was caused by middle-class whites—people who had probably once shaken their heads in judgment at the violence they watched on CNN during the various riots around the country in recent years.

Now, in the early morning hours, it was almost peaceful. But the peace was an illusion. Mostly, it was people hiding—hiding in their houses, hotel rooms, RVs and cars. Those on the ground in the middle of it all weren't fooled. They knew it was only the beginning. Of what, they weren't sure. They knew what was coming from the weather. They knew the Cape was in for it. But the hurricane, as monstrous as it was predicted to be, had been relegated almost to an afterthought. After all, what use was it to worry about the hurricane if they might not even be alive for it? It was the intentions of the terrorists that frightened everyone. They hadn't heard anything yet from them. It was obvious they had a plan. But what? You don't bring down bridges for the fun of it. The terrorists had something more in store for the Cape, and until they heard otherwise, half a million people were going to assume the worst.

By 9:00, people began to venture out into the rain on foot to survey the scene for themselves. The only vehicles on the road were the occasional police car or emergency vehicle. It was clear that cars were useless. Where would anyone go? Besides, sticking close to home seemed prudent, considering all that had happened.

Neighbors, hiding their embarrassment at anything they might have done the night before, began talking to other neighbors. Now the indignation at what "everyone else" had done set in, and it was time to protect themselves. Neighbors quickly formed alliances to guard against future acts of aggression, as did hotel guests. But they all knew it was just a way of doing something. They knew that their real enemies were the unseen terrorists who wielded the real power and could use it at any time.

Those who weren't outside were glued to their TVs, waiting to hear the rescue plans the government had in place. But none came. In fact, what was becoming frighteningly apparent was that the news media weren't even asking those kinds of questions of the authorities.

It didn't take long for people to realize that something was just not right. Not only were the reporters not asking the questions about rescue and the authorities not volunteering the information, there was no activity coming from Otis. Formally known as Joint Base Cape Cod, most people knew it as Otis Air National Guard Base, or just Otis. Covering 22,000 acres on the Upper Cape, it was home to Camp Edwards, a National Guard training complex. Otis also housed a Coast Guard Air Station, an Air Force facility, and other training groups. Despite the large area, the population of the base had dwindled significantly over the years from budget cuts and realignments. Otis had several airstrips, and during the 9/11 crisis, Cape residents could hear the jets taking off like clockwork every day for months. When they reassigned all of the jets to other bases, noise from the base had become only an occasional event.

Today the base was quiet. No military jets or cargo planes bringing supplies, and no helicopters. The only news coming from the base was that they had announced they were opening it to any displaced tourists. Anyone driving or walking to the base would be allowed in and they would also send trucks out to collect those who needed a place to stay and had no transportation.

While that was all good news, it didn't answer the questions on most people's lips: What were the authorities doing to protect everyone, and how were they going to get all the nonresidents off the Cape? And after the hurricane hit, it might be more than just the tourists who would have to be relocated.

By 10:30 the rumblings started on the air. Reporters were well aware that the lack of information was troubling those on the Cape. More importantly, it was affecting their credibility as the source for news. No news station wanted to be the last to report what was really going on. It started as hints by reporters that they were being instructed not to ask certain questions. Once the ice was broken, others became more bold, insisting that something much larger was at stake and demanding that the governor address the situation on air. Finally, a press conference was hastily set up over the objections of the president and shortly before noon, this announcement was made by the Governor:

"This will be a short statement and I will not answer any questions. Yesterday, as you all know, this country — this state — once again became the target of terrorists. Several hundred people were killed when the bridges to Cape Cod fell as a result of bombs planted by the terrorists. Panic by the citizens of the Cape and those who were on vacation there led to a night of violence that resulted in several more deaths. With the ferry docks and airport both disabled, transporting people off the Cape is an option not available to us at the moment, and we ask those stuck on the Cape to be patient. Joint Base Cape Cod was not attacked, and the logical questions have been asked of why we haven't sent aircraft in."

The Governor shifted uncomfortably at the podium.

"We have been in contact with the terrorists. At this time I am not at liberty to tell you who they are or their reasons behind this barbaric attack. What I can tell you is that they have made threats that they will commit an atrocity worse than yesterday's if we attempt to bring in the military or try to land planes at the base, even for the purpose of evacuating people. Judging by what they have

already accomplished, the FBI tells us we have to take their threat seriously. We will be able to make airdrops of food and water in the coming days, and we will do so aggressively. We are well aware of the situation and feel a tremendous amount of compassion for everyone dealing with it there. We are also following the track of Hurricane Chad with great concern and will keep everyone up to date on its progress. Our emergency management team is on the job round the clock making preparations for keeping everyone safe."

He stopped and looked directly into the camera. His frustration at the situation was reflected in his face. He seemed to go off-script at this point.

"I understand your fear and I feel your pain. I also know that the information I've just given you doesn't answer your questions, and for that I apologize. It's a delicate situation that dictates our discretion when talking about it. I ask that you trust me when I say that your health and safety is our number one priority. As soon as I have any more information, I will pass it on. Good luck and God bless."

Not surprisingly, instead of calming the people of Cape Cod, the Governor's speech had the opposite effect. The questions flew: What was the threat the terrorists were holding over the government? What could be so serious as to halt any attempt to come to their aid? "Good luck and God bless" seemed like a defeated response. The prevailing thought was that it had to be a nuclear weapon. With that in mind, what was once an overwhelming fear had turned into total, debilitating terror.

Chapter 23

Ann Lawrence hadn't slept a wink. She had done the neighborly thing by allowing Joe Doyle to spend the night, but now he had to go. Having another person in her house—a complete stranger no less—was frightening. She heard him on his phone shortly after she had gone into her room. She tried to hear what he was saying, but her hearing wasn't what it once was. He was whining about something and she heard him say he was stuck on the Cape. She also heard him say that something wasn't fair. But that was about it. After he hung up, he was quiet for the rest of the night, but it didn't help her sleep any better. Now it was after seven and she was trying to figure out what to offer him for breakfast before kicking him out. She usually had a bowl of oatmeal, but somehow he struck her as a bacon and eggs kind of guy. Well, she had eggs, but he'd have to forego the bacon.

The breaking news just a few moments earlier was a relief to her. Otis had opened up for refugees, and Joe Doyle definitely fit the profile of a refugee. She could drive him to the center of Truro and he could wait for the truck or bus or whatever they were using to pick people up and she'd be done with him. Maybe tonight she'd get a good night's sleep.

If he was at least an interesting person—well-read or well-travelled—it wouldn't be such a dreadful experience. But he seemed so common. She realized how that sounded in her head. Snobby. Hey, she was eighty. She could afford to be snobby. Besides, it wasn't snobbery at all. She was happy to talk to anyone, and often did. It didn't matter if it was a millionaire or a homeless person, she was always happy to talk. Doyle was different, though. It was like he was hiding something.

She opened the door to her bedroom and walked into the kitchen. She looked over at Doyle on the couch. He was sitting up and looked terrible. He didn't look like he had slept at all either.

"Good morning," she said, trying to put a little enthusiasm into her voice—enthusiasm she certainly didn't feel. "Would you like some coffee?"

"That would be fine, thank you."

"How about some oatmeal or eggs?"

"No thank you. I'm not very hungry." In fact, he was starved, but after discovering the item in the bag with the money, he felt like throwing up.

"Suit yourself. I just heard on TV that they've opened up the base to refugees. I think you fall into that category. I'd be happy to drive you into Truro. They are sending busses out to gather people."

"Ann," said Doyle, hoping that the use of her first name would soften her up, "if you don't mind, I'd rather just stay here. I have plenty of money on me and can pay you for your hospitality—in cash."

"I appreciate that Mr. Doyle…"

"Please call me Joe."

"Okay, Joe. Please understand that I'm used to living alone. Having a guest here—especially someone I don't know—just wouldn't work."

"Please?"

"I'm sorry." Ann felt horrible turning him away, but she just couldn't have him staying there. "I'll drive you into town when you're ready."

Doyle got up off the couch. "Ann, you're a real nice lady, and that was nice of you to let me stay the night, but I'm afraid I'm going to have to insist that I stay a while longer."

Ann was speechless for a moment. How dare he say that.

"Mr. Doyle, I'm going to have to ask you to leave … right now. You scare me with talk like that."

"Not as much as with this." Doyle pulled out his gun. Ann gasped and pulled back against the sink.

"I … I don't understand," she said. "I let you stay here the night."

"And I really appreciate it. I just need to stay a while longer."

"If you want to rob me, feel free, but I don't have much to rob." She was regaining a little courage, but not much. "You are welcome to take my Jeep."

"And where would I go? I'm not going to hurt you if you cooperate. You're a nice person, but you don't understand. I'm safer here."

"But I'm not, not with you here. You're pointing a gun at me. I have enough to worry about. I don't need to deal with a gun." And then she thought of the words he used, and asked, "Safer here from what?"

"None of your business." And then thinking that he'd be

better off trying to be friendly, he said, "I'm sorry. There are some people looking for me. No, not the police. If they find me, they'll kill me. I'm safe out here in the sticks. They'd never think to look here."

"And if they do? Then I'm dead too." Now she was just mad.

"They won't."

"My niece calls me a few times a day," a slight exaggeration. "If she can't get through, she'll call the police." That was also not quite accurate. The other item she heard on the news that morning was that the phones were down—landlines and cell phones. Everything was overloaded and they all finally crashed during the night. The authorities had no idea when phone service would resume. No time soon, for sure.

"Then you'll have to convince her that you are fine. But I think you know as well as I do that it's not an issue. I turned on the news too. We are both aware that the phones are down." He realized that his call to Murphy the night before might have been one of the last calls out. In retrospect, he might have been happier not knowing that Flint was aware he didn't make it off the Cape. Ignorance was bliss. Ignorance would also get him killed. No, it was better that he knew. "Seriously, you have nothing to be afraid of. I have no reason to hurt you. I just really need to stay here. Maybe we can even get along. I'm not a bad guy."

Ann was stunned. She had never experienced anything like this. She was being held captive in her own house, and with no way to warn people. She thought of Officer Parker. Normally he would make one more attempt the day before the hurricane to convince her to go to a shelter, but she couldn't count on that this time. She heard on the news all that had gone on yesterday. He'd have his hands full. It would be a waste of time coming out to an old lady who he knew would refuse to move. Better to put his attention on one of the countless other emergencies.

The fact was, she was stuck with Doyle. In fact, he hadn't seemed like a bad guy at all, just not very interesting. Bad guy or not, he had forced his way into her life and she resented that. There had to be something she could do. And then she remembered the gun. She had put it in the drawer next to her bed to keep it close after her experience in the supermarket parking lot. She would bide her time, and when it was right, she'd give Doyle the surprise of his life. In the meantime, she had to make him think she was accepting of the situation.

"You say you're not a bad guy, but you also told me that people were wanting to kill you. How does that make sense?"

"I robbed some money from a crook. The guy is bad news. He deserved to get robbed."

"And you deserved to be the one to rob him?"

"Something like that."

"So what you're telling me is that you are a good guy because you robbed the bad guy? Do you know how stupid that sounds?"

"Hey, don't forget I have the gun," said Doyle, stung by Ann's comment.

"A gun you won't use on me." Doyle started to object, but Ann put her hand up to stop him. She had calmed down considerably and was looking at the situation logically, as she did with most situations in life. "You may think I'm just some old lady you can frighten by waving a gun around—which you can, by the way. But what people your age—what are you, 37

… 38?" He nodded. "What you don't get is that people like me were once your age. I actually remember what I was doing at 37. We may move a bit slower, but we have a lifetime of experiences behind us. So I can take one look at you and figure you out because I've met lots of people like you."

Doyle didn't say anything, so she continued.

"The fact is, you're a punk. You say you're not a bad guy, but that's bullshit." She figured a swearword from an old lady would help make her point. "You're a two-bit loser. You're lazy and not willing to work for your money. Maybe this man you robbed is really a crook, but I can bet he's not the first person you robbed. You had to work your way up to him by preying on people like me. How many honest people did you rob or scam, or whatever it is you usually do, to get to this point? I bet you've been doing this since you were a teenager. Have you ever held a real job?"

"None of your business, lady."

"I'm not 'Ann' anymore? I can see the real you is coming out now…"

"Yeah, I've had real jobs," he said, interrupting her. "They just didn't pay enough. I don't want to go through life wondering what it would be like having money…"

"And look at you," she interrupted right back. "I don't know how much you stole, but you're scared to death that he's going to find you and kill you. Are you enjoying it yet?"

Sometimes Ann liked being old. She could see right through people and tell them, and couldn't care less what they thought.

"Okay, so maybe I'm not such a great guy. The fact is, they won't find me here and when I get off the Cape I'm heading for a Caribbean island and live the way I want. So just shut the fuck up."

Ann, anger mounting, was thinking of the gun in her bedroom. She didn't know if she could really use it on someone, but if things continued at its current pace, she might just find out.

Chapter 24

A little after noon on the 6th, people were thinking clearly ... in a desperate sort of way. The Governor's speech managed to make people believe that they had to get off the Cape any way they could. The bridges were down, so cars were out; the airport was damaged, so planes were out; and the ferries were disabled and the ferry docks were destroyed. That left small boats. It was only the larger docks—large enough for ferries and Coast Guard vessels—that were gone. All of the smaller docks and berths were still there. The answer was to hire a small boat, or appeal to a boater's generosity, to take them to Boston, Plymouth, Fall River, Martha's Vineyard, Nantucket, or wherever the hell they wanted to take them, just so they were off the Cape.

A good idea, for sure, but not if tens of thousands of other people had the same idea. The swarms of people heading for the docks from Bourne to Provincetown actually began long before the Governor's speech. By noon the rain was still coming down and the harbor areas were clogged with frantic people, each hoping to catch a boat ride out of there. They quickly realized upon arriving that their great plan had no chance of working. There were no boats.

The minute the bridges came down, boat owners up and

down the Cape knew that they had the means to escape both the terrorists and the hurricane. While everyone else was running to the stores, the gas stations, and in circles, private boat owners quietly headed down to the harbors with their families and maybe their close friends (if space warranted it). They had gathered precious few belongings knowing that time was their enemy. If they waited too long, they might get to the harbor and find their boats gone.

Not all boats were in the water. Many were still sitting on racks in the boatyards. Boatyard owners, or in some cases their fast-thinking employees, made it down to the boatyards to help people get their boats out—for a price, of course. Nobody on either side quibbled about price. The boatyard people always started their requests high, but not all of the boat owners had a lot of ready cash on them. Some paid as much as five or six hundred dollars to get their boat in the water, while others got away with paying thirty or forty dollars. Still, not all went smoothly. Some boats were hijacked once they were in the water. Some of the boaters and virtually all of the boatyard employees had guns, so some of the potential hijackers ended up face first in the water. In the haste to get boats in the water quickly, some toppled from the forklifts and crashed to the ground, ending those families' escape plans. The people who owned boats on the Cape, but who weren't there that weekend, were both lucky and unlucky. While they didn't have to deal with the situation on the Cape and could watch it all on TV from the comfort of their off-Cape homes, they also lost their boats to theft. In the long run, and considering all that was happening, they were more than willing to sacrifice their boats.

So by noon on Monday the harbors were almost empty. In

many cases, near-empty boats and their owners were sitting in the middle of the harbor looking in dismay at the bedlam on the docks. Some had tried to make money on the deal, selling seats to the highest bidder. Others had a more noble purpose and were willing to ferry people for no charge. Both ideas failed. Every time they got close to the docks, the crowds would stampede toward them, causing them to head back out to the middle. Some people jumped off the docks in the hope of swimming out to the waiting boats. However, there were so many swimmers and the water was so choppy from the rain and wind, the boaters finally left the harbor altogether, in their near-empty and half-empty boats, for fear of getting swamped.

When they could, the boaters picked up individuals in the water who were far from the crowds of swimmers. As long as they felt it was safe to do so, they were happy to help. If they picked up someone particularly obnoxious or demanding, the person went back into the water—not voluntarily. One boat picked up a man in his twenties who stood up in the stern of the boat and did a little dance and gave the finger to the crowds on shore in an "I made it and you didn't" gesture. The man and his finger were helped back into the water by all of the other passengers.

When the news helicopters sent video back to their stations showing the scene at the harbors, emergency management personnel scratched one idea off their list. Someone had come up with a plan to send a flotilla of private boaters down to pick up stranded Cape Codders. While they knew it would be a slow process, it seemed like a viable plan until they saw the video.

By 2:00 on Monday there wasn't a boat to be found on the

Cape. People were using anything that would float to make it off land and hopefully into the waiting arms of crews aboard Coast Guard and Navy ships stationed not too far offshore. But the choppy conditions and rain hindered any attempts to be rescued. Some made it and some didn't. Those using cheap rubber boats or even small beach rafts found themselves either swamped or losing air long before they reached the ships. Many people drowned that day trying to swim and boat to freedom.

Once the realization set in that they would not be able to escape, the crowds at the harbors dejectedly made their way back to their lodgings, feeling the futility of it all. The terrorists—still unseen—were in charge, and there was nothing anyone could do about it.

Chapter 25

Things were getting ripe in the ferry. It had been a rough night for everyone on board. The captain and crew had tried to make everyone as comfortable as possible, but comfort was a relative term. Most of the passengers would have preferred to be out on the deck—desperate to be outside would be more like it—but the wind and rain made it too dangerous. The crew had also insisted on everyone wearing their life jackets, which, while safer, made it all the more impossible to get comfortable. The ferry was rocking steadily and many of the passengers were so sick that talk of the terrorists was long since forgotten.

The engines were damaged beyond repair, so moving the ship was out of the question. And because of the wind and swirling seas, any attempt at rescue by the Coast Guard was deemed too unsafe, and would be until after the hurricane.

With the terrorists an afterthought, the fear now was Chad. If it was this bad now, what was it going to be like during the height of the hurricane? The very real fear the captain was now facing was whether or not the anchors would hold during the storm. The Coast Guard had done their best to help secure the ferry and keep it from drifting, but if the ship did begin to drift, it would almost certainly crash into the rocks.

For the most part, the passengers had settled down. With

very little to do, they tried to sleep. Cell batteries had died by now on most of the phones, but it didn't matter much. Sometime during the night cell service had also died. So most of the phones and tablets had been used to play games. Now, with dead batteries, there wasn't much left to do.

Richard Price was watching the beginning of a scene across the way. An old lady had gotten up to stretch her legs, only to come back to find a thirtyish bruiser of a guy sitting in her seat. Her husband of equally vintage years was asking the man to move to give his wife some room, but to no avail.

"Hey, you move," Richard heard the man say. "I've been on the floor since yesterday. It's my turn."

Richard sighed. Julie knew that sigh. He was going to get involved. But she didn't mind. The old lady needed assistance and there was probably no one on board more capable of dealing with it. Richard had studied the Martial Arts since he was a young teenager, almost twenty-five years ago. He was a master black belt in the art of Tang Soo Do, as well as a long-time practitioner of the Israeli military self-defense system of Krav Maga. Richard was a security consultant, in great demand from corporations, colleges, school systems, and police departments. He had begun studying the Martial Arts after being mercilessly bullied when he was young. Not surprisingly, he hated bullies with a passion. This man was most definitely a bully. She could see that Richard was about to get up and intervene.

"Go for it," she whispered. Hey, if nothing else, it would relieve his boredom. Sophia was asleep and wouldn't have to witness her father's dealings with the bully, which would most likely be extremely subtle. Most of the passengers wouldn't even be aware of it.

Richard got up slowly and walked over to the scene. A few of the people around the man were asking him to move and let the woman sit, but he was telling them—in crude fashion—to mind their own business. He was a massive guy, observed Richard, but very little of it usable muscle. To those around him though, all that was noticeable was the massive part. Richard was trained to see beyond that. The problem of course was ego. Even if the man felt compelled to move, he couldn't now. He had already gone too far in his bluster. His self-respect was at stake. He had already committed himself.

Richard stood over him, steady despite the rocking of the boat.

"Excuse me sir, but I believe you are in this woman's seat."

"You going to do something about it?"

"I'm hoping I don't have to. I'm hoping you will be man enough to recognize that this behavior isn't acceptable and will get up voluntarily."

"Well that's not going to happen."

"Then we have option number two. I drag you off the seat while you cry like a baby in front of everybody on board."

The bully stuck out his middle finger and said, "Fuck y..."

He was on the floor before he got out the second word, Richard holding him by the middle finger.

"Now, in most cases, I would have just broken the finger, but I don't want you disturbing the other passengers with your screams. So you are going to get up slowly, without a word, and come with me. Understand?" As he said it, he exerted more pressure on the finger.

The man nodded, grimacing as he did.

"You will also apologize to this nice woman for taking her seat."

He shook his head no, grimaced again as Richard put more pressure on the finger, then said, "I'm sorry I took your seat."

"There, that wasn't hard. Now follow me."

The big man had no choice, and he followed Richard, bent over in pain, to the delight of the surrounding passengers. The crew had locked the doors to the outside, so Richard took him downstairs to where the cars were parked.

"Here's the deal," he said when they were alone. "I could hurt you so badly you really would cry for your mother. Hell, I could kill you if I really wanted. But I don't. Here's what you are going to do. You're going to go back up there and find a spot on the floor and that's where you are going to stay. You're going to keep your mouth shut. Why? Because you annoy me. You picked the wrong time and the wrong place to be a bully, and I'm the wrong person to be a bully in front of. Got it?"

The man nodded.

"Good." He tapped him in the solar plexus and the man went down hard to the floor, doubled over in pain. "Remember that."

He left him lying there, knowing he'd be fine in a couple of minutes, and walked back up to his wife and daughter.

The rest of the day and night were some of the most uncomfortable hours Richard and Julie had ever spent. And no relief was anywhere in sight. All of a sudden, as nightmarish an experience as it was, Julie's family home on the Vineyard didn't look so bad now. Richard and Julie weren't alone; they were surrounded by hundreds of other suffering travelers. Other than the bruiser, who now sat alone sulking under a stairwell, behavior among the masses was generally good. Fear and exhaustion were the main reasons for the calmness, but seasickness also played a major role. The smell of vomit was overpowering. By evening on the 6th, the toilets had stopped working from massive overuse and the ship's crew was trying to work out an alternative solution. Plans were being made to make use of the car deck for sanitation purposes.

All the crew and passengers could hope for was that the storm would let up the next day. If not, when Chad arrived the day after, they were screwed. Royally screwed.

*****

The ladies of the Lifetime Book Club were on the verge of complete and utter breakdown. Twenty-four hours in the same house together had the women at each other's throats. Mostly, though, they were at Claire's throat. The eighty-four-year-old had worn out her welcome the night before. She talked constantly, complaining about every little thing. She was always hungry and kept asking Gloria if she had any snacks. Short of hitting her with a shovel and using the same shovel to bury her in the backyard, there was little they could do. So they ignored her. Now, they were coming to the conclusion that ignoring her might not have been the best idea. Like a child, Claire saw through their plan and was doing everything in her power to be intentionally annoying, shooting rubber bands and throwing crumpled bits of paper.

Claire was the enigma of the group. She joined with a friend two years earlier. The friend had been an acquaintance of Gloria's, and after discussing books one afternoon, Gloria invited her to join. The acquaintance asked if she could bring Claire, a well-read elderly friend. Gloria saw no harm in that and welcomed them both with open arms. The acquaintance lasted two meetings and then disappeared, never to be heard from again. Rumor had it she moved away, but no one knew for sure. When Gloria asked Claire about her, Claire said she had had a falling out with her and had no idea where she'd gone. Much to the chagrin of the other members, Claire continued to come, never missing a meeting. She always read the chosen book—unlike many of the other members—and always participated in the discussion, but there was something about her that made the others uncomfortable. It might have been her constant use of salty language, or maybe her penchant for saying whatever was on her mind, no matter how inappropriate. No one knew her background, which would have explained a lot. And Claire would have been happy to talk about it, except for the fact that no one ever asked.

Claire was born and brought up on the streets of Boston in a poor, working-class family—when someone was actually working. As a child in the waning years of the Depression, she spent many of her days conning and stealing. She only made it through fifth grade in school—when she went. Then she married a series of sketchy men, none of the marriages lasting more than a few months. During the Korean conflict, she worked as a nurse's aide in a hospital less than ten miles from the fighting. The war changed her, and when it ended, so did her wandering. She somehow made it into nursing school and became a full-blown nurse, working in various hospitals in the Boston area and earning a reputation as someone who was great with patients, but she was not as well-liked by her co-workers. She never had children, and when she retired, she moved to a small apartment in Plymouth and worked at odd jobs to keep herself busy. None of them lasted very long, as her poor Boston upbringing never left her and she managed to rub too many people the wrong way. She was once fired as a Walmart greeter for using crude language in front of the customers.

Her one passion was reading. She read anything she could get her hands on, and had since childhood. A book group seemed the perfect way to kill a few hours every month, and she enjoyed it. So when the others began to ignore her, she took offense, and dealt with it the only way she knew how from her background—retaliation.

Seeing as how no one was going anywhere until at least after Chad left the scene, it was going to be a very long few days for them all.

Chapter 26

Marcus and Sara didn't get out of bed until almost noon, finishing their night together with a long hot shower.

For two no-nonsense, capable people, the first hour of love-making was almost comical. They fumbled around, each trying to please the other, but making a total mess of it. Their long periods of celibacy had made them rusty—although they each secretly wondered if they hadn't always been rusty, and that time had nothing to do with it. Marcus realized quickly that he was no James Bond. It was only when they stopped trying did a natural flow take over. They finally fell asleep around seven. They woke up in each other's arms, and made love one more time before showering.

Marcus watched her dress, feeling none of the awkwardness that sometimes came after making love to someone for the first time. Was it just because he wasn't a kid anymore and had had too many life-threatening experiences to ever be awkward about anything again, or was there something real going on here?

He moved his eyes up her body to her face and realized that she was smiling at him. There was no doubt, it was real. Could it be that he was finally going to experience a normal relationship—assuming, of course, that he didn't die at the hands of the terrorists or in Hurricane Chad?

After dressing they turned on the TV in time to see the governor's address.

"It's not nuclear," said Marcus when it was over.

"Why?"

"A nuclear weapon leaves a trace ... a signature. The military can locate a nuclear device. Most likely, one or more of those helicopters up there has tracking equipment on it. If they had located the device, they would be homing in on it now and might even have them surrounded."

"The Governor's speech couldn't be a decoy to lull them into a false sense of security?"

Marcus shook his head. "Did you see his body language and hear his voice? He was actually afraid. No, whatever it is has to be more insidious than a bomb. It would be something much harder to trace. I think the Governor came on because they aren't even close to finding these guys."

He checked his phone. There was no signal, but there was a new text message. It had come sometime early the previous evening before the phones went down. He read it.

"Hmm."

"Hmm what?" asked Sara.

"A text from the head of the CIA, of all people. Somehow they know I'm here. He's asking me to call him back. Well, that's not going to happen now. Too bad I didn't see the text when it came in. But reaching out to me shows that they have very little to go on. They are desperate for help getting these guys. It also tells me it's bad."

"Chemical or biological?"

"Either one would be my guess. I think we're looking at

something like anthrax. Something airborne, most likely. Whatever it is," he continued, "it's scary and the people here have every reason to be terrified."

Sara made them each a bagel. As they ate, Marcus's thoughts turned to Seth. He groaned inwardly.

"Do you want to look for him?" asked Sara, picking up on his thoughts.

"Hell, no," answered Marcus. "What I really want is for him to walk into the sea and keep on going. However..."

"You're being paid to watch over him."

"Actually, what I'm being paid to do is follow him and figure out what he's up to, which I pretty much did."

"But you have feelings of responsibility for the guy. You let him walk away, you'll feel that the job isn't complete."

"Something like that."

"So let's go find him."

"It's not your responsibility," said Marcus.

"Not yours either, it seems. Let's go."

In all his years as a spy, Marcus had rarely worked with a partner. The one exception had been Skyler. On the one hand, he was skittish about teaming up, especially with someone he obviously had feelings for, knowing how the last one ended. On the other hand, in such a lonely profession as a P.I., and before that as a spy, it was nice sometimes to work alongside someone else. He wondered if it was just because he was getting older and his needs were changing. Up until now he was perfectly happy to work completely alone. In fact, it was the only way he wanted to work. He hated relying on others. If he only had himself to be responsible for, he could be sure the job would be done right.

They went out the door not knowing exactly what they would find outside. Knowing that the phones were down they expected to see a scene similar to the night before. But all was quiet. Very few cars were on the road. Either people were conserving gas or they just had nowhere to go.

"Where to?" asked Sara.

"Beats me. You know this town. Where would he go? We have to assume for the moment that he is on foot, so I'm assuming he'd still be in Hyannis somewhere."

"I guess we have to answer the question: What is his intention?" said Sara.

"We know he's scared," said Marcus. "Almost getting killed will do that. But now I'm beginning to wonder if I missed something. Does he have another reason to be scared?"

"You mean other than the bridges being blown up, the ferry docks being blown up, the airport being blown up, a mysterious terrorist whose intentions aren't known, and a hurricane coming? Other than those?"

Marcus made a face. "Yeah, other than those. No, not other than those. His reaction to almost getting killed seemed normal ... for a while. I know that it was probably a shock for him, but it seemed a little overblown the longer it went on."

"Are you thinking he was faking it?"

"Not really, but what if he's afraid of something even greater? What if he knows more about the terrorists than he told us?"

"Either way he's going to want to get off the Cape any way he can. The most logical way would be by boat. I say we look at the docks."

They took Marcus's car, but he let Sara drive, figuring she

knew the area and could make quick turns and take back roads at a moment's notice if necessary. It wasn't very far to the harbor, and with the lack of traffic, they made it in a matter of minutes. They weren't prepared though for the sight that confronted them when they turned the corner onto Ocean Street. From where they were, they should have been able to see the docks. All they saw was people.

"Holy shit," said Marcus. "Did everybody have the same idea?"

"There must be thousands of people here."

Marcus caught a quick glimpse through a momentary hole in the crowd. "What's not here?" he asked.

"Well, I can't see anything beyond the people, but if I had to guess, I'd say boats?"

"Good guess. So what are they all waiting for? You think there are boats coming?"

"If I had a boat, I sure wouldn't dock here. It would be overrun in seconds."

Sara turned the car around in a driveway and pulled into a parking lot. They got out and surveyed the scene.

"Hey Sara."

Sara turned to see a uniformed officer standing behind them.

"Hey Pete. Crazy times, huh?"

"You said it. Come down here to float away?"

"No, we're looking for someone. Pete, this is Marcus Baldwin. He's a P.I. His subject decided to skip out overnight. We figure he might be here."

"Yeah, well, good luck with that."

"Any word on the terrorists?" Sara asked.

"Nothing. Not a peep from them."

"We think our perp might have some peripheral ties to them. Who do you suggest we go to around here if we can confirm that?"

"If you can find any of the FBI guys, I'd go to them. Locating them might be a problem though. They're scattered all over the Cape. They're based at Otis, but without phones and Internet, getting hold of them is nearly impossible. Maybe we can get through to the base via police band from the station, but then they have to get word out to their agents by cell phone. That part's the problem."

"Is there someone at the station who could help?" asked Sara.

"No way. Total chaos there. You can guess who's in charge, and I say 'in charge' with a whole chunk of salt. Sara, you should know that most of us never believed any of the charges against you. Frankly, I wish you were with us right now. Chandler has no clue how to handle this. He's in so far over his head, it's not funny."

"Thanks, Pete. I really appreciate that. I wish I was with you too."

There was an awkward silence, then Pete furtively looked around. "You carrying?" he asked.

"Why Pete, you know I lost my carry permit when they canned me."

"Yeah, I know." He swept his hand around to indicate the crowd. "You think I care about something stupid like a permit? What I meant is if you're not carrying, I suggest you start. Things could get really bad around here soon. Gotta go. Take care." He went running off to break up a fight between two women.

"What do you think?" asked Sara.

"Gut feeling? He's here. I say we split up and meet back here in fifteen minutes. Hopefully one of us will have him."

"That'll take some luck," said Sara. "See you in fifteen."

Five minutes later Sara had maneuvered her way close to the water, figuring a desperate Seth would want to be on the first boat out. When she saw him, she said "no way" out loud.

"No way what?" asked an older man standing next to her.

"No way I could get this lucky," she answered, not really paying attention to the man. She bullied her way through the crowd until she was standing next to an unaware Seth. She put one hand above his elbow, the other on his wrist, and pushed down on his arm ever so slightly, hyperextending his elbow. He went down on one knee and cried out, "What the hell?"

"I'm going to ease up just a little bit, just enough for you to stand, and then we're going to make our way through this crowd up to the car. If I even sense that you're going to try to escape, I'll break your elbow. I'm not a cop anymore, I don't have to play by the rules. Understand?"

Seth nodded.

"Then let's go."

Getting back to the car was remarkably easy. Had it been a man strong-arming a woman through the crowd, numerous men would have come to her rescue. But a woman escorting a man elicited a different response.

The phrases "You go, girl!" and "Way to go, lady" accompanied her all the way to the car. Once there, she pushed him to the ground, and had him turn his head toward her and stick out his arm. She knelt on the arm and pressed one of her fingers into a soft spot below his ear. He grimaced in pain and stiffened.

"This hurts like hell," she said, "as if you didn't know, but it's doing no damage and the minute I take my finger away it won't hurt. I wouldn't trust you in the back seat of the car, so we'll just wait here for Marcus. You struggle at all, I press harder, and trust me, it'll be excruciating." She looked at him and shook her head in disgust. "That was a really stupid thing to do. You didn't think we'd find you?"

Seth was in too much pain to respond.

A few minutes later, Marcus approached from the direction of the crowd wearing a smile.

"You go fishing?" he asked.

"Caught me a big one." She let off the pressure, helped Seth to his feet, and threw him into the back seat of the car. Marcus climbed in after him while Sara drove.

Seth didn't say a word the whole trip back. When they arrived at Sara's condo, Marcus sat Seth in a hard kitchen chair and stood over him. Seth averted his eyes.

"I could tie you to the chair," he said, "but I don't think it'll be necessary, do you?"

Seth just stared at the floor.

Marcus kicked his leg hard and Seth cried out in pain.

"I said, do you think it will be necessary?"

"No," said Seth, still looking down.

"There's something you haven't told us. Something pretty important. Here's your chance. You can volunteer the information or I'll beat it out of you. Doesn't matter to me. And you know I'll beat it out of you, right?"

Seth nodded.

"Good, so let's start. You know more about this operation than you're telling, right?"

Seth nodded.

"What do you know?"

"Doesn't matter now."

"Why?"

"Cuz it doesn't."

"Want me to hit you?"

"I don't care." He lifted his head and looked Marcus in the eye, a tear rolling down his cheek. "You don't get it. In two days we're all going to be dead!"

Chapter 27

"I assume you're not talking about the hurricane," said Marcus.

"Fuck the hurricane. Of course I'm not talking about the hurricane."

"So tell us what you know."

"I know that no matter how this turns out, I'm a dead man."

"Why?"

Seth just shook his head.

"If you're dead either way, then why not talk to us?" said Sara. "We might be the only people who can help you."

"That's a joke."

Marcus slapped him lightly across the side of his head, more for effect than pain. "Look, it's obvious that you're scared. No offense, but it's also obvious that you don't possess the brain power or the energy to be a major player in all this. Here's what I think: I think you got involved because someone offered you a decent amount of money. And then they filled your head with ideas of some sort of government takeover. As long as you didn't have to get involved in the nitty-gritty of this supposed takeover, you thought it might be fun. Someday you could tell people that you were there at the beginning of the revolution. But then you got more involved than you wanted, and it scared you, and now you want out. When they tried to kill you, you realized that you were just being used."

"You don't know the half of it."

"Then tell me."

"They're in touch with the Feds by email. Guess whose email account they're using?"

"You let them use your email?" asked Sara, amazed at the stupidity of the man.

"I didn't let them, they just took it. They have some computer geek working with them. He took over my email account, so now the Feds will think I'm involved in all this."

"You are," said Marcus. "The Internet is down, so they won't be sending anything from the Cape."

"They're not. The computer guy is somewhere else sending the demand and the follow-up emails."

"One demand?" asked Sara. "That's it? Must be a pretty big one."

"It's stupid. I didn't think so at first, at least not when they sold me on it. It almost seemed reasonable. But the more I thought about it, the more I realized it would never work. The government would never let it happen. It's one reason I was going to back away from it. Turns out it didn't matter. They were planning to kill me anyway."

"So what is it?" asked Marcus, growing impatient.

"Land. They contend that the land the government has given back to the Indians is wrong and that they don't deserve it. They want the government to break up the Indian land and give it to American groups."

"American groups?" said Sara with a shake of the head. "You mean more American than the Native Americans?"

"And money. They want loads of money wired into a

whole bunch of foreign accounts. They'll use the money to fund their group."

"So what is their group?" asked Marcus.

"Citizens for a True America."

"Never heard of them," said Sara. "And trust me, I've heard of most of the fringe groups out there."

"They told me they have a couple hundred thousand members."

"Baloney," answered Sara. "If they had that many members, I'd have heard of them."

"Where do they want this land?" asked Marcus.

"Out west someplace. Montana or Wyoming, I think."

"So how does Cape Cod figure into this?" asked Sara.

"Convenience. Holding all these people hostage was a way to show they were serious about this and show how powerful they are."

"And they really think the government is just going to hand over land to them?"

"That's where I started to have my doubts. I didn't know what their demand was going to be until recently. They just talked about developing their own society out west. Sounded romantic, and, as I said, the guy I talked to was a good salesman."

"So why are we all going to be dead in two days?" asked Marcus.

"Anthrax. They've got a lot of it and if the government doesn't give in, I think they're going to use it."

"Why?" asked Sara.

"Makes sense to me. You don't have that much of something so deadly unless you are prepared to use it. Besides, if the government turns them down and they use it, think how much more powerful they would be the next time they issue a threat."

The room was silent while they considered what Seth was saying.

"Bad news," said Sara.

"Yeah. Did you see it?" Marcus asked Seth.

"I saw the case it was in. Kind of like a briefcase. It was sealed, so I couldn't open it, not that I would have anyway. That shit scares me."

"Something here doesn't make sense," said Sara, looking at Marcus. "They are making a demand that they have to know the government can't give in to. Would they really use it? If they did, they'd be hunted down. They have to know that. Especially with all the state-of-the-art surveillance equipment available."

"Unless they are strictly low tech," said Marcus. He addressed Seth again. "Do they communicate with each other using anything other than the disposable phones?"

"No. They can make a few coded calls to each other before they have to destroy the phone. Nothing has been done by computer other than the emails to the authorities—which can all be linked back to me. They don't leave any traces, which is probably why they wanted to kill me. If I had to guess, when it's all over, they'll kill the geek too."

She turned to Seth. "And why two days?"

"That was the deadline for the demand—three o'clock on July 8th. I think they are going to see if they can bring America to its knees."

"Do you believe the anthrax is real?" she asked Seth.

"The case looked official. Lots of stickers covering it saying things like 'Biohazard'. Looked real enough to me. And I saw a sticker that said D-394. I heard them refer to the anthrax as D-394 a couple of times."

"So who were you in contact with?" asked Marcus.

"A couple of people. A guy I used to know—Harry—got me into it and I went through him sometimes, especially at first. Tanner, the guy you killed, was another one of my contacts. He's the one I went through most of the time. He made me think he was my friend." He made a face. "The other one I think was the head honcho. He met me with Tanner once. He called himself Mason."

"So here's the big question," said Marcus, "you don't happen to know where they are, do you?"

"I'm pretty sure Falmouth, but I don't know where."

Being fairly unfamiliar with the Cape in general, Marcus looked to Sara for help.

"Narrows it down a little, but it's still going to be tough. Falmouth is composed of the town itself and a few surrounding villages. Needle in a haystack territory."

"And we have three days ... maybe," said Marcus.

"Two days," said Seth.

"At least three," countered Marcus. "If it's airborne, they can't do anything with it raining like this and then with the hurricane coming in on the 8th. The soonest they'd be able to do anything with it would be the day after the hurricane. So we have at least until the 9th."

"I don't know," said Seth. "Harry said Mason was real set on the 8th being the deadline."

Sara went quiet for a moment. Marcus noticed and let her

have her space. A good minute passed before she said anything.

"This guy on the outside, the geek. Does he have any decision-making capabilities?"

"No way. Nobody has decision-making capabilities except Mason."

"How do they get in touch with him?" she asked.

"Disposable cell."

"And what if they can't contact him?"

"I don't know. He can't make any decisions on his own though. That much I know."

"With the towers overloaded," she said, "this Mason can't contact the computer geek, which means he doesn't know if the government has responded to any of his demands."

"So," said Marcus, "this guy is sitting on a pile of anthrax, he's got a threat out there to use it if the authorities don't give in, and he's got no way to be in touch with the one person who is in contact with them. My guess is, he's pretty frustrated right now, because I'll bet he didn't anticipate the phones going down."

Chapter 28

"Shit, shit, shit, shit, shit!"

Mason was staring down at his dead cell phone, and then in a fit of anger, threw it against the wall. Even as angry as he was, he threw it knowing full well that he had a supply of them. Had it been his only one, he might have tempered his anger a bit. He couldn't believe it. He had thought of everything. Absolutely everything. He and Tanner had spent countless hours going over "What if" scenarios and felt they were prepared for any situation. So how did they miss this? One of the simplest of all the possible problems.

Since taking down communications wasn't a part of their plan, the possibility of them going down on their own simply eluded them. But of course it was possible. It made perfect sense. You get a half a million people in a small area all trying to make calls on their cell phones at the same time and the system is bound to crash. And that didn't even take into account the millions on the mainland who would be trying to call those half a million cell phones—and landlines, for that matter. The hurricane was one thing. There was no way they could have predicted that. The cell phone fiasco was another altogether. They had gone to great lengths to keep the whole operation under the radar: no emails or text messages between them; phone calls were short and the messages were coded; anything important was discussed in person; not too long living in one place; and all of their "recruits" had to have clean records and a probability of not being on any watch lists. In the early stages, he and Tanner had even communicated by old-fashioned letters when they were on different sides of the country and the information wasn't time-sensitive. There was no chance of any "chatter"; no idiotic tweets or Facebook posts, which seemed to be the downfall of most stupid terrorists; nothing to call attention to themselves.

And now, when they needed their cell phones to make use of—for the first time—email, they couldn't. Mason's computer guy was in Chicago and was waiting for Mason to okay the next email to the Boston outlets. He had a series of emails all set to go. In some cases, the same email had three or four different versions, all labeled uniquely. All Mason had to do was to give the guy a call and let him know which version of which email he needed sent. The whole phone call would take ten seconds. Now the guy was high and dry. He was under strict orders not to send anything without Mason's okay. It meant that the authorities had his demands, as well as his initial instructions about wiring the money (which he was under no illusion that they would actually do) and orders not to allow planes to land or take off, but now they would be awaiting the next set of instructions that would never come as long as there was no cell service.

What now?

He could continue on to his endgame and forget the rest of the plan, but the whole process of getting there was supposed to be the significant factor in all of this. The result would be the same either way, but it would lose its meaning without the buildup. No one would know why, and they *had* to know why. The "why" was what it was all about.

He thought back to when the plan was hatched, the result of years of anger, hurt, and humiliation. And then he drifted back even further, to the day his life ended ... September 11, 2001...

*****

He was thirteen and had just begun eighth grade. A new school and a new town. His father had gotten a job in New York City at an investment firm. Mason hated leaving Phoenix, but his father couldn't find work there. His parents told him that this move would be a new start for them all, so they had spent the summer packing and moving, finally settling in a rented house in suburban Tenafly, New Jersey. The commute into the city wouldn't be a hard one for his father, and the town seemed nice. Mason had already made a couple of friends, but it was still early in the school year. He knew he'd eventually make more.

September 11th. His mom had an appointment in the city—he never did know what it was—but was going to visit his dad at work first. His dad was so proud of that office and had taken Mason there over the weekend, just a couple of days before. They were going to the Museum of Natural History—just a father and son day—but stopped at his office first. They took the elevator up to the 93rd floor of the North Tower and his father showed him his office and—even more impressive—the view. It was breathtaking. He remembered thinking that his dad must have been a pretty important man to command a view like that. He later found out that his father was just one of the many drones who worked in the office. He often wondered later whether his father was happy working there, handling someone else's money day after day. A question he'd never know the answer to.

So on September 11th, it was his mother's turn to gaze out at the stunning view. He wondered if they were standing at the window when the plane hit. Did they see it coming? Were they scared? More questions without answers. He knew they didn't suffer, not like so many others stuck on floors above and below the strike zone. No, his parents' death was instantaneous and surely without any pain. The pain was reserved for Mason.

He was sent to Cape Cod to live with his mother's sister and her three children, all girls, and all older than Mason. His aunt was a single mother who—Mason realized much later—missed her teenage years and was trying to relive them through her own daughters' lives, leaving Mason pretty much out in the cold. His aunt probably tried in her own way to be a good surrogate mother to him, but she just wasn't up to the task, and looking at Mason probably just reminded her of her dead sister.

His cousins, on the other hand, were just cruel—two of them, anyway. The oldest, Cissy, was the kindest of the whole family and treated him decently. But she was older than the others and had her own life. The other two—twins—were two of the most evil people he had ever met. Sandy and Sharon, two years older than Mason, would go out of their way to terrorize him and made his life even more of a living hell than it already was. He was small for his age and the twins were not, each outweighing him by almost double. They beat him when their sister and mother weren't around and constantly played nasty tricks on him. He often considered running away, but could never muster up the courage.

He missed his parents terribly, and like so many others in the country at that time, came to hate anyone of Arab descent and cheered when troops were sent to the Middle-East. When he was fourteen and in his first month of high school, his class was assigned a project researching 9/11. His teacher had no idea that Mason's parents were killed in the attack, and when he found out, was mortified and apologized profusely to Mason. By then Mason was able to take it all in stride to some extent, and tried to reassure his teacher that it was okay. However, his teacher gave him free reign in choosing his topic—a decision that would affect the rest of Mason's life.

Mason had begun hearing stories about what the government knew and what it didn't. He heard about the unheeded warnings concerning a possible terrorist attack in hijacked airliners. From there he moved onto conspiracy theories involving the inferior metal used in the construction of the towers, and others about how much the government knew ahead of time about the attack. The more he read, the more he believed that it could have been prevented and his parents didn't have to die. He became obsessed with the subject, wisely keeping his obsession to himself, and studying everything he could find about the attack.

All the while, he was living in a place he hated, with a family that was becoming increasingly hostile to him. Cissy went off to college the next fall, when Mason was fifteen, giving the other two total freedom to terrorize Mason even more. He couldn't go to his aunt for help. By that time she had sunk into an alcoholic haze that began when it finally dawned on her that she couldn't go back to those carefree high school years.

One weekend night his cousins were having a sleepover with some friends. They told their mother that it was an all-girl sleepover, but the minute their mother retired to her bed and her bottle, they all snuck in their boyfriends. Mason stayed in his room, studying his 9/11 theories.

He had just gone to bed in his pajamas when his door burst open and three of the boyfriends grabbed him and carried him out to the living room. Mason was scared and could see that they were all pretty drunk. He knew something awful was about to happen. The boyfriends ripped his pajamas off and he was standing naked in front of a group of about twelve teenagers, most of whom he knew from school, and some of the younger ones were his classmates. He was embarrassed by his scrawny body and tried to cover up his private area, but the boys held his arms. Then his two step-sisters approached him and took off their tops, revealing their ample breasts. He felt himself growing down below in front of everyone.

"We've seen you looking at us," said Sandy. "So what are you going to do about it?" She reached in and touched his hardness. The inevitable happened amid the roar of laughter from everyone in the room. When the nightmare was over, the two boys let go of his arms. He picked up his pajamas and covered himself, humiliated beyond anything he ever could have imagined. As they all got up to leave, thanking him for the show, his cousin said, "You better clean that up. Mom will kill you for getting it all over the carpet."

And then he was alone with his humiliation, his world

having once again crashed down on him. He despised his life with his adopted family on Cape Cod, he hated what he was believing to be true about his government, and he was no longer willing to sit by and let it all happen. It was then that the germ of his idea of revenge was born.

When he left high school, he joined the Army—not out of any sense of patriotism, but rather, with the hope that he would gather some of the fighting skills he might need in the future. Unfortunately, he never did. While he was highly intelligent, he lacked the physical skills to make it into Special Forces as a Ranger or a Green Beret. He ended up in procurement, ordering everything from uniforms to toilets, experiencing first-hand just how screwed up the military was. It only served to point out how needless the death of his parents was, and to further fan the flames of hate deep inside him. Putting on a convincing performance, along with some self-inflicted injuries, Mason was able to get out on a disability after only three years.

*****

Mason tried to erase the thoughts from his head. It would be a couple of years before his idea would reach the planning stage, but it gave him more time for the hatred to fester. If the government had done its job, he would have been able to live a normal life. Who knows what he would be doing now. But he was robbed of that chance.

Over the years he read just about every report and theory available on 9/11. He wasn't stupid. He knew that some of the crackpot theories were too farfetched to be true. But there were many that he believed—maybe because he wanted to believe them, or maybe because they made just enough sense to be credible. But it didn't matter. He knew beyond a shadow of a doubt that the U.S. government had dropped the ball, and it was time to make them pay.

But he wanted something good to come out of this, as well, so that his parents' deaths wouldn't be in vain. The terrorist attacks on American soil had increased dramatically over the last couple of years and nothing was being done. He was convinced that it was because none of them were large enough. A few people killed from a shooting; another thirty in a shopping mall; ten from a car bomb; all acts of terror but nothing on a grand scale. Nothing to make the government sit back and say, "It's time to do something." Everything was argued endlessly in Congress and blamed on the president, who in turn, blamed Congress. Nothing was going to get done. It was up to Mason.

After the Army he used the GI Bill to go to college, where he excelled, pulling down close to a 4.0 grade point average and majoring in chemistry. Rather than going on to graduate school, he took a job with a government lab that worked with biological and chemical weapons. It was there that he realized how much the U.S. was involved in the creation of these weapons, no matter how often the government said they were only working on ways to defend against other countries' weapons.

The last project he worked on before leaving the lab was D-394, an enhanced strain of anthrax. The spores were finer, allowing for better distribution by air, but also twice as potent. But even better, at least in Mason's mind, was that it was now more water soluble, much more likely to make its way through filters. And being more potent, it was able to stay active in a water supply much longer than conventional anthrax. Its value as a weapon had more than doubled. Stealing a batch of it was ridiculously easy, further pointing out the government's lack of security. He was able to make it appear that the D-394 was lost in transit to another government facility. He stayed at the lab another year, mostly to avoid having any suspicion of the loss of the weapon put on him. When he did leave, his co-workers were sad to see him go and even threw him a party.

The attack was planned with great thought. The first step was money. He needed enough to buy explosives and pay his two explosives experts an advance of their pay—the only payment they would ever receive. He and Tanner also needed money to travel around gathering up their pawns. In retrospect, with the impending hurricane and the unexpected loss of phones, the four others weren't really needed. They were supposed to travel around the Cape after the bridges came down and keep Mason informed of the situation and of any problems that might pop up. Now they were just extra baggage. The money came from a fraudulent crowdfunding campaign for a product that didn't exist and never would. From it they earned enough to cover step one.

The bridges coming down and trapping people on the Cape was step two. He wanted people scared—no, he wanted them terrified. He wanted this talked about more than 9/11, and it was important that people saw it coming. He wanted the whole country afraid. He would follow up the bridges with a series of messages over the next couple of days threatening the anthrax. He knew that at first the government would put a gag order on the news, but he also knew that word would get out, causing panic all over the country. They would know that if it can happen on Cape Cod, it can happen anywhere.

And finally, just as Mason accepted whatever offer the government made—it didn't matter what—he would let the anthrax go into the water supply—not into the air, as would most likely be suspected—killing thousands. The lack of phones made contacting his Chicago man impossible, taking away all of the drama around the event. And with the bad weather leading into a hurricane on the 8th, even his release date of the 8th might have to be postponed a day.

No, he decided. He'd stick to his schedule of the 8th, no matter what the weather. The date had too much meaning for him. Both of his parents were born on July 8th. Although the year of birth was different—his father was two years older—his parents took great delight in the fact that they shared the same day. Mason took that into account when planning the attack. He would have stretched the terror out even a couple of more days, but it seemed appropriate that the country get the message on the birthday of probably the first two casualties of 9/11. The message would still get through though, he'd make sure of that, with the fringe benefit of Cape Cod and his fat cousins, both of whom still lived there, going down with it. He wouldn't have the satisfaction of watching the aftermath though—and this was the part he never told Tanner—Mason would die with the rest of the victims.

Unlike the others though, he would be just one more victim of 9/11.

Chapter 29

Ann's mother used to say in moments of anger that she was so mad she could spit nails. Ann had never been that angry herself ... until now. She was no longer scared of Doyle ... well, sort of. She really didn't think he'd hurt her, but on the other hand, it paid to be cautious.

After their discussion about Doyle being a punk, he had gone silent, almost refusing to look at her. She was right and he knew it. A day earlier he was so proud of himself for having ripped off Flint for a million bucks, but now he was scared. The things he was scared of were mounting quickly: 1) Flint—especially now that Flint knew Doyle was in possession of the other item—and his men; 2) the unknown equation that the terrorists represented; 3) Ann—she was a smart old lady and he knew he was going to have to watch her closely; 4) and finally, the understanding that Ann was right, he *was* a loser. Ripping off Flint was just a step up from ripping off convenience stores and gas stations, and it certainly wasn't something he should be proud of. He was wishing he had picked a different house to hide out in.

All of these thoughts had made Doyle quiet and morose. Ann, on the other hand, was doing everything she could to piss him off. It was clear that Doyle wasn't a killer. Not that he couldn't suddenly become one, of course, or at least become violent, but Ann was pretty sure he wouldn't hurt her. Right after the argument Doyle had confiscated Ann's keys, so escaping by Jeep wasn't an option. He had also taken her cell phone and had unplugged her house phone, in case some service was restored.

So she was left with annoying him until he got fed up and took off. Despite him saying that he wasn't hungry, Ann could see that he was famished, so she made a batch of eggs with onion (so as to fill the house with the smell of food) and sat down at the table and ate it right in front of Doyle.

From Doyle's perspective, she was acting like a little kid. But it was working. He was getting more and more pissed at her. Finally, after about three hours of this, he couldn't take it any longer.

"Okay, you win," he said. "I'm sorry I yelled at you and I'm sorry to be interfering in your life. I really am. This is not where I want to be, trust me. I treated you badly and I apologize. You're a good person and don't deserve this. I'm just in a mess of shit—more than you could imagine—and I don't know how to get out of it. I'm just hoping that if I lay low during this, I might be able to survive. It wasn't my intention to put you in danger, but if I let you go now or if I leave, you'll go to the police and I will be dead for sure.

That's what she was waiting for. With all that had happened, all she wanted (besides Doyle to leave) was an apology. She looked at him and could almost feel sorry for him. He was pretty pathetic-looking at that moment.

"Would you like something to eat?" she asked softly.

"Please," he said, eyes still looking down.

It was lunchtime by now, but she still made him a large batch of eggs and toast that he dug into greedily. When he was done, he sat back and let out a quiet "thank you."

"Can't you just return the money?" she asked. She was sitting across from him.

"Don't want to, but even if I did, I couldn't."

"Why not?"

Doyle realized that he needed to tell someone, and he didn't have a lot of people to choose from.

"It's not just the money. There's something else." When he got no response, he continued. "Do you remember the story about five years ago—I don't know, maybe it was more than that—of the priest in Boston who was murdered?"

"Vaguely."

"You'll remember this. It was all over the national news. He owned a really ornate crucifix that had been passed down in his family for centuries. It had jewels in it and it was solid gold. The thing was worth a fortune, but he refused to sell it. They never caught the guy who killed him and the cross has never shown up. Whoever killed him has never tried to sell it, as far as anyone knows."

"I do remember it now. That story went on for months."

Doyle got up and went to his backpack and pulled out a velvet bag. He brought it to the table and set it down in front of Ann. "Open it."

She knew what was in there and found herself trembling as she opened the bag. She reached in and pulled out a crucifix about eight inches long and six inches wide. It was beautiful! She remembered seeing pictures of it on TV, but they hadn't done it justice. It was definitely gold—it was heavy, very heavy for its size—and jewels lined the front. She could identify emeralds, rubies, diamonds, and a blue stone that escaped her mind for the moment. She glanced up at Doyle with a questioning look.

"This was in the safe with the money. I didn't know what it was, so I just grabbed it and put it in my backpack with the cash. Don't you see? I can't return this," he said. "The very fact that I've seen it makes me a dead man. I looked it up online last night before my cell service crapped out. This is definitely the one. It means that Flint, the guy I stole it from, killed the priest, or had him killed. How else would he end up with it? Losing the money is one thing, but for a guy like Flint it's probably loose change. If all I got was the money, I'm not even sure how much he'd be after me right now. But the cross? Holy shit! My life is over if he finds me."

"As is mine."

"I'm sorry. I really am. But don't you see? This is like the most private place around. He'd never find me here. The minute I leave, he'll find me."

"What about your car?"

"It's down the road in a secluded spot. Besides, he has no idea what I was driving. This is a rental."

Like it or not, Doyle was staying. Ann thought again of her gun next to the bed, but who was she kidding? She couldn't use it on him and if she tried to bluff him with it, he'd just take it away from her. Besides, despite all he had done in forcing himself into her life, she was developing a bit of a soft spot toward him. He was a crook, no doubt about that, but he was also someone who had gotten himself into something way over his head. That made him pathetic and brought out the nurturing instinct in her.

She sighed. "I guess I can't do anything about you staying here, but I'm going to go through my food twice as fast now, and with a hurricane coming, that's not good."

"Trust me, I won't eat much. I'm too stressed. I get your point, though, and I'll live on one meal a day." He thought for a moment. "I wonder how much Flint is freaking out about the cross."

*****

Freaking out was an understatement. At first, in his panic, he had sent his men out willy-nilly in the hopes that one of them would see Doyle. But once the cell phones lost service and he realized that gas was eventually going to run out, he decided it was time to strategize.

So at that moment he was standing next to a map of the Cape pinned to the wall, barking out orders to his men on how to make the search as efficient as possible.

Using his contacts the day before, before the phones went dead, he'd had a picture of Doyle emailed to him. It was a mug shot three or four years old, but it would do. Flint broke one of Vincent's fingers to convince him to give a detailed version of Doyle's current look. He had eight men in on the hunt, each with his own car and a full tank of gas—again, the beauty of being rich. However, one tank each was all they were going to be able to get, so he urged them to be smart and coordinate their search in such a way as to use the least amount of fuel. If one of them happened to run across him, he could bring him back to Flint—preferably alive, but dead would be acceptable—

along with the things he stole.

Flint knew it was a shot in the dark, but not impossible. They were to concentrate their search on the car, not the man. If they found the car, they were to come back and wait for the others, then they would all go back together and search the area in the vicinity of the car. Most of his men assumed it all had to do with the missing money. Only two of Flint's most trusted employees knew the real object of the hunt.

After they had gone, Flint went to take a nap. His doctor had said that at his age a nap everyday was important. This time he wouldn't sleep though. There was too much at stake. He never should have killed the priest and stolen the cross. He should have known he'd never be able to sell it. It became too famous the minute it hit the news. He could have taken out the stones and melted down the gold, but it wouldn't be worth a fraction of what it was now. No, it was now just something pretty for him to look at when he was alone.

He couldn't let Doyle get off the Cape with it. If Doyle recognized it, he wouldn't be stupid enough to talk to anyone about it, so if his men could find Doyle fast, this whole thing could go away.

On the off-chance that he did talk though, whoever he talked to was going to have to die too.

Chapter 30

In Chicago, Hanson the computer geek was freaking out. He was a hacker, yes, but not a killer, and he wanted out. He wasn't totally sure why he got involved in the first place. Probably ego, he figured. Mason had come to him and fanned the flames of his ego, making it hard to say no.

Hanson and Mason were in college together and had formed a loose friendship. Hanson appreciated Mason's intelligence and Mason was impressed by Hanson's magic with computers. As he thought back, though, Hanson began to wonder if Mason's friendship wasn't calculated. In fact, he was beginning to think that all of Mason's relationships were calculated. It seemed that every person Mason befriended had a skill of some kind. He was obsessed with gaining knowledge, and he was always taking notes. He just wasn't normal.

Nice to be having these epiphanies now, he was thinking. *Why didn't I have them before I agreed to do this?* He couldn't just walk away. Tanner made that clear. He didn't like Tanner at all, and he wasn't sure how Mason and Tanner got together. Probably another case of Mason finding someone who served a purpose. Tanner was dangerous and he had made it clear that if Hanson tried to quit, he'd make sure his name was leaked to the Feds.

But things had changed. At least he thought they'd

changed. It was the evening of the 6th and Mason hadn't contacted him. By now he should have sent at least two more emails out to the media. Things were definitely behind schedule. He couldn't do anything on his own—Mason was very clear about that. Mason had the schedule worked out, and the email he had Hanson send out would depend on the situation. So there was nothing he could do.

And then he saw why. He wasn't sure why he hadn't seen it earlier. After all, he spent almost every waking minute online, with much of his attention these days focused on the Cape Cod situation. Maybe they weren't making the information public right away. The government was sneaky about things like that. The phones had to be down. Mason couldn't call him!

He found himself laughing. With all the planning Mason had done, he didn't anticipate the phones being affected? It was almost too funny. This would be a good time for him to shut things down. It would be easy enough to do. After all, they hadn't tracked him after the first email—and he knew they wouldn't—so all he had to do was to jettison the Seth Wakeby email and all traces of the code from his system, and then he'd be done with it all. Totally untraceable. But what if they suddenly got their phones back, however unlikely that was? Mason would call and Hanson would have to tell him that it was shut down and couldn't be revived. That wouldn't bode well for him. Mason would have Tanner on his ass the minute it was over.

Hanson struggled with those thoughts for the next two hours, coming to no clear conclusion. He was driving himself crazy, a feeling he wasn't used to. Being a hacker—and a good one—he was used to being in control. People needed him and he was able to dictate his own terms. That's what was wrong with this. He had no say. Mason told him what to send and when to send it. Mason was in total control. Well, screw him. That wasn't how he worked, and he couldn't believe he had let himself get blindsided like that. He had to give Mason credit though, he was good.

And then he saw his out.

He was wandering through the FBI secure website looking for information on the terrorist attack, when he came across an item about a body found near a cranberry bog on the Cape on July 4th. It was discovered with two bullets in it. There was a link to the crime scene pictures. Somehow, Hanson knew that it was related to Mason's operation, but it was just a gut feeling. It wasn't going to be Mason in those pictures, because Mason called him on the 5th, but he just had a feeling…

It was Tanner! Yes! Someone had done away with Tanner. Hanson felt a surge of excitement run through his body. With Tanner out of the picture, it changed everything. Hanson was pretty sure, based on the emails Mason had left for him to send out, that Mason had no intention of surviving this thing. He had assumed though that Tanner and the rest of the crew would be gone by the time Mason pulled his last move. Now it didn't matter. Mason and Tanner were the only two who knew who he was. The rest of the crew just knew that Mason had hired a computer expert to take care of the communications. The only one he feared was Tanner, and now he was gone.

Now Hanson would be gone, as well. He spent the next fifteen minutes deleting from his system everything pertaining to Mason, Seth Wakeby, or the emails to the media. When he was done, his computers were squeaky clean—well, except for all the other illegal stuff still on them. He even deleted the phone number that Mason called.

When it came to the Cape Cod operation, he was out of it. Even if Mason got back his phone service, it would be too late.

Hanson was out of the killing business.

Chapter 31

Hanson wasn't the only one who was questioning the operation. Mason's two explosives guys, Danielson and Packer, were beginning to have serious doubts. But in their case, it had nothing to do with second thoughts about killing people. They enjoyed that part. Their concern was getting paid. Through little things that Mason had said and done, they were beginning to wonder if they had been told the whole story. They weren't stupid like the other four recruits. They knew there was no movement afoot to take over the government. And the ransom demands were laughable. There was no way the Feds would give them Indian land. And as far as the deposits into foreign accounts was concerned, they might do it, but with all kinds of tracers. The minute someone tried to access one of those accounts, agents would be swarming all over him. None of that mattered to Danielson and Packer, because they had been paid a portion of their fee in advance, and were told that they would be paid out of a different account as soon as the job was complete. The sharing of the ransom would come later. Well, their part of the job *was* complete. It was time to go see Mason.

Their work had begun a few months earlier, scouting the Cape. They had taken many boat rides up and down the canal to determine just where they needed to plant the charges on the bridges for the greatest effect. The ferry docks were easy—they did all that underwater with scuba gear. The ferries themselves proved to be a bit complicated, getting down to the engine room without being seen. But with a little luck and using the four idiots as diversions, they were able to accomplish it. The airport was the toughest one of all. Even though it wasn't a major airport, there were still security measures to get around. Stringing the bombs along the runway proved the trickiest, again having to use the others as diversions and the dead of night as cover.

But now it was reckoning time. Time for Mason to pay up. They drove to Mason's in the rain and wind with dollar signs in their eyes and guns in their belt.

*****

Mason had been expecting them. Not necessarily at that moment, but soon. He had heard them grumbling about not being paid after the last group meeting and knew it wouldn't be long before he'd get a visit from them. He was at the kitchen sink when he saw a car pull up to the curb a half a block down. That usually indicated that whoever it was, was up to no good, especially with none of the other houses currently occupied.

This is where Tanner would have come in handy. He could have dispatched these two clowns with ease. Mason figured that Tanner probably would have used a knife. Well, he wasn't as crude as Tanner. He'd be a little classier in his method. But just in case things didn't go as planned, he kept a gun within reach around the corner of the kitchen.

He was standing in the kitchen doorway when they entered through the back door.

"Howdy boys. What brings you out on such a rainy night?" Danielson and Packer, by virtue of their more important role in the operation—and the fact that they were smarter than the others by leaps and bounds—had the freedom to visit Mason anytime.

"Thought we should have a talk," said Packer, a small man with a bald head and tattoos that covered almost every inch of his body from the neck down.

"And I know what we're talking about. Beer?"

Both men nodded and Mason opened the fridge and opened two bottles of beer—two bottles that he had already opened and recapped minutes earlier—and handed them out.

"You want to know when you're getting paid." He took a swig of his beer and waited for the others to drink before he continued. "There's been a slight change of plans."

"Change, how?" asked Danielson, also bald, but much larger than his partner, with long arms and biceps the size of watermelons.

"I actually don't have the money." Mason talked slowly. The timing was going to be crucial. "We pretty much used up everything we had to get this far. I've got nothing left."

"So now you're planning on paying us from the ransom?"

"Oh grow up. You know there won't be any ransom money. There never was going to be any."

The two men looked at each other, then back at Mason.

"So you were never planning on paying us," said Packer.

"That would be correct."

"Everything we put into this and we get nothing out of it?"

Mason could see it now. Packer was rubbing his stomach and looking gray. Danielson would follow in a minute.

"Nobody was getting anything out of it. Only me, and my reward wasn't material. I had a plan, but I needed others to help me carry it out. You two and Tanner were the most important. The other four not so much. Even Tanner didn't know my real plan. I don't know if he's dead or in jail. Doesn't really matter. If he's alive, he won't talk, and if he's dead, he can't talk. Either way, he was never destined to live—none of us were." Both men were in obvious distress now. He had to pick up the pace a bit. "I will die when I let out the D-394 on Wednesday. The other four will die that day as well. I'm afraid you two won't last that long, however. I put some poison in your beer. You should be dead in about fifteen seconds."

They both lunged off the couch at Mason. Or rather, they tried to lunge. They barely made it upright, didn't even make it two steps before falling to the ground. They both threw up and a few seconds later they were dead.

"Sorry, boys," Mason said to the air.

It was time to leave. He had a second place rented that he hadn't told anyone about, even Tanner. He figured it was where he was going to stay his last day on the earth. The plan was that by the time he was ready to move to his secret location, everything would be in motion and he could just sit back and watch the chaos—the people panicking and the government totally helpless. It was a beautiful plan. It sucked that they had missed something as simple as overloaded phone lines and it wouldn't go as he'd hoped. Hopefully though, the end result would be the same.

He gathered just the few things he needed—most

importantly, the D-394. He had been careful not to keep anything else around that could give the authorities any clues if they happened upon the place.

He took one last look at the two men on the floor in their contorted positions and pools of vomit and went out the door, locking it for no particular reason.

He had just one stop to make.

Chapter 32

Mason stood at the end of the street and looked down the block at the ugly ranch-style house in East Falmouth. The neighborhood had seen its best days—if it ever had any—back in the '70s. Two homes on the block were well-kept, but it was a losing battle for the homeowners. All of the surrounding houses were rentals, occupied by people who took little pride in their houses. It was one of those that his cousins called home.

Six months earlier, Mason had hired a sleazy P.I. to check in on Sandy and Sharon, so he could take stock of their situation. He hit gold. Neither had children (*Thank God they couldn't ruin anyone else's life*, he thought) and each had been through a divorce. They now lived together, worked part-time jobs, and barely made ends meet. It was a fitting life for the two people who helped ruin his.

He had parked his car around the corner and now started to walk toward his cousins' house. It was dusk and the rain continued to be steady. With only two street lights on the whole road, he was pretty sure he wouldn't be seen.

He'd had numerous arguments with himself over what he would do when he saw them. Would he kill them outright? Would he make them suffer? But what finally won out was neither of the two.

He knocked. He had already determined that both were home, and he could hear a TV blasting. The door opened and he was confronted by an even larger version of his cousin than he remembered. She wasn't grotesquely fat, just had the body of someone who didn't care one iota about her appearance. A cigarette dangled from her lips.

"Yeah? What?" Mason had no idea if he was looking at Sandy or Sharon. For that matter, he really didn't care.

"You don't recognize me?"

"Should I?"

"Maybe I should take my clothes off. Maybe then you'd recognize me."

He had her stumped now. She was thinking back through all the men she'd had sex with and trying to picture him. It was too much for her brain.

"What are you talking about?" Her twin had joined her now. Mason figured they could be the whole front line for the Patriots.

The first cousin looked to the second for help. "You recognize him?"

The second one put up her hands in defeat, and then looked more closely. "It's Mason."

"Holy crap," said the first. "We haven't seen you since we left high school. How the hell are you doing?"

Mason could see through that one like a plate glass window. She was going to be nice until it was determined that he had nothing for them. The other one wasn't as smart.

"If you need a place to stay, we can't help you. We're full up."

"I don't need a place to stay, thanks. Just figured I'd come and say hi."

"Come in. We don't have anything to give you. We have to ration."

"I wouldn't expect that you would give me anything." He sat down on a hard folding chair, not wanting to trust the couch. He looked around. "So you two look successful."

They didn't pick up on his sarcasm.

"We're doin' okay."

"Not that it matters, but which one is which."

"I'm Sandy," said the door opener. "That's Sharon."

Well, duh, thought Mason.

"What have you been doing since high school?" asked Sandy, obviously hoping to hear that he'd won the lottery and had come to share with his beloved cousins.

So Mason told them. They seemed unimpressed.

"What are you doing now?" Her interest was waning. Mason figured it was time to ramp it up a bit.

"I'm doing a project that involves you."

They perked up. That might mean money.

"How's Cissy?" he asked.

"Living in Oregon. Married with a couple of kids. She's a doctor."

"Good for her." Mason was genuinely pleased. The only one in the family to show him kindness deserved to have a good life.

"We never hear from her."

I wonder why?

"How's your mom?"

"She died two years ago."

"No great loss."

"What? How can you…"

"Let me save you the trouble. Your mother was a drunken loser. If she'd been a real mother, she wouldn't have let you terrorize me the way you did. I had just lost my parents, but that didn't matter to you. I was just someone you could practice your cruelty on."

Suddenly they were scared. They came from a segment of society that practiced revenge. Was he there to kill them?

"We think you should go."

"Oh, believe me, I want to be here even less than you want me here. I wasn't going to stop by at all, but I decided today that I had to tell you about my project, so you'll know what's in store for you."

Silence.

"Here's the thing. You know the bridges falling down and the terrorists threatening the Cape? Well that's me, and I wanted to come by to tell you how you are going to die."

Their eyes were wide open now.

"The day of the hurricane—assuming you are still alive and this place hasn't blown away—I will let out a whole batch of anthrax and everyone on the Cape will die."

Sharon had a tear rolling down her cheek.

"And here's the best part: Your death will be very slow and painful. You'll be vomiting blood. You'll be gasping for breath, but none will come. I sincerely hope that your last image before you choke to death on your own bloody vomit is of me, standing there naked, having been totally humiliated by the two of you in front of people I had to see every day. It's because of you that I chose Cape Cod as my target and the reason so many people are going to die."

It wasn't really the only reason he chose Cape Cod, but he wasn't going to tell them that.

They were both crying now.

"We're sorry," said Sharon. "We were just stupid girls then…"

"…Who have grown up to be stupid women."

"What makes you think we're not going to go to the police?" asked Sandy.

"Be my guest. They'll never find me. But it's a moot point. The police force has their hands full, you don't have any way of calling them, and the junk box I saw in the driveway is probably out of gas."

He paused for effect, then said, "In two days you will be dead. I hope you made the most of your life."

He stood up and walked out the door.

July 7th

Chapter 33

Chad was taking his time coming up the coast, as the experts figured he would. Off the Maryland coast now, he was sucking up the unseasonable warmth of the ocean, replenishing his arsenal for an assault on Cape Cod. The strong Category 3 storm had left the Outer Banks in ruins and the tourist industry in limbo for at least a couple of years. It was assumed by most that cleanup would take weeks, but they were wrong. It would be months. And after the cleanup would come the rebuilding, followed by the media campaign to get the tourists to come back. It would definitely take a couple of years to return to normal. But what would normal be? The smaller businesses, even with government help, wouldn't be able to survive that long without a good tourist season. So by the time everything was back up and running, it would be full of new businesses, the old ones having finally given up.

There were only two deaths from the storm, simply because practically everyone had been evacuated, so the toll was going to be measured mostly in dollars—in the billions, most likely.

The Maryland coast was feeling the effects of the storm, but it was far enough out to sea to only result in humongous waves, much to the delight of the surfers. In fact, Maryland, escaping all but the fringes of the storm, actually had a higher death toll than the Outer Banks. Five surfers had seriously misjudged their skills and had been swept out to sea.

Meanwhile, New England meteorologists looked toward Cape Cod in frustration at their impotence. There was nothing they could do. Absolutely nothing. Boaters were being warned about the danger of trying to ferry refugees out. "If you try, you could die" was the unofficial slogan going around. There was a minor effort being attempted in a few of the harbors, having Coast Guard personnel standing guard in a Coast Guard vessel while the small boats loaded up passengers. In the places it was being tried it was fairly successful, but everyone knew it was only a drop in the bucket. There were just too many people to get off the Cape.

All the meteorologists could do now was to keep the updates coming. As far as anyone knew, they still had TV reception on the Cape. That would end quickly enough as soon as the first power line came down in the storm.

No, the Cape was screwed. It would only be a matter of time before they learned exactly how screwed.

*****

President Landau and family arrived in Washington in the morning of the day before the storm. He had insisted that he be able to stay on the Vineyard to lend moral support to those caught by the hurricane. It all sounded good and made for some heartwarming sound bites, but no one was fooled. In fact, his approval ratings plummeted immediately after the announcement. He knew—as did most of the American public—that the Secret Service would never allow him to stay on the island in the path of a major hurricane. He hadn't even wanted to make the announcement, it was the brainchild of his chief of staff. With the swift negative reaction of the public, he was beginning to think it was time to rid himself of the man and go in a different direction. But that would have to wait. He had to make it through this crisis first.

Upon landing at Andrews AFB, he was whisked by helicopter to the White House, where he went immediately to the situation room, facing the same people he had seen earlier on the Vineyard.

"Where do we stand?" he asked the assembled group.

"The same as before," came the reply from Charles Kent of the FBI, who had flown back from vacation and replaced Wiggins at the table. "We've heard nothing more from the terrorists—no demands, no … nothing. They've gone totally silent."

"How about the source of the email?"

"We tracked it only so far. My experts say it's been totally shut down. We won't be getting any more messages from that source, which doesn't mean they couldn't change it. The feeling, however, is that we're not going to hear anything else from them."

"So do we make a move now, before the deadline?" asked the president. "Send in troops? A full frontal assault?"

"Against whom?" said Kent. "While I said the feeling is that we're not going to hear anything more from them, it doesn't mean we won't. We still don't know who they are. We don't know who we're looking for. We have to give them at least through today to contact us. If we hear nothing, then we make a move as soon as the storm ends. We're in agreement that they probably won't try anything in the storm because of the violent weather and the fact that they would never be able to disperse the anthrax in the rain, so if we don't hear anything today, we move at the end of the storm."

It didn't make sense to Landau, since the current weather also made it impossible to release the anthrax into the air. They could have a thousand troops on the ground in just a few hours. But he remained silent, the sting of the shopping mall incident still weighing heavily on him.

"So we're agreed," he finally said, "that if we don't hear anything more from them, we send in troops the second the storm has passed?"

He got a unanimous approval. Leaving the room, all he could think of was that he had once again agreed to a terrible choice. They could send in troops the morning of the 9th, but in his heart he knew it would be too late for the people of Cape Cod.

Way too late.

Chapter 34

It was only a matter of time before word of the anthrax slipped through the cracks and made its way to the general public. And it just took one person. A camera operator for one of the Boston TV stations lived in Plymouth with his wife and two young children. Up until that moment, the only people at the station besides the station heads who knew about the anthrax were the senior anchors of the morning and evening news broadcasts, who were all sworn to secrecy. The camera operator just happened to hear two of the anchors whispering next to one of the news trucks. When he thought he heard the word anthrax, he inched closer, only a few feet away on the other side of the truck. What he heard next terrified him. Plymouth was a few miles away from the (former) Sagamore Bridge on the mainland side of the canal. He knew that it would be easy enough for the wind to transport the spores all the way to Plymouth, so he called his wife. Rather, he tried to call his wife and couldn't get through. It made sense. He knew cell service was out on the Cape, so the chances were it would be out in the outlying areas. However, unlike on the Cape, landlines were still active, so he called the home phone from a landline in the station, relaying the message to her that she needed to leave and go stay with her sister in Vermont. And for God's sake, don't tell anyone or he'd be in big trouble.

It didn't take long at all for his wife to call everyone she knew and for them to call everyone they knew. A few short hours later the rumor had flooded Twitter feeds and Facebook pages all over the world. Not to be left bringing up the rear, the Boston stations announced the rumor as being true. The hostages on the Cape, thus far still having power and TV reception, heard the chilling announcement around noon on the 7th.

The reactions took two directions, both fueled by panic. Some chose to hunker down in their houses, duct-taping every possible crack to the outside, effectively hermetically sealing themselves inside their home. It amounted to not much more than a poorly thought out time-waster, since Chad was probably going to cause major damage to most of the houses the next day.

Many in the second group chose a much more immediate and life-threatening route—escape by water, no matter what it took. If the weather had been clear, boats numbering in the hundreds would have been sitting offshore, either full of gawkers looking at the Cape hoping to see something blow up, or waiting to pick up anyone trying to escape by raft or any other floating device. But the weather wasn't clear and the sea wasn't calm. The storm that had been affecting the northeast the past couple of days had been pushed out by the leading edge of Chad. Although the hurricane wasn't due until the next day, the storm was so huge the clouds and rain were already being felt. But for some, tackling the rough seas was preferable to dying a painful death from anthrax.

Coast Guard cutters and Navy ships were patrolling the

seas off the Cape, and the hope of many of the foolhardy escapees was that they could time their escape to the appearance of a ship. They used anything at their disposal to create makeshift rafts. Many never made it beyond the waves that were crashing onto the beaches, finding themselves tumbling back toward the beach and landing head-first in the sand, embarrassed, but still alive. Many of those who did make it beyond the breakers died when their rafts broke apart in the choppy water and they found themselves foundering without a boat in sight.

Others got in their cars—conserving gas be damned—and headed up to the canal, often having to use back roads with the highways still jammed with abandoned vehicles. The plan was to cross the canal using makeshift rafts. Some of the stronger swimmers decided to forego the rafts altogether and swim across. After all, it wasn't that far to the mainland—maybe a football field and a half.

The results were disastrous. In normal conditions the current in the canal constantly changed direction and could be hard on even small boats. In stormy weather it was even worse. A swimmer stood little chance of making it. Some tried to use the remnants of the bridges to swim to, hoping to make the crossing less hazardous, but the currents pushed them against the jagged metal beams, tearing the skin right off their body.

A few made it safely across, greeted by cheers and helping hands on the other side, but far too many perished in the canal, their bodies washed out to sea. The problem was compounded by the absence of law enforcement to talk them out of their foolhardy schemes. Police in every town on the Cape were too busy dealing with the panic in the towns to worry about stupid people who had death wishes. The swimmers were on their own, and most of them were going to die.

Chapter 35

Doyle was in a deep sleep. It was far from restful, though. He was dreaming of Flint. In the dream he had been caught by Flint's men and taken back to the mansion. Flint was waiting for him, an evil gleam in his eyes. Somehow, in the dream he looked even more evil than in real life. He was younger and not as frail, and in his hand was a baseball bat. Doyle was pleading for his life, tears soaking his shirt. His sobbing only helped to make Flint enjoy the process more. He swung the bat, shattering Doyle's knee. Doyle cried out in agony. Now Flint was feeling Doyle's shoulder, trying to find the right spot to hit. He kept pushing on it. Now he was yelling at him, yelling at him to wake up.

His eyes opened and he was looking up at Ann.

"You were dreaming," she said. "To be more precise, you were screaming in your sleep. It must've been a doozy of a dream."

Doyle just nodded. He hadn't yet come back to reality and was still breathing heavily. Slowly the breathing returned to normal.

"Sorry," he said in a hoarse voice. He wasn't sure what else to say.

"Well, get up," said Ann. "If you're going to stay here, you're going to pull your weight. The hurricane is hitting tomorrow. We need to get this place boarded up and ready for the blow and I can't do it alone."

"Yeah, okay. Give me a minute to use the bathroom." He suddenly realized that the place had a wonderful smell to it. He sniffed.

"Pancakes. You need something in your stomach if you're going to help me. So go do your business and get to the table."

She watched him shuffle to the bathroom, probably a little faster than he would have without pancakes waiting for him. She couldn't help thinking what a sad case he was. He wasn't stupid by any means. He probably thought of himself as street smart, but she wasn't sure he even had that going for him. He looked like someone who never got enough hugs as a child. He just seemed lost. He had told her a bit more about how he planned the heist from Flint and seemed genuinely proud of the whole thing. She wasn't a crook, but even she could see the gaping holes in his plan. She didn't say it to him, as he had already had enough things go wrong, but in reality, his plan had succeeded by pure luck alone. She'd tell him another time.

Another time? What was she thinking? She wanted him out of her house as soon as possible. There wouldn't be another time. But if she wanted him out of the house so badly, why didn't she try to steal back her Jeep keys while he slept?

They had spent the previous evening playing cards to pass the time. It was the only thing Ann could think of. She taught him hearts and cribbage. While they played, he talked a little bit about his childhood—as she suspected, it was pretty loveless—and she talked about her life. She talked about her early experiences and about her solitary life on the dunes. He seemed to show genuine interest in her paintings, so she described the process. All the while she was trying to figure out her feelings for him. Was he her captor or just some lost soul who had wandered into her life?

He came to the table looking somewhat awake. He had splashed water over his face and looked like the dream of a few moments before was gone from his head. She placed a stack of six pancakes in front of him. Butter was dripping down the side of the stack. He poured maple syrup onto the pancakes and dug in. Ann noticed that his appetite had returned.

"These are delicious."

"You'll be working them off in a few minutes, so enjoy them now."

"I notice you talk to me in a mean voice, but you do nice things for me. Why is that?"

Why was that? Deep down Ann knew the answer to that and to the reason she didn't take her keys while he slept. In a strange way she kind of liked him. Liked him or felt sorry for him? Either way, she felt the urge to do some nice things for him. And yet, technically, she was still a prisoner in her own house. She should hate him for that. *I must be getting old and soft*, she thought.

"Just eat."

When he was finished and the dishes had been cleaned up, she gave him his instructions.

"In the shed out back I have some large pieces of plywood. They'll cover the two front windows. I don't cover the other windows. They have shutters, but I like to look out at a storm, so I don't usually use them. I can always close the shutters if it gets bad. After that, I have a lot of things—chairs, tables, and the like that have to be put in the shed. You ever been in a hurricane?"

"No, I grew up in Upstate New York. We had blizzards, but not hurricanes."

"Completely different animal. Depending on which side of the hurricane we end up on, we'll either have more wind or more rain. Either way we'll get plenty of wind. And if this turns out as big as they say, this place is going to be rocking—literally rocking. I might even lose the house. Make sure you nail those pieces of wood really well. If the wind catches a loose corner, it'll rip it right off the house. Happy you picked my rundown little cottage now?"

Doyle didn't respond. He took the hammer and nails Ann handed him and went out the door. He was pissed at her for ordering him around. *He* was the one with the gun. *He* was supposed to be in charge. And yet, he didn't mind being pushed around by her. She was kinda like a grandmother. Isn't that what grandmothers were supposed to do? He didn't actually know. He had no memory of a grandmother in his life. Same with his father. And he'd only had his mother once in a while. He shook his head. He didn't like thinking about that. The fact was, he liked Ann and was feeling bad that he scared her in the beginning. He had no right to do that. If all had gone as planned, he wouldn't even be there now. Most likely, he would be in the Caribbean sitting on the beach, if his car hadn't crapped out.

Doyle spent the morning getting the little house ready for the hurricane. He was surprised at how good it felt to be doing some physical labor. In truth, he appreciated anything that would keep his mind off the cross.

By noon the house was as ready as it ever would be. Ann

stood outside and looked around, then gave him the "thumbs up."

The hours spent working on the storm preparation had given Doyle time to think. Ann was a good person. Understandably, she was pissed at him for keeping her captive. Hell, who wouldn't be? On the other hand, she had been decent to him despite what he had done. And it wasn't a decency from fear; he wasn't even sure she was afraid anymore. In fact, she was a pretty gutsy old lady. She knew he wasn't going to hurt her, and knowing that, she could have tried to steal her keys back and slip out while he was asleep, but she didn't. Why was that? He had to admit that he didn't understand people. In his worldview it was the people who stole and the people they stole from. It was pretty simple.

Well, he'd be gone soon enough. He wasn't exactly sure, but once the hurricane was gone and the terrorists had been taken care of, they'd have to come up with a way to transport people onto the mainland. Until then, he would try not to do anything to piss off Ann. He needed to stay there. He needed to be where Flint's men wouldn't find him.

*****

A few hours later as the dusk was beginning to fall, a car drove slowly up Ann's road. Flint's man had spent the day checking out the parking lots in Provincetown, coming up empty. As it hit the dinner hour, he was on his way back, frustrated by his lack of success. But he didn't just hop on the main road. It occurred to him that Doyle could have found an out-of-the-way place to hide out, so, mindful of wasting gas, he made side trips up some of the more remote roads just on the off-chance. It was raining steadily, the outer fringes of Chad making the dusk come more quickly.

It was fruitless and he knew it, and for the sixth time in an hour he told himself to head back and call it a day—until he passed the car pushed off to the side of the road. He had been following a small road in Truro that led along the ocean. He almost didn't see it, tucked away in the tall beach grass. He stopped suddenly and carefully looked around before getting out. No one was around. He went over to the car. Right make and color. He checked the license plate.

"Oh my God," he said under his breath.

He looked around at the houses standing in the rain. There were only two that he could see, and one of them, quite a ways up the road, looked like a wreck. As desperate as Doyle must be, he wouldn't be hiding in that one. He would need food and water. The closer one had lights. He saw an old lady in one of the windows.

Flint had given them the option of capturing Doyle when they saw him or returning with more men. He chose the second. He figured with the storm almost upon them, Doyle would stay put. He also didn't like the idea of going into an unknown situation alone. Too dangerous.

He got back into his car, closing the door quietly. He turned his lights out and crept down the road past the occupied house, only turning them on when he felt he was a safe distance away. When he reached Rt. 6, he sped back as quickly as he could on the near empty road.

Flint would be happy.

*****

Flint was ecstatic.

"You're sure about the car?"

"Checked the plate and everything. It's his car. I'm guessing he either ran out of gas or had an engine problem by the way it was pushed off to the side. He was trying to hide it as best he could, but it wasn't good enough."

"And the house?"

"Gotta be in there with the old lady I saw in the window, unless he broke into the wrecked one up the road. At any rate, they are only a few hundred yards apart, so if he's not in the occupied house, we can just move on to the other one."

"Any chance you're wrong?"

"Hell, no ..." He stopped. Flint was giving him a look.

"I mean, no sir. It's the boonies out there. He'd have to walk miles to get to any civilization. He's there. I'm convinced of it."

"Okay, then you guys head out tomorrow around noon."

"Uh, boss? That's when the hurricane is supposed to hit."

"Exactly. You get my money and the other item, you kill him, then you torch the place. Everyone will think Chad caused it."

"But it means we have to drive through it."

"What are you, a fucking wuss? We've been given the perfect time to kill him. You're going to complain about some rain and wind?"

I notice you're not going with us, thought two or three of the men simultaneously.

"By this time tomorrow," said Flint. "Joe Doyle will be dead."

Chapter 36

By the time they had finished interrogating Seth the day before, it was too late to try to find Mason. In order to keep an eye on Seth, Marcus had once again slept on the air mattress in the living room, much to his chagrin as well as Sara's. They were up early the next day, discussing their plans at breakfast.

"Can we find him in a day?" asked Sara.

"That depends on how helpful Seth is," answered Marcus, giving Seth a hard look. "Do you have anything you can give us that would be useful?"

Seth thought for a minute, was about to say something, stopped himself, thought for a moment more, and finally said, "I know where two of them were living."

"You what?" asked Marcus, incredulously.

"Are you kidding me?" said Sara. "You just happened to think of it now? We could have done something about it last night."

Seth was silent.

"He didn't just think of it," said Marcus. He turned to Seth. "Did you?"

"Not exactly."

"Why didn't you tell us?"

"I don't want to have anything more to do with them."

"Even though it might help us find them and stop this, you still didn't want to tell us? The fact that it might save your life didn't factor into your decision? You were willing to waste even more hours of valuable time?"

Seth didn't say anything.

"Whose address?"

"Two of the guys. It's just a cottage. One of those summer rentals."

"Let me guess," said Sara, "in Falmouth."

He nodded.

"How do you know?" asked Marcus.

"I was there."

"Explain."

"I told you before that there was someone who got me involved in this—someone I knew. In the beginning he was my contact person until Tanner took over. One day, I was supposed to bring a load of supplies down to the Cape—stuff they didn't want to be seen buying. I got lost, so I called my friend Harry to let him know I couldn't find the meeting place. He tried to describe it, then said, 'Ah, hell, just bring it to my place.' I got the feeling that he wasn't supposed to do that, but I think he was just being lazy. I think he forgot I was coming, because he hadn't even left for the meeting spot yet. Anyway, he directed me to this house in Falmouth. I delivered the stuff, we had a few beers, and then I left. He had a roommate, and the guy seemed nervous that I was there. That's why I think my seeing it was against the rules."

"When was that?"

"I don't know. Maybe three weeks ago. Maybe a month. I don't even know if they are still there."

"Do you at least have an address?" asked Sara.

"No."

"Of course you don't. Would you know how to find it?"

"If I got close enough, I could probably recognize some landmarks. It was near the water. I've gotta go pee."

"I've got the bathroom window alarmed," said Sara. "Don't think about crawling out."

He hesitated, then walked into the bathroom and closed the door.

"I think that's just what he was planning," said Sara.

"I think I'm just going to kill him now," said Marcus.

"You can't. There's a law against killing stupid people."

"They should repeal it."

"I agree."

His escape plan botched, they heard Seth flush, then come back into the room.

"I'll help you try to find the apartment," he said, "but that's where my involvement in all this ends."

"Ends?" said Marcus. "You are one of the reasons we are all in this situation. You are one of the reasons so many people are dead. Do you really think you can bow out of this now?"

Seth was silent.

"I'll tell you what we will do, though. If you can lead us to the correct location, you can stay in the car while we check it out."

"Okay," he mumbled.

"It's almost ten o'clock," said Marcus, looking at his watch. "I say we go find this place and sit on it for a bit to see what kind of activity there is." He looked at Sara. "Do you still have any handcuffs?"

"I do, but you don't strike me as a handcuffs kind of guy," she said. "I imagine you getting things done in a different sort of way."

Marcus smiled. "These are for Seth, to keep him in the car."

"I wouldn't go anywhere," said Seth belligerently.

"Of course you wouldn't," said Marcus. "I say we should get on the road. How far to Falmouth?"

"With no traffic we could do it in a little more than a half hour from here. I don't anticipate many cars on the road, but who knows what's out there."

Sara went back into her bedroom and came out carrying her gun and holster, in addition to her handcuffs. "Feels good to carry it again," she remarked. "Wish I was legal."

"As your cop friend said, I don't think it matters anymore."

They left the condo to the sound of hammering. The noise seemed to be coming from all around them, and mixed with the rain seemed almost muted.

"Hurricane preparations," said Sara. "I'm sure people don't know which disaster to pay the most attention to: Being stuck on the Cape; not knowing what the terrorists have in mind; or Hurricane Chad. Chad is the one thing they have even the slightest control over at this point. Putting the plywood up over the windows at least gives them something to do."

The wind had picked up from the day before, but they knew that this was only a hint of what they were in for. They opened the doors to Marcus's Pathfinder and Marcus ushered Seth into the back seat. He held his hand out for the cuffs. Sara opened them and gave them to him. He secured Seth to a metal bracket that ran down the back of the seat for anchoring infant car seats. All the while Seth wore a scowl.

"Do you mind driving again?" Marcus asked Sara. He had grabbed his case of equipment as they went out the door and now put it in the back of the SUV. He opened it and took out his silencer, closed the back, and climbed into the passenger seat.

Sara gave him a look.

"This might come in handy."

She nodded and put the car in gear.

They drove through Hyannis, almost a ghost town at this point. Word of the anthrax threat hadn't yet hit the airwaves, so things were still calm. All the way down Route 28 to Falmouth they passed houses and businesses in various stages of hurricane preparation. For the most part the roads were empty of vehicles. Occasionally, though, they came upon a crash site a couple of days old. The manpower didn't exist during the height of the panic to clean up after the accidents.

"Seems kind of eerie," said Marcus. "Different from a usual summer day, from what I've seen."

"This isn't even a usual winter day," replied Sara. "These days, traffic here on the Upper Cape even in the winter can be pretty heavy at times. This is just plain spooky."

They reached East Falmouth and Sara turned to Seth and said, "Okay, start talking."

"This doesn't look familiar. Definitely not here."

"Okay, we keep going."

As they approached downtown Falmouth, there was more activity, mostly with shop owners preparing what was left of their businesses for Chad.

"Ever been in a hurricane?" asked Marcus.

"Hurricane Bob," Sara answered. "I was still in high school

and was on the Cape for the summer. It was right toward the end of the summer and I was getting close to going home. I was staying here in Falmouth and Bob hit us head-on. It wasn't big as hurricanes go. I think it was a Category 2, but those numbers don't mean anything to me. It was strong. It blew down massive oaks and blew boats right onto land. We lost power for a week. Funny, you know what I remember the most? The bees. With all the trees coming down, I think massive numbers of bees lost their homes. People were getting stung all over the place. I was stung four times over that week. Bees and the sound of chainsaws, those are the things I remember the most." She paused. "That hurricane was scary and it was a relatively small one. If Chad does hit as a Category 4, I can't imagine what this place will look like."

Seth broke into her reverie.

"Here. This road. I definitely came down this road."

They were in the center of downtown Falmouth.

"Shore Street," said Sara. "It leads to the water."

They drove down the road in silence. When they reached the water, the road bore right, running parallel to the beach.

"Still look familiar?" asked Sara.

"Yeah, this is definitely it. There is a side road somewhere up here."

"Pick the right one. There are a few side roads."

"I will. This all looks familiar. Here. This one. Turn right."

"Well I'm certainly not going to turn left, or we'll be driving across the water to the Vineyard."

Sara turned the car slowly onto the side road. On either side were summer cottages, including a whole strip of connected units that looked almost like a motel.

"Slow down," said Seth. "There it is. On the right, about three houses up."

Sara stopped the car.

"The gray one with the old lobster traps out front."

"They're all gray and they all have lobster traps," said Sara.

"Okay, the one that doesn't have an upside down broken boat in the yard."

Marcus and Sara spotted it. All the shades in the house were drawn.

"What now?" asked Seth.

"We sit for a bit and see if there is any movement," said Marcus. "Then we go introduce ourselves. All of these cottages look empty."

"They've all gone to shelters," said Sara. "Anyone with any sense knows that by tomorrow night, these houses will most likely be gone. It's why they didn't bother bringing in the lobster trap decorations or the skiffs. It doesn't matter."

"It'll make it easier for us to do our job," said Marcus. He opened his door. "Forget waiting. I've spent too many hours over the last week sitting and waiting. It's time to make something happen. You with me?"

"Gladly."

Marcus turned to Seth. "Now you sit quietly and behave yourself and maybe you'll make it out of this alive. Take a nap."

He closed his door before he had to listen to Seth's response.

"Front or back?" asked Marcus.

"I'll take the front and distract them," she replied. "You can take them from the rear. Boy, do I miss this."

They separated, with Marcus going down the side of the

house next door, then coming around the back to the house Seth had pointed out. Sara, meanwhile, waited a minute to give Marcus time to get into position, then strode up to the door and knocked with the butt of her gun.

"Falmouth police. You need to evacuate. A major hurricane is headed this way."

No answer from inside, so she pounded on the door again.

"We know you haven't evacuated yet. It's too dangerous to be here. This house will get destroyed tomorrow. If you stay, you will die."

Those were the words that finally did it. The door opened a crack and a skinny man in his twenties peered out at her. He looked scared.

"Is it really going to hit?"

"A head-on collision without air bags. All of these cottages will be swept away. If you're still here you will not survive it."

The minute he heard them talking, Marcus picked the lock on the back door and let himself in. The cottage was small, and he saw two men standing near the door. One was talking to Sara, using the door to hide the gun in his hand, and a second man was hiding behind the door with his gun drawn. At that moment he saw Marcus and raised his gun. Marcus shot him in the leg, the loud pop of the suppressed gun echoing in the house. The gun dropped and the man screamed.

The other man looked back in fear, and as he did, Sara kicked open the door, slamming the man in the head. He was momentarily dazed, and Marcus took two long strides and brought his gun down hard on the man's arm. He cried out in pain and dropped his gun. Sara picked up both guns and set them down on a table.

The man with the leg wound was groaning in pain.

"Stop being a baby," said Marcus. "I didn't shoot you any place that will kill you. It'll hurt and you'll lose some blood, but you'll be fine."

"I'll sue you and the police department. I've seen how it's done," he said, slumped on the floor.

"And you call yourself terrorists?" asked Sara. "You're going to sue us?"

The one with the bad leg suddenly jumped up on his good leg, whipped out a hunting knife, and threw himself at Sara. Marcus put two bullets into the man's skull and he dropped to the floor dead.

That scared the other man, and he threw his hands in the air. He kept looking down at his dead friend on the floor.

"Don't shoot me!"

"We won't need to if you answer our questions. We want to know where Mason is.

"I don't know who you're talking about."

Marcus rapped him on the side of the head with his gun and the man hit the floor dazed.

"Something you need to know," said Marcus. "We're not cops. We don't have to follow any rules. Are you Harry or is the dead guy Harry?"

He was silent, so Marcus raised his gun hand, as if to hit him again. The man tried to cover his head and said, "I'm Harry."

"Well Harry," said Marcus. "You want to know how we found you? Your friend Seth. Unfortunately, Seth didn't like our interrogation techniques and he is not doing so well. He's in a lot of pain and one arm will never be right again. He could have saved himself a lot of trouble if he'd just told us what we wanted to know. Now, there's only one way you will live and that's if you tell us what we need to know. Where's Mason?"

"I can show you where he lives, but I don't know if he's there."

"Close enough."

"Did you kill Tanner?" asked Harry, his voice cracking.

Marcus looked at Sara, then said, "Tall skinny guy with a big Adam's apple?"

Harry nodded.

"Fraid so. Your friends don't live too long. You'd better hope you're not from the same gene pool."

Harry looked even more scared than before.

"Before we go for Mason, how about you tell us how many are involved," said Sara.

"What do you think we are involved in?"

"We have zero patience," said Marcus. "Zero."

"Eight," said Harry. "Six now, since you killed Tanner and Carson. Mason is the boss. Tanner was too, but I think Mason had all the ideas. The explosives guys are Danielson and Packer, and then there's Holt and Jones. Like us, they are the eyes. They go all over the Cape and report. You were lucky to find us here. The cell phones going down kind of screwed up our ability to report, so we came back. We were going to go report to Mason in person in a while."

"You still can. You'll just have company."

They escorted Harry out of the house to the waiting car and threw him in the back seat, causing him to land on top of Seth. He moved to the empty seat, all the while staring at Seth.

"What the fuck?" said Harry. "They said you were beat up.

Hell, you gave me up willingly, you asshole." He lashed out with his fist and smashed Seth's nose. Blood spurted all over the back seat.

"Hey," yelled Marcus. "Not on the leather."

Sara found some tissues in the glove compartment and passed them back.

"You keep your hands to yourself," said Sara, "or your nose will look like Seth's."

Harry dropped his head.

"So where are we going?" asked Sara.

"Turn right here. It'll lead up to Main Street, then hang a left."

The rain was fairly steady, with the wind keeping pace. Unlike earlier, however, people were out, and they seemed frantic about something. Marcus and Sara glanced at each other and Sara turned on the radio to a local station.

Repeating the breaking news, it has been reported that the terrorists holding the Cape hostage are in possession of a powerful strain of anthrax and threaten to disperse it if their demands are not met. It is unknown to the media at this time what those demands are, or the authorities' reaction to the demands.

Marcus turned off the radio and looked back at Harry.

"Seth told us the demands. Did you really think the government was going to give in to them?"

"Personally, I don't care about the land. I just want the money."

"And you think they'll do that?" asked Marcus. "You know the old 'we don't negotiate with terrorists' saying? I can tell you right now that there is no way you'll ever get what you want."

"Mason says we will."

"Mason's an idiot."

"No, he's smart."

"Then he's got his own agenda. Anyone smart would know that there is not a chance in hell that the government would give in to those demands. Turning over Indian land? That's ludicrous. Either we're dealing with someone monumentally stupid, or you guys are getting screwed over. Have the authorities responded yet?"

"I don't think so." Harry looked uncomfortable. "The phones are down, so Mason hasn't heard anything yet."

"I vote for stupid," said Sara.

"Turn right," said Harry. "Halfway up the block is a small house. Sara pulled the Pathfinder off to the side of the road behind a nondescript Toyota.

"Hey, that's Danielson and Packer's car. That means Mason isn't alone. Those guys are ex-military. You're going to need more than just the two of you."

Sara looked at Marcus and smiled. Ignoring Harry, Marcus went to the back of the SUV and lifted the hatch. Opening his box of "tools of the trade," he pulled out a roll of duct tape, then closed the box and the hatch. He opened the back door and—none too lightly—bound Harry's wrists behind his back and then his ankles.

"Okay then, you boys be sure not to go anywhere," said Marcus, slamming the door and locking it.

"I say we take the direct approach," said Marcus, as they cut across a neighbor's lawn. "No knocking. We just go in. How about you do the back this time and I'll do the front."

"Works for me."

Like before, they took their positions at the doors. This

time they coordinated their entrance, both smashing in their doors as their watches hit thirty seconds.

Marcus knew from the moment he entered that they wouldn't find Mason here. The smell was overwhelming. He looked around quickly to make sure they were alone, then looked down at the two bodies.

"Clear up here," he called out.

"And back here, too," came Sara's response. She appeared in the hallway. "Being a former homicide detective, that's a smell I miss. Brings me back."

"I could do without it."

They looked down at the bodies and Sara gave them a once-over. Marcus took a picture of each of them on his cell phone.

"Poison. This wasn't a sudden falling out among crooks. This was planned," she said.

"Which means Mason has a scheme of his own that doesn't include these guys."

They took another look around. They had already checked each room thoroughly for Mason, so they concentrated on his belongings. They decided almost immediately that Mason had cleared out for good. They found just enough to know that he had been there, but nothing to show where he'd gone. There was no briefcase of D-394 and no explosives. There were a half a dozen new cell phones still in the boxes. Marcus tried a couple. They had been activated, but there were no numbers stored in memory.

They continued their search, hoping to find something ... anything ... that would give them an indication as to where Mason had gone. But there was nothing.

"What now?" asked Sara.

"He's most likely out of touch with his computer guy, so he hasn't had any contact with the Feds, which means he has no idea if they've responded to his threat. My guess is he's improvising."

"Or not," said Sara.

"Go on."

"It goes back to what you said earlier to Harry. The idea that the government would ever give them Indian land. It's stupid. There's nothing about that demand that makes a bit of sense. And the money? I suppose it's possible, but highly unlikely. He's got to know that he'd never make it off the Cape alive. In fact, in some ways, by bringing down all the routes of transportation, he's made it easier for the authorities to control the evacuation. It may take a while, but they can check each person who leaves. They would be in total control of the process."

"Which points to an alternative plan."

"The real plan."

"Which is?"

"Hey, you're the former spook. This kind of double-crossing stuff was right up your alley."

"Well, if I had to guess, I'd wager a bet that he has no intention of getting off—that he never had any intention of getting off. I think he was going to string the Feds along until the last minute and then say, 'I was just kidding. You're all going to die anyway.'"

"Something like that," replied Sara.

"Let's assume he really does have D-394. He can't do much with it today or tomorrow, so Thursday would be the day.

Where's the highest point on the Cape?"

"Wow, you're really not from around here, are you? There is no highest point on the Cape. I mean, sure, there's a sign near Hyannis on Route 6 that informs people that it is the highest point on the Cape, but it's kind of ridiculous. Take my word for it. There is no high ground here. My guess is that he'd go to the highest building—again, nothing to shake a stick at—and let it go from there. There's only one thing wrong with that."

"The wind," said Marcus. "He can't pick his launching spot until he knows which way the wind is blowing. So maybe we pick the tallest buildings in the different places on the Cape, and the morning of the 9th we see which way the wind is blowing…"

"…And hope we're not too late."

Chapter 37

"I say we talk to Harry again and see if he knows where the others are living," said Marcus on their way back to the car.

"Let's hope, because otherwise the plan is pretty flimsy—waiting until the morning after the hurricane and hoping we find Mason."

"Never said it was a good plan."

They got to the car—the rain still coming down at a steady rate—to find Harry slumped over in the back seat, blood all over his shirt and pants. Seth was sitting up and breathing heavily, blood dripping from his right hand. One look and both Marcus and Sara knew what had happened. Seth, with his one free hand, had decided to give Harry a taste of his own medicine and had pounded on his face until Harry lost consciousness. Being taped up, Harry had no way to defend himself. Blood was all over the seat and floor.

"So much for not getting blood on the leather," said Sara.

"So help me, Seth," said Marcus. "If he's dead, so are you, and I don't give a damn that I'm working for your uncle."

"He deserved it," said Seth, still catching his breath. "Not just because he hit me, but because he got me involved in all this. He's not dead, but I should have killed him."

"You got yourself involved in this," replied Marcus. "You

knew it was illegal—hell, you were stealing from your own uncle. You just didn't like the fact that it blew up in your face. So don't give me the 'innocent man in the wrong place at the wrong time' shit. You bought a ticket to this show. You're going to have to see it through."

Meanwhile, Sara was checking on Harry.

"I'll need a wet towel to clean him up, but it's all pretty superficial, despite how it looks. Just for the record, Seth didn't come close to killing him. My grandmother could have done more damage."

Marcus went back to Mason's house for towels and wet them in the sink. When he returned, Harry was conscious and shouting out a string of obscenities. Marcus heard Sara say, "Shut up, Harry, or you'll see what a real beating is like."

Marcus and Sara cleaned him up and sat him back in the seat. Other than a broken nose, a loose front tooth, and a cut on his forehead—the source of most of the blood—he was fine.

Marcus pulled out his phone and brought up a picture of the two dead men he took. He showed it to Harry. Harry started to gag and Sara pulled him out of the SUV. He immediately threw up.

"Imagine that on your leather," Sara said to Marcus.

"I have a feeling I'll be getting a new car when this is all over."

When Harry had recovered, Sara pushed him back in the vehicle.

"Two of yours, I assume," she said.

Harry just nodded.

"Which two?"

"Danielson and Packer, the explosives guys. What

happened to them?"

"Your boss poisoned them and then split. Like I said before, he never intended to collect any of that ransom money and he knew the government would never give over any land to you. He's had his own agenda all along and you guys were just pawns in his scheme. Any idea where he might have gone?"

"No clue. He does what he wants and goes where he wants."

"Do you know where the last two guys live?"

"Their place is in Hyannis."

"I guess we're going back home," said Sara.

They were on their way in minutes. Driving down Main Street in Falmouth, there was ten times the activity that had greeted them earlier. Mostly it was small groups of people talking amongst themselves, all hoping that someone out there had a good plan to protect all of them from the anthrax. They passed a number of pickup trucks heading down to the water carrying homemade rafts.

"They're going to try to escape the anthrax," said Marcus.

"They're going to die trying," said Sara. "They're not going to survive those waters in this weather."

Other than the pickups, traffic was almost nonexistent. As they approached Hyannis, Sara said to Harry, "Where to?"

He led them through a series of turns and side streets, until they reached an older apartment complex.

"Second floor, third door from the left," said Harry.

Marcus and Sara didn't try for any finesse. They got to the door and kicked it in. It took them five seconds to determine that the place was empty, and another five to understand why.

"They left a note," said Sara.

"You're kidding me. Where did Mason find these people? What does it say?"

"Mason, you asshole, you lied to us. We're not going down with you. We hope you rot in hell."

"Please tell me they didn't sign it."

Sara just smiled.

"I think they were expecting Mason to come looking for them," said Marcus.

"Then they wrote the note in vain. I think Mason knows he's on his own. The last thing he would do is come here. In fact, I think Mason has known from the beginning that in the end it would just be him."

"I agree with you, but it brings up a big question. We know why he brought in the explosives guys. That's obvious. We know why he had Tanner in on it—he needed someone to help him plan it. But why these four clowns? If he was going to release the D-394 anyway, why the production of the demands and having these four monitoring what was going on across the Cape? What purpose could that solve?"

Sara had no answer ... and then she did.

"We know the ransom demands were bogus," she began. "And we can be pretty sure he intended from the beginning to release the anthrax no matter what. What was the purpose of the bridges coming down?"

"Fear and panic."

"And word of the anthrax has now gotten out, so he had to know it would get out. And the result?"

"Further fear and panic. Probably complete and utter terror."

"I think his purpose was the fear. He had a reason for instilling that fear. It was like a kid who goes in and shoots up a high school. A big part of the reason is to see the fear on his classmates' faces. I think it was that, but on a much larger scale."

"You may be right. I don't think we'll ever know his reasons, and frankly I don't care what his reasons were..." He stopped. "But I do have a question. The four clowns. Harry said they were supposed to monitor what was going on. But what about before that? They've been here a while. Sure, maybe they did some grunt work, but they had to have more of a reason than that. Let's search this place, then go out and talk to Harry. I think there's something he forgot to tell us."

Going through the small apartment took no time at all, but yielded rewards. Unlike Mason, who wanted to cover his tracks so he could complete his job, Holt and Jones couldn't have cared less. From out of a beat-up backpack Marcus pulled a large map of the Cape. They spread it out on the card table that had doubled as a kitchen table. There were several spots circled, one in almost each town.

"Any clue?" asked Marcus.

Sara didn't respond, her fingers moving over the map as if it was written in Braille. When she moved over to Falmouth, she had her answer.

"Anthrax is effective in water, right?"

"Right. And if this some kind of souped-up anthrax, it might be even more effective." He looked at her intently and saw a small nod.

"All this time we were figuring he would disperse it into the air, which gave us an extra day," he said. "But he's going to put it into the water supply, isn't he?"

"He's got most of the public wells circled," Sara answered. "Most of the Cape gets its water from an aquifer—water going through the rocks and sand underground—and there are various wells throughout the Cape that tap into it. If he was able to dump some into those wells, it would get into the public water supply. He must have had his guys keeping an eye on those spots where he could introduce the D-394." She looked troubled. "But I don't think they were his main targets."

"Because he put idiots in charge of watching them?"

"Precisely. I still think he was planning on targeting them, but they were his second choice. In other words, if his first target was successful, then he could move on to the secondary targets."

"And what is his first target?"

She put her finger on a large reservoir in Falmouth. "Long Pond. It provides the only drinking water on Cape Cod that comes from a pond—an above ground source. Mason has been based in Falmouth. If he can distribute the anthrax in Long Pond, it will affect the drinking water of the whole Upper Cape. It would be his easiest target by far, and he'd try to get that one out of the way first. Even if he never made it to the other spots, he would have done monumental damage. He's not waiting for the 9th. He's going to carry out his plan tomorrow."

Marcus looked at his watch. It was 8:00. They had spent all day tracking down Mason's men. Normally it would still be light outside, but it looked like the middle of the night because of the clouds and rain.

"We need help," he said. "By the looks of the map, it's way

too big for just the two of us."

"There is a water station at the pond. If he wanted to guarantee success, that's probably where he'd go."

"Everything else has changed. Do you think he'd change the date and do it now?"

"I suppose that's possible. Maybe Harry knows."

They headed out to the car, map in hand. It was now raining harder and the wind had picked up. Marcus wasn't looking forward to the next day and Chad. He climbed into the passenger seat, while Sara got in behind the wheel.

"How was Mason going to distribute the D-394?" he asked Harry.

"At first, we didn't think he would at all. We figured that if the government came through with his demands, he wouldn't have to use it. Then we started to think he was going to do it anyway. Now I realize he was always going to do it, and if we died in the process, so be it."

"You didn't answer my question."

"He had us scouting out wells. I don't know exactly how he was going to access them—maybe explosives? But definitely water."

"Did he talk about the pond in Falmouth?"

"No, there was a lot he didn't talk about to us."

"His original date on the demand was tomorrow," said Sara. "Would he change it to tonight, or to the day after tomorrow, after the hurricane?"

"I don't think so."

"Why?

"He's kind of a stickler for schedules. That's all we ever heard—'I need this done by a certain day'. The other thing is that there was something important about tomorrow's date—something personal, I think."

"We need to go to the pond in Falmouth," said Marcus. "Think the Falmouth police will help?"

"I don't think they can," said Sara. "They are probably spread out pretty thin. Besides, they don't know you from Adam, and I don't have the best reputation anymore." She sighed. "As much as I hate the idea, there's only one place to go where we might be heard."

She put the Pathfinder in gear and stomped on the gas.

Chapter 38

At that moment, Captain Chandler was wishing he had gone on vacation, far, far away from Cape Cod. The wind and rain had picked up, and yet forecasters were saying that the storm was still twelve hours away. Ten minutes earlier, Chandler had called all the cars back to the station. There was no need for them to be out there. There was no one to protect. Everyone was holed up in their homes or in shelters.

Not everyone was in agreement with his decision, however. After speaking amongst themselves for a few minutes, several officers approached Chandler.

"We think you're making a mistake."

"Oh?" Chandler looked around at the dozen or so stony faces. He knew he was in trouble. Most of them had spoken to the chief on Sara's behalf when all that shit was going down, and most suspected that he had planted evidence. Well screw it, he thought. He was still in charge.

"We think we should be out there all night. Even a few cruisers. There might be people who need help."

"It's a waste of time."

"Don't you think we should make our presence known?"

"Presence to whom. There's no reason anyone should be out there, and there's nothing else to loot. We should conserve our gas."

"We have about four shelters in town and not one cop on duty. That's not right."

Chandler had forgotten to assign people to the shelters. More of the organizational crap that he hated so much.

"I think each one has an ambulance assigned to it."

"They're not cops. What if someone starts trouble. That's not their responsibility to do something about it."

"Okay, okay, you're right. I dropped the ball. I'll assign two people to each shelter. But I only want a couple of cars on the streets. It's already bad out there. By morning, I want everyone in here. Once the storm hits in earnest we'll have to be under cover. When it's all over you can go out on patrol, but not until then. As for anyone who happens to be out there during the storm, they're on their own."

The doors burst open and Sara stumbled in, followed by a man unknown to Chandler escorting two men bound together with a pair of handcuffs.

"We need your help," said Sara.

"What are you doing here?" demanded Chandler. Seeing her once again brought up all of his regrets, but he pushed them aside.

"These two men are involved in the terror plot. They are pretty low-level, but the leader, a man named Mason, is still out there, and we know where he's going."

"That's the least of our concerns right now. We have a hurricane coming."

"What do you mean, it's the least of your concerns? If he accomplishes his mission, you'll be dead soon after the hurricane ends. We need some of your officers."

"You don't work here anymore. And who is this guy?"

Marcus stepped forward and held out his hand, which was ignored. "Marcus Baldwin. I'm a P.I. and long-time operative for the CIA. I suggest you listen to Sara." Marcus absolutely never brought up his background, but Sara had convinced him in the car that it would help sway people—not necessarily Chandler, but some of the others.

"Well, whoop-di-do. That's supposed to impress me?"

"Nope," said Marcus. "Just giving you my credentials. You have a terrorist who's about to release D-394, a highly effective strain of anthrax, into the Cape's water supply. You don't help us, it's on you. You want to take on that responsibility?"

Chandler hesitated. Then he sighed. "Fill me in."

They laid it out for him, starting with their encounter with Tanner to the discovery of the map.

"If you had all this, why didn't you come in earlier? Why didn't you try to contact the FBI?"

"Contact the FBI with what?" asked Sara. "All communications are down, and from what we understand, even you are having trouble knowing where they are. Based on what we've seen out there, all the police departments on the Cape are flat out trying to deal with the panic. As for why we didn't come in here, why do you think? How much credibility would you have given me, especially knowing as little as we did before tonight? You would have blown me off."

Chandler looked uncomfortable, mainly because he was surrounded by Sara's friends and former co-workers. He felt very alone.

"We have reason to believe—good reason to believe—that Mason is going to dump his load of D-394 into Long Pond. We also have reason to believe that it will be tomorrow..."

"Not with the hurricane," interrupted Chandler.

"Yes, even with the hurricane. Besides, the hurricane isn't due until around noon." She looked at her watch. "The 8th officially begins in a couple of hours, which means—assuming his man was right about him being a stickler for time—he could dump it in anytime in the next twenty-four hours, although supposedly he gave a three o'clock deadline. Can I make a suggestion?"

"As if I could stop you," Chandler mumbled.

"Send some of your officers out to keep an eye on some of the public wells. Not all of them, just those close to this area. Then let me have some of your people to head to Falmouth and try to get this guy."

"Why didn't you go to the Falmouth PD?"

"Because I know the people here. I really don't think Falmouth will care about territorial issues. I don't think any of that applies anymore."

"So you're saying you want me to send my people into the woods during a major—and most likely, devastating, hurricane?"

"That's what I'm saying ... asking."

"No way."

"Yes, way," said one of the officers. "My wife and kids might die if we don't do this. I don't know about you, but I could never live with that." He looked at Sara. "Count me in."

"And me."

"And me."

Chandler had lost them, and he knew it.

"Okay," he said. "We'll help. But I'm going too. I'm not

going to force anyone to go. It'll be on a volunteer basis only." He turned to his people. "Your families come first, so I expect you to be there for them. But anyone who wants to do this suicide mission is welcome to come. We'll leave as soon as everyone is suited up. Automatic weapons and vests."

He gave Sara a look. "You'd better pray no one gets hurt in this wild goose chase of yours, or I'll have your ass."

"You already took care of that," Sara replied, staring him down.

Chandler turned away uncomfortably and strode into his office.

"We doing the right thing?" she asked Marcus.

"Sometimes you don't have a choice. Chandler might not be wrong. It could very well be a suicide mission, but what's the alternative? The hurricane might kill us, but if Mason really has the D-394, it will definitely kill us."

He continued, "All things considered, my old life is beginning to look pretty good."

July 8th

Chapter 39

It took a while to get everything together, but they were on their way at two in the morning. Seth and Harry were locked up and a force of five men—including Chandler—and one woman accompanied Marcus and Sara. Marcus again let Sara drive his Pathfinder. Chandler and his troops followed behind in two police cruisers. The rain and wind had picked up considerably from the night before.

"Just for the record," said Marcus, "I'm really sick of the weather."

"Noted. I know you're not used to the Cape, but we really do have better weather than this most of the time."

"I'll take your word for it. Changing the subject, I'm not particularly impressed by your friend Chandler."

"No? How odd. Hard to believe I rejected his advances, isn't it."

They lapsed into silence while Sara tried to fight the deteriorating conditions of the drive.

"It's going to be really bad in a few hours, isn't it?" Marcus finally said.

"That's right, this is your first hurricane. In truth? I think it's going to be worse than even I can imagine. It's going to be hell in those woods."

It took them over an hour to reach Falmouth. When they were opposite one of the entrances to Long Pond, they parked their vehicles across the street in a secluded lot and gathered around Sara, Chandler having already been demoted in the minds of his officers.

"I contacted Falmouth PD," said Chandler, trying to maintain some illusion of control, "and let them know what we were doing. They're spread even thinner than we are and gave their blessing to the operation."

"Why didn't we drive straight to the water station?" asked one of the younger officers.

"It's going to be hard enough to keep Mason from knowing we're here," said Marcus. "If we advertise our presence, he will bolt. If he does, there's no telling what he'll do. At that point, his timetable will be out the window, so he'll become unpredictable. He might let it loose in the air in a day or two."

"You're assuming he's going to make some sort of precision strike at the pumping station, but what's to stop him him from just dumping it in the pond at some random spot?" asked Chandler. His voice had an edge, and Marcus knew it was because Chandler recognized that his authority had been watered down. Normally, Marcus would have made an effort to include him in the decision-making, but knowing what he did to Sara lost him any consideration in Marcus's book.

"There is nothing stopping him." He addressed the assembled waterlogged group. "Understand something. Everything we know about Mason has been learned in just the last twenty-four hours. There is a lot more we *don't* know about him than what we do. We were told he has a fixation on sticking to schedule and that July 8th has a special meaning to him. But is that a fact? We have no idea. For all we know, he could have already released the D-394 into the pond. My gut says he hasn't, but nothing is certain. Our best guess, based on all the information we've run across, is that he will release the D-394 at three o'clock today, with the assumption that it will be here at Long Pond. In my other career, would I have carried out an operation with information as sketchy as this? No way. But we're in a different situation here, and we don't have a choice."

When he got no objections or arguments, he continued. "Sara and I will proceed to the pumping station. I suggest you break into three groups of two and take positions on different sides of the pond, and each pair hunker down in a spot that affords you the best viewing area, but also keeps you safe from the hurricane. Near some big rocks or under a stable fallen tree would be good. The public won't be out here today, so if you see anyone moving, chances are it's Mason. A 'shoot first, ask questions later' attitude might be the best one to take. All of your normal rules of law-enforcement are out the window. We're here to stop a terrorist from killing half a million people. We do what we have to do."

Getting no objections from Chandler, he said, "I don't know the area, so I'll let Sara and Chandler tell you where to go."

He left them to figure it all out and opened the back of his Pathfinder and retrieved his rifle from a case. He quickly put it together and pulled out a couple of magazines of bullets. He and his rifle had been together a long time and it had seen much use in its youth. Marcus had spent time aplenty calibrating it to his own specifications, resulting in a fairly light, but extremely accurate sniper rifle.

The others were ready to go, so they said their goodbyes

and headed off in different directions. Sara led the way to the pumping station. A flashlight was necessary so they didn't kill themselves in the process of getting there; they had no choice. Marcus was counting on Mason not yet being there. It took almost an hour to find the right spot, one that afforded them a good view of the pumping station, but was also fairly safe from the storm. They made themselves as comfortable as possible in the steady rain and waited, hoping that they had made the right assumption.

Either way, it was going to be a long wait.

Chapter 40

"...*Going to be a direct hit on Cape Cod. And due to the unusual circumstances caused by an act of terrorism, tourists who would normally be gone in advance of the storm are stuck, with no place to go.*"

"No shit," said Doyle. "I could have been long gone."

They had turned on the TV to get the latest updates on the storm, secretly hoping it would go out to sea. Ann had never seen the Weather Channel reporters look so serious. It was their job to look serious, but this time it was different. They were almost scared for the people on the Cape. Normally there would be dozens of news people covering the storm from the ground, but because it was difficult to get onto the Cape and since cell service was down, there were only a handful, all using the same satellite feed from the one truck capable of getting a signal out. It was a truck from a Boston station that had sent a team down to the Cape to do a story about sharks.

"*Shelters have been set up all over Cape Cod and we urge anyone not already in a shelter to make your way there. This is a very dangerous storm. By the time it hits later today, it is predicted to be a Category 4. We expect that soon after Chad hits, major power outages will occur, plunging the Cape into darkness.*"

"Well, that was cheery," said Ann, turning down the sound.

"What time do they expect it to hit?" asked Doyle.

"Noon." She changed the subject. "My niece must be so worried about me being out of touch like this."

"You're a tough old bird. I'm sure she knows that."

"'Tough old bird.' That's an old expression. Never had it used about me though. Not sure I like it. Makes me feel like an overcooked chicken."

"It was a compliment."

"I'm sure it was." Again she changed the subject. "Are you familiar with the Stockholm Syndrome?"

"Something about kidnappers, right?"

"Sort of. It has to do with kidnapped people forming a bond with their captors, forgetting that their captors kidnapped them in the first place. Sometimes I wonder if I have it. I should be fighting you tooth and nail for what you've done, but I'm not. Why is that?"

"My charming personality?"

"Hardly. Frankly, you need to work on your personality. How much schooling did you have?"

"I dropped out of high school when I was sixteen."

"Why?"

"I don't know."

"You don't know? You dropped out of school and you don't know why?"

"I guess I wasn't much of a student. I was pretty much failing every class. I smoked a lot of weed and got into trouble—shoplifting, fighting, little stuff. I guess I didn't see the need for school."

"Suppose you get away with this robbery. What then?"

"I told you before. I'm heading to the Caribbean."

"And then what?"

"I don't know. Be a beach bum or something."

"Which island?"

"What do you mean?"

"Which Caribbean island would you head for?"

He was clearly uncomfortable. "I haven't thought about it. Bermuda maybe?"

"Bermuda's not in the Caribbean."

"You're starting to piss me off."

"I'm making a point," she said.

"Which is?"

"Do something with your life. You're still young. Get an education. Get a job. Something. If you keep going like this, in five years you will either be in jail or dead."

"Already been in jail, and I think it's too late to get an education. I know what I need to know."

"Like how to rob people?

"You're not my mother."

"Thank God."

"Why do you care?" he asked.

"To be honest? I don't know. As I said, I should be fighting you, but I'm not, and I don't know why. I even wondered what I'd do if the police came by to urge me to evacuate. Would I turn you in? I don't think so. But I don't know why I wouldn't. After all, you kidnapped me. You're holding me hostage in my own house. That should be reason enough to scream for help. It's a puzzle, that's for sure."

Doyle didn't say anything. The silence lasted for five minutes. Then he said, "so where is Bermuda?"

*****

By 11:00 the wind had started to howl and the rain increased in intensity.

"I think they were wrong about the time," said Doyle.

"No, it's not here yet. This is nothing. This is just the outer edges of the storm. You ain't seen nothin' yet."

They spent the next hour in relative silence, watching the wind and rain pick up. Every once in a while a strong gust would come up and the cottage would shake and the lights would flicker.

"Think we'll lose power?" asked Doyle.

"I know we'll lose power. I lose power in smaller storms than this. The only question is when."

The "when" came two minutes later.

"Well that was quick," said Ann. "Time to ration water." They had filled the bathtub earlier in the day in anticipation of the outage.

"Don't you have some kind of backup generator for the water pump?"

"I used to, but it always broke, so I got rid of it. Usually we get our power back within a few hours, so I don't worry about it. Not today." She gave a worried look. "Honestly, with things the way they are, I don't know when we'll get it back."

By 2:00, they were experiencing the full fury of Chad. The house was shaking badly and Ann started to worry about her roof, which was creaking loudly.

"Maybe I should have gone to a shelter," she said, but then realized that Doyle wasn't listening. He was sitting quietly on the couch, staring into space. And then it dawned on her, Doyle was scared. No, he was petrified. She had to do something to snap him out of it.

"Hey," she shouted. Doyle jumped. "It'll be okay," she said. He nodded vacantly.

She stood up and walked to the kitchen. Even though it was mid-afternoon, the house was almost dark. She turned on the battery-powered lamp on the kitchen table and went to the counter to pour herself a glass of water. She looked out the unshuttered window and all she could see was rain and blowing sand. Even wet, the sand filled the air.

And then she saw movement, movement that didn't belong. It wasn't something blowing or falling. It was something else. Was it a person? She went to the table and turned off the lamp, then returned to the window. All she could see was sand billowing past. No, there it was again! Definitely a person. Someone in trouble? Suddenly she got a shiver up her spine. A second person. Both were approaching the house, but they were coming from different directions. A particularly strong gust of wind blew them both over. They struggled to get up, but once up continued on toward the house. They definitely weren't lost. What could they be…? And then it hit her.

They were Flint's men. And they were coming for Doyle!

Chapter 41

The last thing Flint's men wanted to do was venture out into a hurricane, but they had little choice. What the old man wanted, the old man got. He sent four of them. His last words to them as they bundled into rain gear was, "If the four of you can't take care of a two-bit loser and an old lady, don't bother coming back."

The men checked their weapons. They only carried handguns. Rifles would be overkill. Besides, they were pretty sure anything they had to do would be at close range. Of the four, only one of them had ever killed a man, and that was when he was drunk. He had very little memory of the incident. The step they were taking was a big one. Their loyalty to Flint was being sorely tested. It was strong, but it was being made even stronger was the promise of $10,000 each if they accomplished their mission. They had never known Flint to be so free with his money, which meant that he was seriously worried about something. None of the four knew about the cross—just that there was an item in a small box, and it was more important than the stolen money. Ten thousand was a lot of pocket change. They would do what they had to, each one secretly hoping that one of the others would end up doing the actual killing. After all, killing Doyle was one thing, killing an old lady was another altogether. And what if there was a third person? It could all get messy.

They left long before noon, feeling like idiots. The storm was in the process of ramping up and it was looking very tropical outside. Only a lunatic would be making this drive. They likened themselves to four clowns in a clown car. Travel had been banned for the duration of Chad, but that was kind of a joke. Because of the terrorists nobody was driving anyway. With everything that had gone on in the past few days, the cops wouldn't be on the road either.

Chatham to Truro was about a forty-five minute drive this time of year—more on busy weekends—but they could tell from the get go that even without traffic, this ride was going to take far longer. As they drove, it became more and more difficult to see. It was so dark from the low hanging clouds, it seemed almost like night. Added to that was the rain, which was steady and getting progressively heavier and all but impenetrable by the headlights. The wind was so strong the rain was coming from a sideways direction, making the wipers almost useless.

"This is totally fucked up," said one.

"You think?"

"I think we should go back," said the first.

"And how are you going to explain it to Flint," asked another one. "Sorry, but we were scared?"

"I'm not scared. I just think this is fucked up, that's all. We can't even see where we're going."

"I can see well enough to drive," said the one at the wheel, "if you guys would shut up and let me drive."

"I'm just sayin'…"

"Yeah, we know. It's fucked up. We get the idea."

They went silent for a while, each one dealing with his own fears about getting there safely, and what they were going to do once they did arrive.

The further they went, the slower their progress. Branches, some the size of small trees, littered the road. Several times the driver had to slow to a crawl while trying to make out what was littering the road. In many places large puddles had formed, causing the men to cross their fingers every time they went through one, as if that would keep the engine from stalling.

Over two hours later they reached Ann's road, having passed it three times before finding the turnoff. They found Doyle's car a few minutes later and parked behind it. The one who had discovered it the day before pointed out Ann's house. The electricity was out but they could see the slight glow of a lantern. They had assumed, from having seen no lights on anywhere during the whole trip to Truro, that there was a massive power outage. A Jeep was parked in the driveway. Someone was definitely home.

"We split up and approach the house about fifty feet apart," said the one in charge. "When we get there, we kick in the door and take care of whoever is in there."

"What if Doyle isn't in there?"

"He will be," answered the one who had found Doyle's car.

"I'm just sayin'..."

"Yeah, you're always just sayin'," said the leader. "He'll be there and we'll take care of him. Just nobody shoot me in the dark, okay?"

None of them wanted to think what they would do if it

turned out to be an old lady alone.

They spread out and started toward the house, at times being literally blown over by the wind. The wind this close to the water was stronger than any they'd encountered on the ride there. The rain and blowing sand came at them horizontally with such force it stung. As such, the walk from the car was slow and painful.

Finally they reached the house. As they rounded the corner toward the ocean side front door, they were hit with a wind that took their breath away. They each bent over to avoid the worst of the wind and felt along the house so as not to get lost. Two of them tumbled and struggled to regain their balance. When they reached the front door and found it open, the leader said, "Shit! They saw us coming."

"I think I just saw one of them crossing a dune," yelled one of the others, barely able to be heard by the others. He fired his gun.

"Don't shoot unless you have something to shoot at," screamed the leader. "You three go after them. I'll stay here in case they double back."

The other three looked at each other, shook their heads in disgust, and ventured out across the dunes, all sharing the same thought.

They suddenly didn't care about the $10,000. They just wanted to survive.

Chapter 42

Hurricane Chad smashed into the Cape as if it was being pushed by the hand of God. All of the other hurricanes in Cape Cod's history, including Bob, Carol, and the Hurricane of 1938, paled in comparison, and none affected as many people. All of the Cape was going to take a major hit and everyone knew it. Residents right along the shoreline fortified their houses as best they could, knowing it wouldn't be nearly enough, and took advantage of the many shelters set up in the schools throughout the Cape. The shelters were pleading with people to bring as much food with them as possible. With the bridges down, supply trucks weren't available. As a result, between more schools than usual being used and supplies being in short supply, there just wasn't enough to go around.

Almost exactly on schedule, and as a Category 4 storm, Chad landed around noon. The southern-facing areas on Buzzards Bay, including Woods Hole, Falmouth, and Bourne, took the first hit, with sustained winds reaching almost 140 mph. Trees toppled like matchsticks, hundreds of homes lost their roofs, and less structurally sound buildings were flattened. Surf Drive in Falmouth, running along the beaches facing the Vineyard, had been destroyed during Hurricane Bob, but rebuilt soon after. The concrete of the road was once again pushed aside with surprising ease and the few beach houses whose owners had been allowed to rebuild after Bob were gone in minutes.

The pounding rain flooded the streets, and the wind compounded the problem by bringing down trees—even the biggest oaks—which covered storm drains and stopped the flow of the water, creating small lakes all over the area. Downed trees blocked almost every road in the area. Emergency vehicles didn't even attempt to get out—not that they were receiving any calls with the phone lines down. Within minutes of Chad making landfall, power across the whole Cape was out. After Hurricane Bob, power company vehicles from all over the east coast showed up to help restore power. With the bridges down, there would be no hope of that happening. Officials knew that it could easily be months before power returned to most areas.

From Falmouth and the Upper Cape, Chad rumbled through the Mid-Cape, including Barnstable down through Dennis, and finally the Lower and Outer Cape of Chatham, Truro and Provincetown. The coastline of the Cape Cod National Seashore would be redrawn.

As dangerous as the winds and rain were, what made Chad a truly catastrophic event was its speed. Some storms hit and were gone in a matter of a couple of hours. Chad was so massive, and so slow-moving, that the Cape was going to be under its control for many hours. What Chad didn't destroy in the first violent minutes still had plenty of time to feel his wrath. With an almost human-like zest for revenge, it seemed that Chad was going to make Cape Cod pay for something. For what, no one exactly knew.

*****

For the passengers stuck on the ferry outside Woods Hole's harbor, Chad must have been feeling fairly benevolent. But it didn't seem that way at first.

Fifteen minutes after the storm hit, the anchor chains were severed, one by one, until the ferry was adrift and a near certainty to crash on the rocks at the edge of the harbor. But fate had different plans for the passengers and crew. For several weeks, crews had been dredging the channel, creating more and deeper space for the ferries. But the job wasn't done and there were shallow areas at the edge of the dredge sites. The ferry, now free of its anchors, plowed into the shallow water and became mired in the sand. The more the wind blew, the more entrenched the ship became, until it was apparent to everyone on board that they, in fact, were going nowhere. The ferry became nothing more than another building in the storm, and being made of steel, it wasn't likely to sustain any significant damage.

Before it settled, however, terror gripped the ferry's crew and passengers. The ship was being flung by the waves and wind, and everyone and everything on board was being flung with it. The cars below deck bounced and crashed into each other like bumper cars.

Richard and Julie Price, like everyone else, were trying to hold onto something for dear life, while at the same time, trying to keep hold of Sophia. Both were bruised and bloody from being slammed into the wall they were gripping onto so tightly. They had found an area that had a couple of metal poles protruding from the wall. Knowing the bars would be stable, they did everything possible not to let go.

And then a particularly violent wave slammed into the side of the ship, breaking the final anchor chain and sending the ship rocking wildly toward its eventual resting place in the sand. The hit was so powerful that Richard lost his grip on Sophia and she screamed and sailed across the floor, now at a 45-degree angle, and was about to smash into the wall on the other side. At the last second, a pair of enormous arms reached out and plucked her from certain death. It was the bruiser Richard had beaten earlier. He pulled Sophia to his chest and—now no longer able to hold onto anything himself—ducked his head and rolled into the wall with a loud thump. Obviously dazed, he didn't move for a moment, but still retained a tight grip on Sophia.

When the ferry momentarily semi-righted itself, Richard slid across the floor. The bruiser had set Sophia down next to himself against the wall. Richard grabbed his sobbing daughter and held her close.

"Thank you," he said to the man.

"Didn't do it for you," came the answer. "Did it for her."

"Thank you nonetheless. You saved her life."

He nodded and looked away.

Richard, with Sophia under his arm, made his way back to his wife on the opposite wall just as the ferry hit the sand and ceased moving.

The ferry, now secure in its bed of sand, finally stopped the rolling the passengers had had to endure for the past several days, and the violent rocking of the past hour. The danger of them sinking was now gone, but drowning was still on the table. Waves were cresting over the ship with an incredible strength and water was pouring down the stairwells and through the many broken windows. Someone momentarily inattentive could easily get caught up in a wave and sustain a head injury while under water. So while not as gravely dangerous as everything had been an hour earlier, they all knew they had a long way to go.

*****

Things were a little more desperate at Gloria's house. Moments before, a portion of her roof blew off, exposing the attic and the upstairs. Within minutes water was flowing down the stairs into the living room. Two of the women were hysterical and Gloria couldn't shut them up. Finally, Claire walked over to them and slapped each of them across the cheek.

"Would you shut the hell up?"

They immediately stopped and looked at Claire with confused expressions.

"You really think that's going to help? You think your screaming will keep the hurricane away? It would certainly keep me away, because I don't want to hear it. But I think the hurricane is here and it's not going to leave until it gets good and ready to. So how about you show just a tad bit of bravery and shut up?"

They shut up.

"Thank you, Claire." Gloria was gaining some respect for the old lady. She still wanted to kill her, but she promised herself she'd do it respectfully.

The house was shaking and creaking incessantly. The problem was, outside was even more dangerous, so they had nowhere to go.

"Grab all of the mattresses and pillows you can find," said Gloria. She pointed to a corner under the stairs in the center of the house. "I suggest we all go sit in that corner. It's probably the safest one in the house. We'll cover ourselves with the mattresses and pillows. If the house comes down, it might save us. It's our only chance." She saw some hesitation. "Ladies, we don't have a choice."

That got them moving. They pulled the cushions and pillows off the couch, and three of them carried in the mattress off the spare bed. It wasn't worth getting the mattress from the bed in the master bedroom upstairs. Besides being soaked by the deluge, it was just too dangerous to go up there with the wind and the associated projectiles.

So only an hour into the storm, all nine members of the Lifetime Book Club were huddled under some manner of protection, all scared to death and none quite sure they would survive the day.

*****

Chandler was miserable. What was he doing sitting in a puddle in the middle of a massive hurricane, looking out at the pond. Looking out? Hell, there was nothing to see. The rain was coming at them sideways so hard it actually hurt. The pond was being whipped up by the storm with such a fury, it looked like the middle of the ocean. Branches and large tree limbs were falling all around them. For what? On the off-chance that they might see a person standing by the pond emptying some powder into it? Sara and that superspy she had with her could watch the place all they wanted. He was leaving and bringing his people with him. Not even a terrorist would be stupid enough to be out on a day like this. He keyed his walkie-talkie.

"Mission aborted. We're going home."

"Is Sara with you?" came the broken up response.

"This is my decision."

"Sara, are you there?" said the voice.

"She's not there. I tried calling her a couple of times. They must be in a bad reception spot. She didn't respond. I've had enough of this place. We're going home."

"But Sara felt…"

"Fuck Sara. I said we're going home, so get your asses over here. That's an order."

The officer with him was looking doubtful about Chandler's decision. "You going to give me a hard time too?"

"I'm just wondering," the officer replied. He had to yell to be heard. "We're in a relatively safe spot. We've got a hurricane the strength of Katrina barreling through here. Wouldn't we be safer staying put? It's a long ride to Hyannis in this."

"What did I say? I said we're leaving. If you want to give me your resignation, you can stay as long as you like."

The officer went silent, fuming inside.

An hour later the other two groups showed up.

"Boss," said Pete, the friend Sara had seen on the waterfront, "I've got serious concerns about this. I don't want to tell you what to do, but…"

"Then don't."

"We're backup to Sara and Marcus. If something happens, we won't be there to help."

"Nothing will happen."

"You were in the military. You don't abandon your comrades in the field."

"They're not my comrades. And you forget, Sara was caught dealing drugs."

"That was bogus and you know it," said Pete, trying to be heard over the screaming wind.

"Are you accusing me…"

He never finished his question. With a crack that sounded more like an explosion, a tree broke in half and plummeted to the ground. Everyone scattered as it hit. Slowly, they all got up, some of them getting blown over again by the wind. Suddenly, someone called out, "Man down!"

Pete ran over to find one of the other officers holding his leg and grimacing.

"You okay?" Pete yelled.

"Fell on a rock trying to get away from the tree. Don't think it's bad. Bruised, probably."

And then another one called out, "It's Chandler. He's down."

They all hurried over to Chandler, who had taken the brunt of the tree. It was laying across his chest. Working together they lifted the tree enough so that he could be pulled out.

When Chandler was free, Pete leaned over him. "You okay?"

Chandler's eyes were open, but he was having trouble speaking.

"We'll get you help as soon as we can." Pete knew that was a lie. There would be no help anytime soon.

Chandler shook his head weakly. He knew it was the end. Blood was beginning to seep out the corner of his mouth.

Pete glanced up at his fellow officers, then said to Chandler, "You're right, no help is coming. Not in this storm. I think the tree crushed your chest. But you can do one right thing before you die. In front of all of us, tell us, did you plant the drugs in Sara's car?"

No response. Chandler was dead.

Chapter 43

Ann ran into the living room and slapped a still catatonic Doyle across the back of his head. That did the trick.

"What the fuck?"

Ann continued on to the battery lamp in the corner and turned it off.

"Your friends are here," she said.

She couldn't believe how calm she was. She made her way to her bedroom in the dark and opened the drawer that held her gun. She grabbed it and pulled her raincoat off the coatrack.

She heard Doyle shuffling around. "Where are you?" he said.

"I'm right here."

"We can't stay in here," said Doyle. "They'll get us for sure."

"I saw them out the back window, which means they're coming from the road. If we're lucky, there won't be anyone out the front door yet."

"Where do we go?" Doyle picked up his backpack.

"Hide in the dunes. It's our only chance. Hold onto the back of my raincoat. I know where to go."

"I can't find my gun."

"Leave it," said Ann.

She tried to open the door cautiously, but the wind caught

it and flung it open, slamming it against a wall mirror with a crash. "Close the door behind you," she said, but her voice was lost in the shrieking of the wind. She took a quick look back and saw the door wide open. Flint's men would know soon enough that they had left.

She struggled against the wind, suddenly feeling every bit of her eighty years. It was hard to breathe and so she put her face down inside her raincoat for a moment of relief. Behind her Doyle was struggling, so much so that he was actually pulling Ann back, severely slowing her progress.

Between her and the ocean were a dozen or so dunes. Of course, she didn't know exactly how much the ocean had risen from the storm at this point. She could hear the crashing of the waves over the sound of the wind. That wasn't a good sign. She had a brief image of a typical sunny day and having to chase tourists off the dunes. The sea grass was a vital part of the ecosystem, and trampling it was not only bad for the environment, it was illegal. Now she had absolutely no problem crossing the dunes if it would save her life.

"Don't pull me back." She shouted to Doyle.

"What?"

He obviously couldn't hear a word she said, so she fought on through the sand toward the first dune. A strong gust hit her head-on, knocking her to her knees. She felt Doyle's hands in her armpits, lifting her to her feet. She heard him say something, but the wind drowned out the words.

She thought she heard a cry in the distance and looked back to see the beam of a powerful flashlight attempting to penetrate the wall of sand. She heard a second cry, followed by a gunshot. It was faint in the storm, but it was the unmistakable sound of a gun.

They reached the first dune and hid behind it for a rest. It was ever so slow going. Doyle said something, but his words were lost in the wind and the pounding rain.

"What?" yelled Ann.

"Where ... are ... we ... going?" Doyle yelled back, spacing his words so she could understand.

"Away ... from ... here." What else could she say? She had no escape plan mapped out. All she knew was that they were there and the men with guns were right in back of them. There was no place to hide except behind the dunes. No! There was one other place. About a quarter mile from her house in the direction they were going was a town beach parking lot. Between the parking area and the beach was a boardwalk that wound its way through the dunes to the beach. Its purpose was to keep people from walking on the dunes. If they could make it, they could hide under the boardwalk. If Flint's men didn't know the area that well—and she was pretty sure they weren't the beach-going types—she and Doyle could hide unseen for the duration of the hurricane. It might also give them a place of safety from the storm itself.

"Keep walking," she yelled. "I know where we are going."

He gave her a thumbs up in response.

They were almost over the third dune when Doyle stumbled and fell on top of her, knocking her to the sand. She reached back to push Doyle off when she felt something wet. It wasn't rain, it had a different consistency. She looked down at her fingers. It was something dark. Blood. Doyle had been shot. She hadn't even heard a shot. She looked back, but couldn't see anyone. A lucky shot, it had to be.

Now she panicked. She had never seen anyone get shot before. In fact, she had never personally been around a victim of violence.

"Joe, are you okay?" Her voice had taken on a pleading tone.

"I'm okay, I think. They got me in the leg. It hurts like hell." He had to yell to be heard. "I don't think it's bad."

"Then get up. We have to go."

"What?"

"Get up!"

If anything, the storm was getting worse. She heard a faint crash. Most likely her shed. It wasn't as strong as her house. Almost as loud as the wind was the pounding of the waves. They were getting closer. She was pretty sure the water wouldn't come up this far, but it was scary nonetheless.

She grabbed Doyle's hand and helped him to his feet. With his free hand he still gripped the backpack. She knew now precisely where she wanted to go, if she could find it in the maelstrom. She held his arm and pulled him along, fully aware of the pain he was in. She would take a look at it when they arrived at the boardwalk. She didn't know how much she would be able to see, or for that matter, what she could do even if she could see. Didn't matter, the important thing was to get out of sight. It was clear that these people would kill them both without a second thought if they caught up to them.

She looked behind her. Nothing. But then, she really couldn't see more than thirty feet before it became a wall of blackness. And here it was, mid-afternoon. It could have been midnight, and there could be a hundred of Flint's men behind them for all she knew. She also noticed she was hunched down as she walked. Part of it was due to the storm, but she knew that the other part was fear of being hit by a stray bullet. As if ducking would make a difference.

Doyle stumbled and she heard him cry out in pain. Was he hit again? She stopped, but he waved her on. It was just a stumble. She turned her head again. Nothing. For a brief second she thought she heard someone yell, but it could have been her imagination.

They kept on. They had to be getting close. She felt it. Amazingly, Doyle seemed to be gaining strength. Maybe it was desperation. Whatever the reason, she wasn't going to question it. There, she heard it again! It was a voice. They were close. She just hoped she was going in the right direction and hadn't gotten turned around in the storm.

She crashed into something and she felt a sharp pain in her right shin. She fell forward onto something flat. It was the boardwalk! Right behind her Doyle also hit the wood and fell right next to her. She heard him cry out.

"We're here," she said. Whether he heard her or not, he didn't answer. She crawled across the boardwalk, Doyle in tow, and half-fell into the sand on the other side. She tried to picture the boardwalk in her mind and where she might be between the parking lot and the beach. She took a chance and turned toward the parking lot. It made sense to her for two reasons: 1) some of the higher parts of the walk were closest to the parking area; and 2) she didn't know how far up the beach the ocean had come. The last thing she wanted was to get trapped by the sea.

She followed the wood of the boardwalk for about ten minutes, going excruciatingly slowly and catching splinters in her fingers. Doyle just held onto Ann's raincoat and let her lead the way. Then she felt a space between the wood and the sand. It wasn't much of one, but she knew she was getting closer. Another five minutes of crawling brought them to a space about three feet high.

"In here," Ann said. She wasn't sure Doyle heard her, but he followed anyway.

Under the boardwalk the noise diminished dramatically. Ann figured the sand helped muffle the screaming of the wind. It was still loud, but now she didn't feel she had to yell. Sand came whistling through the hole, but at a lesser rate. Now they were sheltered under the boardwalk, in a small space that felt like a cramped cave.

"How's your leg?" she asked in almost a normal voice.

"Still hurts like hell, but I don't think it did any damage." He struggled to take off his rain-sodden shirt, with Ann helping. He lifted his pants leg and Ann could barely make out a dark patch. He wrapped the shirt around the wound and tied it tight.

"I think I'll live." He tried to sound confident, but Ann knew he was anything but, so she tried to keep him talking.

"I can't believe you brought your backpack."

"Had to. At this point I don't care about the money—well, not too much—but I don't want them to find the cross. It's the only leverage I have over Flint."

Ann turned on her side and reached behind her back, pulling out her gun. Doyle's eyes grew wide.

"You've had a gun all this time?"

She nodded.

"You could have used it on me."

"Would you have used yours on me?"

"No."

"Well then," answered Ann.

They went silent. Two minutes later they heard a noise above them. Someone had found the boardwalk and was following it. Ann looked to the left and saw a hand. The man had the right idea. He was looking for space where someone could hide between the sand and the boardwalk. She saw shoes. He had found what he was looking for. She saw him go down on his hands and knees. In one hand was a flashlight and in the other his gun. Ann gripped her gun with both hands, hoping she wouldn't accidently pull the trigger. She was shaking. She looked over at Doyle. He had passed out. She was essentially all alone. Her heart was pounding and her hands were sweating. Now she was wondering if the gun would slip out of her hands if she tried to shoot it. Shoot it? Could she really point it at someone and pull the trigger? No way.

And then the flashlight was pointed right at her. She heard an exclamation of surprise at suddenly discovering them. She pulled on the trigger with all her might—it was harder than she thought it would be—and her gun went off. Just like that. The noise was deafening and she dropped it into the sand. With the explosion, Doyle jerked to consciousness and smacked his head against the wood above him.

There was no movement from the man with the flashlight. The light lay unmoving in the sand. Tentatively, Ann reached over and picked it up. She brushed against some fingers when she did, almost causing her to drop the flashlight. She turned it toward the man and this time dropped it for real. The man had a hole in his forehead. It almost seemed to be smoking, but maybe that was her imagination.

Doyle reached over and picked up the flashlight and again pointed it at the man.

"Holy shit, Ann," he said. "You got him almost right between the eyes." He spied the man's gun and leaned over and picked it up. "You think they heard it?" he asked.

Ann barely picked up what he said. She had a ringing in her ears and had developed a massive headache.

"Maybe, but I think this is still the safest place."

"What if they see the body?"

"If anything, the storm is getting worse. I don't think they'll find him. There's not enough room to pull him in here."

Suddenly, Ann was very tired. She could hardly keep her eyes open. She leaned back in the sand, determined to stay awake. If another of Flint's men came by, he'd kill them if he found them. She couldn't help it though. She closed her eyes just for a minute.

A second later she was sound asleep.

Chapter 44

At noon, as predicted, Chad hit full force. Marcus and Sara had spent the last seven hours huddled together in the pouring rain. The spot they had picked would have been ideal had the rain not been blowing sideways. They'd found an enormous tree trunk that had fallen securely onto a boulder, providing them protection from other falling branches and trees, while also giving them a wall of rock to hide behind. Broken parts of the boulder gave Marcus a platform to lean his rifle on for a clean shot. The pumping station lay twenty-five yards in front of them.

However, the rain had made it a most uncomfortable seven hours, and now it was about to get a lot worse. Marcus had been in many of the worst trouble spots in the world, having experienced blistering heat and bone-numbing cold, but this was entirely different. This was frightening on a whole different scale. All around them they could hear branches and tree trunks snapping and crashing to the ground. And those were only the large ones. Thousands of smaller ones were breaking and flying through the air, but those they couldn't hear over the roar of the wind and the pounding of the rain.

Marcus could still see the pumping station, but barely. If it got any worse, they'd have to move closer, and there wasn't any cover closer. Sara said something, but Marcus couldn't make out the words. She pointed to the ground and he immediately knew what she had been saying. Their spot under the tree trunk was in a slight indentation, like a shallow foxhole. It was now rapidly filling with water. Again they were faced with the prospect of moving and becoming exposed. The hole was shallow and there was no way they could drown. The worst that could happen would be that they would be even more uncomfortable than they already were. He motioned that they would stay and Sara nodded her head in agreement.

The next two hours were hell. Their rain gear had become useless once the hurricane arrived, becoming more of a hindrance than a help. Besides being awkward and bulky, it was stiflingly hot. Removing the gear gave them freedom of movement and cooled them down considerably. Conversation was reduced to the occasional shout. Eventually that became tiresome and they went quiet. Occasionally, one of the groups would try to call on the walkie-talkie, but the reception was terrible and the frequency of the calls diminished and eventually died out.

A few minutes after 2:30, Marcus, who had closed his eyes for something resembling a rest while Sara kept guard, felt her poking him. He looked up to see her pointing toward the pumping station. Instantly he was alert, pushing himself up from the sucking mud that had been his bed. They watched for a moment while a figure came out of the gloom and approached the fence. He was hunched over in the wind, carrying a backpack and moving slowly. Finally he arrived at the gate and set down the backpack. He reached in and took out wire cutters.

Meanwhile, Marcus was looking through the scope of his rifle. It was an easy shot, one that he had made countless times in the past. He squeezed the trigger. The whole nightmare could have ended with one bullet right at that moment. But it wasn't meant to be.

A millisecond before the gun fired, a small limb fell and nicked the barrel of the rifle. The gun fired, the noise almost unheard in the storm. Marcus knew that the bullet would miss its mark because of the branch, so he immediately aimed and fired again. But in that brief second, his target had disappeared.

*****

Mason was beginning to wonder if his obsession with timeliness had finally reached the ridiculous stage. He had been smart enough to leave his apartment before noon and the height of the storm so he wouldn't face the prospect of a road blocked with debris. Even then, getting to the pond took forever as he dodged thick branches littering the road. If it was this bad now, he thought, whatever would it be like during the height of it? But there was a part of it that excited him and made him glad he had decided to stick to his schedule. It somehow made the process even more meaningful.

He thought of the aftermath of the Twin Towers—the firestorm raging in the towers before they fell, and the storm of dust, ash, smoke, and paper rolling down the avenues after the buildings collapsed. He was finally experiencing what so many others felt, both inside and outside of the buildings. He wasn't sad for his parents at that moment, because they never experienced any of this. It was already long since over for them.

This was his 9/11, and it was exhilarating!

He was no longer frustrated that he was unable to send the rest of the emails outlining the reasons for all this—the government's failure to stop 9/11, and in fact, their complicity in the event—and detailed descriptions of how the residents would die. It didn't matter anymore. The people were already panicked enough and the government would get the message that they'd once again failed. He did get satisfaction knowing that he had been able to pay the visit to his cousins and let them know exactly how they were going to die and who was going to do it.

He parked his car deep in the woods where it would be hidden in the unlikely event that a police car happened by. He pulled a .45 from his backpack and set it on his lap. If a police car did happen by, it would be the cop's bad luck. Killing his two explosives men had been easier than he thought it would be. Firing a gun into the face of a cop would be no problem at all. But he hoped he wouldn't see one. He wanted to sit in his car for the next couple of hours and just enjoy in silence the anticipation of what he was about to do.

When Chad hit in all its fury and the car rocked from the wind and the rain pounded on the roof, Mason was in heaven. All around him trees were snapping in half and limbs were falling to the ground like concrete from the towers. His intention was to stay in his car until about 2:45, but at two o'clock an enormous tree limb crashed down on his hood, completely obliterating the front of the car. It suddenly dawned on him that if the same thing happened on the roof of the car, he'd be smashed and none of his plan would happen. It was time to leave.

He tried to open the door, but it was stuck. The branch landing on the hood had crumpled the metal so that it interfered with the door. Oh, that was too funny, he thought. He would end up dying in his car, minutes before he was scheduled to launch the D-394. He tried the passenger door with the same result, so he climbed into the back seat. As he did, another tree fell onto the hood of the car, shattering the front windshield and replacing it with the tree. It was getting dangerous. He had to move. He tried the back door on the driver's side. It was stuck. He kicked at the door with no luck. Finally, he took the butt of his gun and smashed the window. He cleaned off as much of the glass as possible and shimmied out, landing head-first on the ground. He stood up and was immediately blown to the ground. The force of the wind was more intense than he had thought. He found it hard to breathe and felt a ringing in his ears. He was now regretting not waiting until the next day.

He slowly got to his feet, bracing himself against the side of the car. He had become slightly disoriented and had to think for a moment which way it was to the water department building. Once he had his bearings, he reached into the car for his backpack and started on his way.

It took forever. Keeping his balance was hard enough, but he also spent half his time looking up, making sure a heavy branch wasn't dropping on top of him. He knew it was stupid. Even if he saw one headed his way, he wouldn't be able to avoid it. But it gave him a little sense of control, imagined or not.

After falling for about the thirtieth time, he resorted to crawling, making no less time than when he was walking.

Finally, he saw the fence to the pumping station ahead. He got back to his feet and shuffled along bent over. He reached the fence and held on. Around him was a large open area. The chances of being crushed by a branch had lessened, but in the open space he could feel the full brunt of the wind. He opened his backpack and pulled out his wire cutters. At that moment, something whipped past his face and crashed against the fence. Even in the roar of the wind he could hear it. At the same moment a massive gust of wind threw him to the ground. He felt another something whip past his head and clang into the metal. Bullets! They knew he was here.

Had the gust of wind not knocked him down, he knew the second bullet would have killed him. He was suddenly scared. He had been willing to give his life for his cause, but it had all been theoretical. The appearance of the bullets, however, made death suddenly very real. He started crawling. No more bullets sailed by. He realized he was in a small ditch. The shooter probably couldn't see him. There was no way he was going to get into the pumping station. He had two choices: One would be to head for the pond and empty the D-394 into the water. It might take a while before people would begin to feel the effects, depending on how quickly it entered the pipes that would carry it into civilization. Or the second choice would be to hide and wait until the rain let up and let it loose in the air. It figured that he was in the woods, away from people. It would still kill a significant number of them, but if he was going to let it go in the air, he would have found a more central spot to get the maximum number of victims. Besides, with someone—he had no idea how many of them—on his trail, he might not last until the storm ended. No, he had to try for the pond.

The pond was to his right. He was in the ditch on the left-hand side of the dirt road that ran around the pond. He was probably fifty to a hundred feet from the water. Somehow, he had to get across the road. If he could do that, he'd again be in the safety of the woods and could easily make it to the water. Once he dumped it in, he'd be dead very quickly anyway as he breathed in the powder.

How was he going to get across the road? The shooter was good. He could tell. It was only sheer luck that he wasn't dead. The guy was probably using a sniper rifle. Whatever he did, he had to do quickly. They could be sneaking up on him right now. And then he saw the tree. A tall one had fallen from the woods across the road. If he could stay behind it, he might be safe. He might get this done after all.

*****

Marcus was cursing himself for missing the shots. He had missed very few in his life, and those were early in his career. Since then, his record was perfect. This was not the one to break the streak.

"He's got to be by the side of the road," he yelled to Sara. "Probably a ditch."

She nodded her agreement and took off, gun in hand. Marcus followed behind, still holding the rifle. It would still be more accurate than a pistol unless they were right on top of him, and he could sight and shoot in a second.

Marcus and Sara were both bent over in the wind, and both had been blown over twice already. A branch came out of nowhere and slammed into Sara's shoulder. Marcus heard her cry out in pain. She was on the ground clutching her arm. Marcus caught up to her.

"Can you continue?" he yelled.

"Help me up," came the response. She held out her good arm and he pulled her up. "Hurts like hell," she said at the top of her voice, "but I'll live. Might have to shoot left-handed."

They continued on. Marcus couldn't see Mason, but he knew that he had to be crawling along inside the ditch. Then he saw his head pop up just for a second. Sara took a shot, but his head had already disappeared.

They had reached the road now, and Marcus pointed to a tree lying across it further down. Sara understood. Mason had to get to the pond, but to do so he had to cross the road. The tree was the perfect spot. Marcus waved Sara on. She diverted her path more toward the woods, hoping to catch Mason as he crossed the road. They were still about seventy-five feet away from the downed tree, but moving at a snail's pace. With the protection of the ditch, it was possible that Mason would beat them to the woods, and then to the pond. Marcus couldn't let that happen.

He had been trying to inch closer to the ditch to see if he could get a shot right down the middle of it, but he realized he wasn't going to make it. He knelt down in the road and took aim for the spot where the tree met the ditch. Mason was going to have to climb out. If Marcus could even see a part of him, it might be enough to get a bullet into him and slow him down.

He waited, rifle pointed at the spot. Mason must have anticipated it, because when he climbed out, he was fast, almost jumping out of the ditch. But not fast enough. Marcus took the shot.

*****

Mason screamed as he felt the impact and then the bullet burn its way into his leg. Nothing had ever hurt so much. He turned his head and saw the blood turning his pants leg dark. If he lost too much blood he was going to pass out. But he couldn't stop now. He had to make it. As he crawled along the downed tree, he berated himself once again for not waiting a day. What a difference it would have made.

He was almost across the road. A second longer and he might lose them in the woods. He was trying to calculate how far it was from the edge of the road to the water. Twenty-five feet maybe? He was getting very tired. He could stop here and open the canister. Some of it might be taken by the wind. Probably not though. The rain wouldn't let it fly. It would soak into the ground. No, he had to make the pond. He was across the road and in the woods now. He found himself scrambling faster, climbing over branches like a snake. He was losing steam. Now he could see the water. Only a few feet more. As he crawled, he reached into his backpack for the canister. He had taken it out of the case before he left the house to make the job easier. Almost...

"Stop right there!" A woman's voice yelling at him. Must be a cop. He almost didn't hear it. Things were beginning to get fuzzy. She couldn't stop him now. His .45 was in his belt. He reached for it. He heard her yell again, but he didn't understand what she was saying. He almost had it out of his belt. And then he felt the bullet hit his side. It was like he was hit by a truck. It turned him onto his back. He looked up at a wet, muddy woman pointing a gun at him, and he knew. His plan wasn't going to happen. He wasn't going to make it to the pond. He tried to lift his gun to point it at her, but it was suddenly heavy. He grabbed it with both hands. She was still screaming at him. He tried to point it, then felt something smash into his chest. His hands fell to his side, the gun lying in the mud. He heard a noise. It was coming from him. It was a whimper. He was crying. And then he wasn't.

*****

Marcus had heard the gunshots, so he knew he was close. He rounded a big tree and saw Sara standing there, gun at her side, looking down at a dead man. A canister was by his side, unopened.

Sara turned when she felt Marcus's presence, and then fell into his arms. They collapsed into the mud. After a few minutes, Marcus picked up the canister and half-carried Sara to the base of a large tree, where they stayed wrapped in each other's arms for the remainder of the storm. A few feet away at the edge of the pond lay Mason, eyes wide open in a stare of death.

ANDREW CUNNINGHAM

July 9th

Chapter 45

Ann slept soundly in her cramped space under the boardwalk. When she finally woke up, she was disoriented, but seemed to know enough about her surroundings not to sit up and whack her head on the wood. She stayed still, coming to grips with her situation. She looked out at the man she'd killed. He was half covered with sand. And then she remembered Doyle. He was lying next to her, not moving. She shook him, but he didn't stir. Tears came to her eyes. *Please God, don't let him be dead.*

She felt his pulse. He was alive! Suddenly he groaned and opened his eyes. "Where the fuck am I?"

"Still alive."

"Good to know."

"We both fell asleep." And then she noticed the wind. There was none. Well, there was some, but nothing like what they had experienced. They had slept through Chad. "The hurricane is over."

Doyle looked at the dead man. "This guy doesn't care. One hell of a shot."

"I had my eyes closed. You're lucky I didn't hit you." She realized that the dead man no longer bothered her. Maybe it was her age, she thought. Maybe she was just able to get over things faster. She also had enough experience in life to know that you made your own decisions and had to live—or die—with them.

"What do we do?" asked Doyle.

"How are you feeling?"

"A little sick, and my leg still hurts like hell. Otherwise, I'm peachy."

"Then it's time to go. I think we should head back to the house."

"They'll be waiting for us ... for me."

"Maybe, maybe not. We don't know how many of them there were. Maybe they hid out in my house to get out of the storm, or maybe they got lost in the dunes and died. Or maybe they didn't like that one of their men didn't make it back and they took off when the storm ended. Whatever, we can't stay here."

"Where does this boardwalk lead?"

"To a public parking lot, but there won't be anyone there. Remember, people aren't driving because of the terrorists. The only people we might run into would be Flint's men. No one else is around here right now. All the other beach cottages near mine are falling down, owned by people who haven't used them in years. They're probably gone altogether by now. My cottage is our only option. It's also where my Jeep is, in case I have to take you to the hospital."

They crawled out the side opposite the dead man. Ann unwrapped Doyle's shirt from his wound. It was the first time she had been able to see it. There had been a lot of blood, dried now, but the wound itself didn't seem bad. There was an entrance and a clear exit, so the bullet wasn't in there. It wasn't a flesh wound, but at the same time, it wasn't deep either, and the bullet definitely hadn't hit a bone or an artery. He'd live. The shirt was a mess, so it wasn't worth putting it back on the wound. Since it had clotted and scabbed over pretty well, she suggested to Doyle that he not cover it for the walk back.

"The air might be good for it and we're only a quarter of a mile from the house. I can put a bandage on it there."

"Assuming they don't kill us first," said Doyle.

"Then a bandage won't matter." Ann was amazed at how cavalier she'd become about everything. It was daytime and she could now see. That relieved the fear of the unknown they had faced the day and night before. She could think and plan, and she was pretty sure she was smarter than any of the men Flint had sent.

She looked at the backpack Doyle was clutching and had an idea.

"Can you part with that for a while?"

Doyle looked down at it, as if it was his child. "Hell, no."

"Suppose they are waiting for us at the cottage? If you bring them the cross, they'll kill you ... us ... without a second thought. If you don't have it, you can use it as a bargaining chip. We can bury it right where we spent the night. Nobody will find it. Nobody's here to find it. We'll move the dead man farther away so we don't draw anyone here. Chances are, you can get it later today."

Doyle thought about it for a moment, then conceded that Ann was right. While she dug the hole under the boardwalk, Doyle dragged the man behind a mound of sand, then proceeded to cover him up. Then he brushed the sand so the drag marks would be invisible. They met back at the boardwalk.

They were in a hollow between dunes. Ann climbed one of the dunes and looked over the top. Nothing. No movement anywhere. She couldn't see her cottage because of another dune a bit higher that blocked it from view. The sun had come out for the first time in days and was a welcome sight. She climbed back down and suggested to Doyle that they get back on the boardwalk and head toward the water until they found a flatter spot to get off and head across the dunes to her house. She was thinking of Doyle's leg and what the climbing might do to the wound.

It was a good idea, but short-lived. Not fifty feet down, the boardwalk was gone. Sand heavily covered it, making the walking no better than traversing the dunes. A little further down from that Ann could see spots where the waves had come up and completely taken the boardwalk away. They turned left and started across the sand.

Dunes were fluid, always at the mercy of the wind, but this time, the wind had really done its job. Ann was wrong. She didn't have to worry about Doyle having to climb. The rest of the dunes were essentially gone—flattened by the wind, or for those nearer the water, the surf. She could see the cottage clearly, which of course, meant that anyone in the cottage could see them clearly if they were standing outside. The boards were still on the windows. She did her best to take a route that afforded them a little cover by some of the slightly higher remaining dunes. Doyle was limping badly, but not complaining.

As they approached the house, she could see that someone had closed the front door, which meant they were probably in the house. Her Jeep was still outside, half-covered in sand.

"Why don't you hide around the corner of the house and I'll go in. After all, it is my house. You can be the cavalry if I need it."

Doyle agreed and moved out of sight around the corner. Ann took a deep breath and opened the door and instantly heard scrambling. Then she heard two guns click as the triggers were pulled back.

"Who the hell are you?" came a voice from the gloom. With only two small uncovered windows for light, it was hard to see.

Ann tried to look appropriately frightened. "Who are you and what are you doing in my house?"

She could now see. There were two of them, both behind the couch, both pointing guns at her.

"If you're here to rob me, take whatever you want and leave."

"We're looking for someone and we think he was with you."

"Look, I just spent the night on the beach. I got disoriented in the storm and couldn't find my way back to my cottage. I'm tired, dirty, hungry, and very much alone." She looked around. "And from all appearances, I'm going to have to do a lot of cleaning. So the storm is over. If you're not here to rob me, could you please leave?"

They glanced at each other, now confused. They were sure Doyle was here, but the one person who had seen the car and deduced his hiding place was missing.

"We lost one member of our search party. Did you see him, by any chance?"

"All I saw was sand, and I think I swallowed most of it."

Ann was thinking she had them ready to leave, when

Doyle's body filled the doorway and he walked into the cottage. Ann inwardly groaned that he could be so stupid as to walk in, when she realized he wasn't alone. There was a man behind him and he was holding a gun to Doyle's head.

"Look who I found outside."

One of the men who had been talking to Ann shot her a mean look. "You were lying to us, you old bitch."

Ann had taken off her raincoat before arriving at the cottage and had it draped over one arm, covering the revolver she held. If she had to use it, she knew she could.

"I have no idea what you're talking about. I've never seen him before."

"Forget about her," said the man behind Doyle. He pushed him to the floor and Doyle cried out in pain. "Where's the stuff you stole from Flint?"

"I have no idea what you're talking about."

The man kicked Doyle in the leg near his wound and Doyle screamed.

"You still have no idea what we're talking about?"

"No idea," said Doyle, crying now.

The man grabbed Ann by the arm—the arm without the raincoat—and pulled her to him. He put a gun to her head.

"Do you care about her?"

Ann looked at Doyle and gave him a look to say, *don't do it*, and thought he would deny knowing her, but then he caved.

"Don't hurt her. I'll take you to the stuff."

The man still held on, but Ann could feel him lighten his grip just slightly. She dropped her other arm and pointed the gun in the general direction of his leg. She gripped the gun hard, remembering that the trigger was stiff and that she'd had to use both hands the night before. She pulled with all her might and the gun went off. And then all hell broke loose.

Her captor screamed and fell to the floor clutching his leg. Between the sudden noise of the explosion and the total shock of Ann's actions, the other two were momentarily paralyzed. Doyle took that opportunity to pull out the semi-auto he had taken from the dead guy and he shot at one of the two men. It was a wild shot, but it hit it's mark, shattering the man's kneecap. Ann lifted her gun and pointed it at the remaining man, still standing as he started to lift his gun, and she said, "Go ahead, make my day!"

He dropped his gun in a panic and knelt down with his hands in the air.

Doyle looked at her, grimacing in pain. "Did you really say that?"

*****

"What do we do now?" asked Doyle. He had just finished using Ann's duct tape to secure their prisoners' hands behind their backs. Ann was busy cleaning and bandaging the two of Flint's men, having already done Doyle's wound.

Ann couldn't help but to notice the change in him. He had already come to respect Ann for her age and knowledge, but now it was different. He was now looking at her as some sort of superstar. As long as he kept that up, she was going to remain in charge of the situation.

"We've got to get them to the police station. The police can see about getting these two to a doctor. You've got to see one too."

"Are you going to turn me in?"

"For what? For seeking refuge in the storm? You need to get that cross turned in to the police. I think they'll believe that you took it from Flint as evidence. After all, he sent his men after you."

"What about the money?"

Ann thought about it for a moment, then said, "What money?"

There was a hint of a smile on Doyle's lips.

Chapter 46

It was still dark out when Marcus opened his eyes. But now it was the dark of night, not blackness caused by the hurricane. He looked at his watch. It was after midnight. Next to him sat Sara. She was talking into the walkie-talkie.

"We got him," she was saying. "We tried to reach you a few times earlier, but the storm cut off the reception." That was not exactly true, thought Marcus. They'd tried once before falling asleep.

"Did he have the stuff?" came the question.

"He did. It's safe. You can find us by the pond over near the pumping station. We're not moving. I think my arm might be broken."

"We have some news too. Will tell you when we get there."

"Let me see your arm," said Marcus.

"I'd be happy to, but I can't move it. You'll have to do the work."

He got the flashlight and shone it on her shoulder. She had on a short sleeve shirt, which should have made examining her easy, but when he tried to lift the sleeve, she cried out in pain. He pulled out his knife and cut the sleeve away. The shoulder was black and blue. He touched it gently and she stiffened.

"Don't know if something is broken or just chipped," he

told her. "But it looks like it might hurt."

"You think?" she said with a grimace.

A few minutes later they saw the bobbing of flashlights coming down the road. Marcus flashed his on and off until he got a similar response.

There were five of them, one limping badly. They plopped down next to Marcus and Sara, their eyes going over to Mason, still staring sightlessly at the dark sky—now filled with stars instead of clouds of debris.

"You got him. Unbelievable. You know, Chandler wanted to leave you here. He said that no terrorist would come out in this."

Sara looked around. "Where is he?"

"Dead. A tree fell on him. Crushed his chest. We left him over there. We can get him on the way back to the cars. A little bit of good news though. As he was dying, he admitted that he set you up, that he placed the drugs in your car. We were all witnesses to it. I'm sure the captain will let you back on the force if you still want it."

"To be able to work again with you guys?" she responded. "Of course I do."

Marcus, meanwhile, was watching the eyes of the others. He knew that Sara would have seen the lie in their eyes had she looked. Maybe she purposely didn't want to look. But he knew. He knew that she had just been given an amazing show of respect from her fellow officers. And she deserved every bit of it.

Epilogue

Life on Cape Cod resumed to some extent on July 9th. The officers got word to the FBI contingent on the base that the terrorists had been neutralized. They, in turn, got word to the president, who informed the media, who immediately broadcasted it on every channel. The only ones who couldn't get the word were those most affected by it—the people on Cape Cod. Power was out and would be for weeks to come. However, through the police, fire, and rescue personnel, word eventually made its way across the Cape.

Supplies began to arrive at Otis by C-130 military cargo jets, beginning almost immediately and continuing every half hour throughout the day. With the supplies came rescue crews and vehicles from all over the country to help the people of the Cape dig out from the disaster. The National Guard was also sent in with orders to make this the most orderly rescue operation in U.S. history. Katrina and Sandy would not be repeated in any way, shape, or form.

The death toll was numbering in the high hundreds, so far, with more to come. Those numbers, though, were far lower than what the authorities had estimated, based on the strength of Chad—which was officially classified as a Category 4 hurricane. What was on everyone's lips was what the death toll would have been had Mason succeeded.

The Cape was in shambles. Thousands of houses were

destroyed completely or made uninhabitable and most roads were impassable. Just getting to a supply zone was a major chore for people, so the National Guard made as its top priority opening the roads. Many of the downtown areas were flooded, the looted stores now just washed out hulks, unrecognizable as the businesses they once were. The same neighbors who, only three days earlier, were looting the stores, were now working together to return to some sense of normalcy. Neighbor checked on neighbor, sometimes finding the worst possible results. Many weeks would pass before everyone was accounted for.

That desire to return to life could be heard in the thousands of chainsaws at work clearing roads, sidewalks, yards—and in many cases, living rooms and kitchens—of tree branches and whole trees. The promise of gasoline becoming available gave homeowners added incentive to fire up the chainsaws.

Water was the first emergency supply to make it to the Cape. Knowing the situation of the roads, water drops were made all over the Cape with police and fire personnel there to help distribute it to those in need—which included most of the people.

Immediate work was started to rebuild the ferry docks in Woods Hole and Hyannis, with the first of the ferries arriving from New Bedford the next day. The plan was for ferries to be running around the clock from New Bedford to the Cape, as well as ferries from New Bedford to Martha's Vineyard and Nantucket. Cars were not allowed on these trips. The first priority was the people. The cars would have to wait. A massive intake center was set up in New Bedford, with buses waiting to take people to Boston, New York, and Hartford, where more help would be offered to get people home.

For a spur-of-the-moment plan, it was well thought-out. Of course problems would crop up, but given what they had just gone through, most of the people were accepting of the situation.

Everyone knew that it would take weeks to even sort out what needed to be done, and then many months to implement all of the plans. It would be a long time before the Cape would show definite signs of progress.

The Army Corps of Engineers was already planning a temporary bridge across the Cape Cod Canal, for emergency vehicles and supply trucks at first. Over time, it could be used for tourists and residents alike to take their cars across to the mainland. It wasn't going to be easy, and it certainly wasn't going to be quick, but over time the job would get done.

The nine women of the Lifetime Book Club were ever so grateful when the first emergency vehicle arrived on the scene of Gloria's former house. Amazingly, no one was seriously hurt when the walls came down after the roof was blown off. Even more amazing was that no one had killed Claire. When she breezily announced that she would be at the next meeting, as soon as someone could figure out where to have it, Gloria quickly informed her that the Lifetime Book Club was being disbanded. Claire was going to have to find a new club in which to spread her cheer.

Despite the demand by Julie's father for them to come back to the Vineyard and stay with Julie's family, Richard and Julie Price and daughter Sophia got off of what was left of the ferry as quickly as they could, with the help of the Coast Guard, and headed to New Bedford and eventually home. If they never saw Julie's family again, they'd be just fine. As they were departing the ferry, Richard looked for the bruiser he beat up, and who eventually saved Sophia, but he was nowhere to be seen. Richard wanted to thank him again, but he realized he had probably embarrassed the man the first time he thanked him, considering the same person who was thanking him had also beaten the crap out of him, mentally even more than physically.

Emerson Flint used his vast influence to get a message sent out on a secure channel to one of his subordinates to pick him up by helicopter at a local school field. The moment he was airborne, he pumped his fist in the air. He'd made it! Obviously the cross had not yet been turned over to the authorities, but once it was, they'd come after him. Since his men didn't return from their mission, he could only assume that it was a failure. Whether his men were dead or not was not a concern. It was time to use his money to get himself to a non-extradition treaty country immediately, if not sooner. Unbeknownst to Flint, Doyle, along with Ann Lawrence for moral and credible support, had made their way to the Truro Police Department—the more barren land had made driving easier than in other parts of the Cape—and turned over the cross to the police the morning after the hurricane. Remembering the story, the police turned it over to the FBI. But with everything going on with the terrorists, they filed it for another day. When it was observed that Flint was leaving the Cape, however, they had the State Police waiting for him when he landed in Boston. Flint wasn't going anywhere.

*****

Sporadic cell phone service appeared on the 10th. For most of the people on the Cape, it was too little, too late, as their phones had long since run out of juice, and with no electricity available to charge them, they weren't in any better shape than before.

Ann had wisely turned off her phone when service disappeared, and was now turning it on once in a while just in case. When she turned it on around noon on the 10th and saw close to fifty voicemails and texts from her niece, she hit "call back" on her phone and crossed her fingers. Marie picked up on the first ring.

"Ann, it's you! I can't believe it. I've been so worried. Are you okay?"

"I'm fine, dear. I'm sorry I've been out of touch, but it's been kind of windy here."

"Windy, ha!" Ann could hear in Marie's voice that she probably had tears running down her face. "I'm so relieved. Between the terrorists and the hurricane and the stories that were coming from there, I didn't know if I would ever see you again. All I could think of was you all alone in your cottage."

"Well, I wasn't alone. I had a young man staying here whose car died right near my house. He was very helpful."

"You let a strange man inside your house? I'm glad he turned out to be okay, but Ann, were you out of your mind? What if he had turned out to be a crook or something? You could have been in great danger."

"No, I was fine. But Marie, you know that little gun you made me keep?"

"Yes."

"I'm running low on bullets."

*****

A manhunt was quickly established for the two remaining terrorists. Using a sketch provided from descriptions given by Harry, officials scoured every face boarding the ferries. The men were found two days later, standing in line for water in Hyannis. Harry and Seth were transported by plane to Washington, where they would be interrogated. Marcus knew that Seth was facing major jail time, but Harry's sentence was likely to be much stiffer—maybe even death.

When Marcus got a clear line out, he called Seth's uncle and brought him up to date. While sad for his sister having to deal with a felon son, he took it all in stride, apologizing to Marcus for giving him such a crummy assignment. He promised to make up for it—he already had a major problem within his company that needed handling. Marcus told him that he would contact him after he took a vacation.

As soon as word got back to the Barnstable Police chief regarding Chandler's "confession" and the job Sara had done preventing the worst terrorist attack in U.S. history, he immediately offered her her old position, with full back pay, a major apology, and a bonus from the Town of Barnstable—most likely in the hopes that she wouldn't file a lawsuit. She accepted the offer, but informed them that she was going on a long vacation first.

Marcus and Sara were going to be honored later in the summer by the president and were going to be given some medal—Marcus wasn't sure which one, and didn't really care.

The CIA contacted him to let him know that he'd brought honor to the agency and wanted to know—based on the events on the Cape and his previous track record with the agency—if he would like to come back in a supervisory position. Marcus politely turned them down.

*****

Joe Doyle stayed a couple more days with Ann, helping her to clean up the mess from the storm. Her shed was gone, but he helped her collect what things they could find and clean the sand out of the house.

Ann drove Doyle to the temporary docks when she felt he had done enough to help her. She stood in line with him.

"I appreciate you bringing me here," he said.

"I figured I may as well finish off the strangest experience I've ever had—see it to the end."

"Again, I apologize for involving you in all this," said Doyle. "It wasn't fair of me and I know it."

"It wasn't, but in retrospect, I'm happy to have met you. And let's face it, I wouldn't have ever met you any other way."

"And I want to thank you again for saving my life."

"Are you going to do what I suggested?"

"I'm going to open a few bank accounts and also get a safe deposit box to hide some of the money. Then I'll deliver Murphy's cut to him and head out of the country for a while. You sure you won't take some of it?"

"Absolutely. I didn't know you were still thinking of leaving the country, so one question: Do you have a passport?"

He looked at her and cocked his head. "Uh, do I need one?"

She sighed, exasperated at his lack of worldliness. "Yes, dear, you need a passport to travel outside the country. You can pick up an application at the post office. They can help you fill it out. Do you have a place to live in the meantime?"

"I have an apartment. I was just going to skip out on the rent, but maybe I should stay a while longer, now that I don't have to worry about Flint and Murphy will be paid back."

"Good plan. With all that money, maybe you should look into starting a business. There are places that can help you with that. And instead of a Caribbean island, try the Florida Keys. You don't need a passport."

"Hey, maybe I could open a business down there, maybe a bar. No more illegal stuff for me. Thought you'd like to know that."

He looked suddenly lost.

"Tell you what," Ann said. "I'll probably live to regret this, but here's my phone number." She handed him a piece of paper. "If you have any questions, call me."

He gave her a sly smile. "You already had this written down. You were going to give it to me anyway."

"I was thinking about it, but hadn't decided. Obviously, you can't even tie your shoes on your own, so you better keep it with you, just in case."

The line started to move and Ann walked a little further with him. When they got to the gate, he gave her a hug. "Thank you for everything," he said. "Don't be surprised if you hear from me."

"I won't be." She hugged him back. "Take care of yourself."

Ann watched the stuffed ferry leave the dock and felt a momentary sense of loss. She knew it would pass and she would return to the solitary life she so treasured. But she was also pretty sure she hadn't seen the last of Joe Doyle.

*****

"So where do we go from here?" asked Sara after a night of careful lovemaking—the careful part being due to her shoulder, which had been diagnosed as having a nasty chip that had been cleaned up during a quick arthroscopic surgery. She knew she was going to have to endure a barrage of "chip on your shoulder" jokes for weeks to come when she returned to duty.

"I don't think I could live with anyone, and I'm sure you couldn't either. I have my career, as do you ... so I think we are perfect for each other. What could be better for two loners?" he asked. "I can come to the Cape as often as we want—my clients will take care of letting me use their helicopters until the bridges are back—and I'm sure no one will object to you taking as many vacations as you want. The fact is," he said, turning serious, "I've fallen in love with you and I want you in my life."

Her smile told him all he needed to know. He pulled her close, getting a couple of yelps of pain from her in the process. "First things first, though. We need to go to a nice vacation spot for a couple of weeks and decompress. Preferably not Cape Cod."

Sara put her good arm around his neck and kissed him deeply.

"Why? What could you possibly have against the Cape?"

The End

ABOUT THE AUTHOR

Andrew Cunningham is the author of 21 novels, including the *"Lies" Mystery Series*: **All Lies, Fatal Lies, Vegas Lies, Secrets & Lies, Blood Lies, Buried Lies, Sea of Lies,** and **Maui Lies;** the post-apocalyptic *Eden Rising Series*: **Eden Rising, Eden Lost, Eden's Legacy,** and **Eden's Survival**; the *Yestertime Time Travel Series:* **Yestertime, The Yestertime Effect, The Yestertime Warning,** and **The Yestertime Shift;** the disaster/terrorist thriller **Deadly Shore,** and the *Alaska Thrillers Series*: **Wisdom Spring, Nowhere Alone, The 7th Passenger,** and **Lost Passage.** As A.R. Cunningham, he has written a series of five children's mysteries in the *Arthur MacArthur* series. Born in England, Andrew was a long-time resident of Cape Cod. He and his wife now live in Florida. Please visit his website at **Arcnovels.com,** his Facebook page, **Author Andrew Cunningham,** and his **Amazon Author Page.**

Made in United States
North Haven, CT
07 July 2025